Staffrider Series

The *Staffrider Series* aims at bringing new books at popular prices direct to the readers of *Staffrider* magazine. Ingoapele Madingoane's *Africa My Beginning* (*Staffrider Series* No. 1, banned May 1979) and Mtutuzeli Matshoba's *Call Me Not A Man* (*Staffrider Series* No. 2, banned November 1979) showed the way. News of other forthcoming titles will appear regularly in *Staffrider* magazine.

FORCED LANDING

Africa South: Contemporary Writings

Edited by Mothobi Mutloatse

RAVAN PRESS · JOHANNESBURG

Published by Ravan Press (Pty) Ltd.,
409 — 416 Dunwell, 35 Jorissen Street,
Braamfontein, Johannesburg 2001, South Africa.
© Copyright (individual stories, articles and graphics): the authors/artists.
© Copyright (this collection) Ravan Press.
First Impression March 1980
Cover Drawings: Nkoana Moyaga
Typesetting: Anne Robertson

ISBN   0 86975 109 3

Printed by ABC Press (Pty) Ltd., Cape Town.

ACKNOWLEDGEMENTS

The Editor expresses his grateful thanks to all
the contributors as well as the publishers of
Marang, The Classic, Drum, Heineman
Educational Books, *The Voice* and *Staffrider*
for allowing him to publish these writings and
thus make *Forced Landing* a reality.

forced
landing . . .

in dedication
to mme-masediba lilian ngoyi
auntie fatima meer
for their resilience and resourcefulness
black mothers who
forever inspire us lost souls
azanian sons and daughters
and
to don 'bra zenga' mattera
for your illuminating pen
of courage and the boldness in your
as well as our
struggle for liberty
justice
and peace!

CONTENTS

INTRODUCTION

. . . do not ask me to use moderation in a cause like mine.
— *Dr Nnandi Azikiwe*

A situation such as that existing in southern Africa compels the black artist to use all avenues available to him in expressing the black experience, and whether it be autobiographically, sociologically, dramatically, poetically or otherwise, is not so important. What is of vital importance is that the black artist, in particular the writer, should understand that he has a purpose. And that his writings have a rôle to play in the black man's life. It is history in the making. This time it is a cultural history penned down by the black man himself. No literature can emerge out of nothing, and, therefore, no black writer can afford the luxury of isolation from his immediate audience, which is what has happened in the white world.

In a race-obsessed country like South Africa the part the black writer has to play is rather demanding — but nevertheless worth it. It seems to me that he is expected to be a jack of all trades — and a master of all! He has to be tradesman, docker, psychologist, nurse, miner, *matshigilane, tshotsa*, teacher, athlete, toddler, mother, musician, father, visionary, *imbongi* and — above all — oral historian.

That's *Forced Landing* . . .

The black community is hungry, and hungrier since 16 June 1976: ever-ready-and-willing to lay its hands on 'relevant' writing, writing by blacks about blacks. The overwhelming response to poetry recitals held in the townships is proof of this bond between the writers and their audience.

1

That's *Forced Landing* . . .

It is an age of experimental literature — vibrantly expressing communal experience. This is a time when black writers should not feel ashamed of portraying the black experience, even though outsiders may hammer them for talking too much about apartheid instead of about the 'nice things'. This is not to suggest that black writers should totally ignore the white world. No! All I am saying is that the black writer should concentrate primarily on his immediate audience. What goes on in the community forms the basis of his writings. He is deeply rooted there — and his authenticity is there or not there for one to see, hear and feel. Otherwise, he would be faking it, condoning all the lies broadcast by the outsiders. The recognition of his work as authentic by the black community — that is the vital link in the creative process, without which all attempts are virtually useless. The outside world is still okay, but it is not that essential, as one must first have a solid foundation where it counts most in the final analysis — at home. For a black writer, and in particular a black writer in Southern Africa, what good is international fame when your own thirsty community is unable to feel, hear and experience your writings, which also happen to involve and affect them in so many ways? The writer has to make the all-important decision: which comes first — one's home audience or the world at large (which is so remote)?

Inevitably he has to opt for the home audience first, to avoid becoming an aloof and lonely figure in his own community. But then some view this as setting one's own trap, so to speak. What with having to maintain independence as an artist on the one hand, and with the political axe that is censorship hovering hawk-like over one's head on the other. The former is not really insurmountable and depends on the writer's personality and skill. With the latter it is, admittedly, a different kettle of fish. And there can be no compromise here.

The black writer has to guard his rôle as an independent thinker jealously in order not to fall into the same trap as the Afrikaanse Pers, which has been doing nothing but echoing its master's voice. Even if the Afrikaanse Pers finally decides to extricate itself from the jaws of Nationalist Party ideology, it is going to discover that the damage is well beyond repair. And so, black writer take note.

That's *Forced Landing* . . .

Nigerian author Kole Omotoso, in his paper 'Politics, Propaganda and the Prostitution of Literature', has just about summed up the rôle of today's writer in Africa with the declaration: 'African writers are not just writers alone.' And it may be added, will continue to be more than 'writers alone' for a long, long time in South Africa's case, right up to liberation (and beyond).

The reason, explains Omotoso further, is that young writers in Africa are still in the process of 'picking up the bits and pieces to build something new and enduring.' Therefore the young black writer cannot afford the 'white' luxury of indulging himself in art for art's sake as if it were a game for selfish, self-centred and hermit-like persons, shunning day-to-day contact with the masses at all costs! Omotoso goes on to say: 'We have a commitment to educate our people. We also need to create myths for ourselves. This,' he insists, 'is an historical duty.'

Mbulelo Vizikhungo Mzamane has put it tersely: 'Since the most important lessons for South Africans are in the political sphere, a writer . . . is unimportant, irrelevant and probably alienated unless he is political.' He expounds in his paper, 'Literature and Politics Among Blacks in South Africa', that art and politics in South Africa, as in many African countries, have 'become inseparable for the simple reason that politics pervades all aspects of a black man's existence.'

In fact one may go further and say that for somebody to state that he is apolitical is a lousy political lie. In South Africa, in the beginning of the Big Fraud, the word was Politics and through this word the black man was robbed of his land, his birthright and even his own name! He dare not call himself African in Afrikaans, as the word is already the sole property of a Euro-tribe.

Frankly, black writers have a limited readership among whites, and this seems unlikely to improve as the majority of whites are complacent, and chiefly interested in escapist literature. They don't like their dream-world to be interfered with. They hate being brought back to reality by cheeky chaps calling themselves writers of conscience, or some such bunk. They are submerged in their hedonism, and so, who the hell dare spoil it with political mumbo-jumbo? We know there's dissatisfaction among a certain section of our black people, they'll tell you, but then Rome was not built in a day. Just be patient . . .

Again, the limited white readership consists mostly of people over 30 as the youngsters are more interested in discos and the buying of a motor-bike. This 'vroom' generation has virtually never heard of black writers, and is unlikely to trouble itself to find out how the other half — the majority, ma'an — lives in South Africa.

And since the literature being produced by black scribes today is uncompromising and does not appeal to the white man for recognition, it is possible that the white readership will remain stagnant, or worse, dwindle because of political apathy among whites in general. Therefore, it would be foolhardy to expect literature in South Africa to transcend racial barriers when white people — 90 percent that is — have barricaded themselves in their fantasy world, and armed themselves to the teeth for good measure. The late Chief Albert Luthuli tried to show them the way, but his hand of friendship was spurned, and he was called all sorts of names. So many other black heroes and heroines tried to do the same but their missions were fruitless. But why? The simple reason is that the white people thought these black heroes and heroines were begging for a living! They deliberately misread all those attempts, and knew they were lying to themselves. And are still lying to themselves. In spite of 16 June 1976, very few whites have ever sat down to question themselves about their attitudes towards black people. Mainly because they are in power . . . they've never seen the need to 'love thy neighbour'.

The majority of white people can ignore work by today's black writers only at their own peril. June '76 is one classic example, and yet the same explosive blunder is still being committed. Ironically, committed with some great help from our honourable super-moralists. And if whites think all is well in South Africa — because SABC says so — then they are living in a fool's paradise, and they only have to read the writings of black writers to grasp some of the reasons why this is so. In fact, each time a book by a black writer is banned, the people of South Africa, especially the whites, are being denied the right to be informed about burning issues. This also means they are being lied to when they are told that the black man is not angry; that repression is the only way to handle dissidents. No wonder that the average white person does not know (or care to know?) that the black man is prepared to sacrifice his own life to achieve his birthright — freedom.

We live on the verge of dictatorship, and if creative writers, in the main black writers (who have now become the last bastion of freedom in South Africa, as James Matthews put it recently) are silenced permanently, all hell will break loose. And all of us would be the losers, becoming puppets of propaganda, for the Press seems to have given up the fight for freedom of thought and expression, so as to survive financially.

Some writers may pull through this forced landing, some may not, but there will always be others from the community, because what we are involved in is something much bigger: the freedom of humanity. And that humanity is personified in the voteless masses of South Africa.

All in all, the material contained in *Forced Landing* covers about two and a half decades in the black man's history, ranging from the early '50s with James Matthews' still-as-fresh 'Azikwelwa', through Mongane Serote's Sharpeville to Mtutuzeli Matshoba's 1976. To a degree this anthology succeeds in narrowing what others have referred to as a generation gap in black literature. Yet it cannot claim to be comprehensive since black life has so many facets that it would require several volumes to collate it, a project that need not be as academic and far removed from the casual reader as it sounds. In another way, this anthology is like a perennial newspaper-cum-journal-cum-book, but with the difference that it is distributed by writers themselves through the trusted *Staffrider* magazine network. It thus becomes another bulletin to the people from the writers.

We are involved in and consumed by an exciting experimental art form that I can only call, to coin a phrase, 'proemdra': Prose, Poem and Drama in one!

We will have to *donder* conventional literature: old-fashioned critic and reader alike. We are going to pee, spit and shit on literary convention before we are through; we are going to kick and pull and push and drag literature into the form we prefer. We are going to experiment and probe and not give a damn what the critics have to say. Because we are in search of our true selves — undergoing self-discovery as a people.

We are not going to be told how to re-live our feelings, pains and aspirations by anybody who speaks from the platform of his own rickety culture. We'll write our poems in a narrative form; we'll write journalistic pieces in poetry form; we'll dramatise our poetic experiences; we'll poeticise our historical dramas. We will do all these things at the same time.

We'll perform all these exciting, painful, therapeutic and educative creative acts until we run out of energy!

That's *Forced Landing*!

In the next anthology (*Reconstruction*) we hope to include a much broader spectrum of works including pieces from 1884 (Jabavu's *Imvo*), Walter Rubushane, Sol Plaatje, the *Drum* writers and the *Staffrider* generation. The last volume in this Azanian trilogy will reach back to the 1770s. And as I write this let me state that we constantly recall, and remember at our recitals the muzzling of Alex la Guma, Can Themba, Dennis Brutus, Lewis Nkosi and all the others.

One of the factors that delayed the publication of this anthology for two years, was the lack of an ideal publisher. Ideal in the sense that as editor I was concerned about the two important aspects of book-publishing in South Africa: distribution and the book's price.

Since I believe in the *Staffrider* dictum that black literature is the property of the people loaned to creative writers, I had to ensure that *Forced Landing* was accessible to the masses. Not only that, but the price of the book had to be reasonably within the reach of even the casual reader. Meaning, in short, a drastically cut price not exceeding R3.

But because it is the concern of all Staffriders to take our contributions to our rich black heritage back to the people, who've loaned it to us spiritually, we've decided to charge a 'skeleton' price. What is more, to distribute these works ourselves, an unheard-of phenomenon in the literary world, in which the writer also doubles up as a mobile bookshop!

In this manner, the reader or potential reader does not have to hunt for our literary work: it is always there on his doorstep or near his elbow in the train or on the bus. And in this way, too, an intimate relationship between writer and audience is established, instead of writers keeping to themselves — writing their stuff and not being concerned about where their works finally end up! Elsewhere this is unimportant, but in Azania it is MOST important that a writer follow up with distribution what he's penned down. Otherwise he stands accused of dereliction of his duty as a mass-communicator.

That's *Forced Landing* for you, people!

This anthology covers a wide spectrum of black life, which is obviously far from entertaining because the black man is still in chains.

The stories herein are arranged alphabetically to avoid lining up the contributors as if they were participating in a beauty contest! *Ach, banna . . .* In this *Forced Landing* arrangement the reader does not have to start with Story One. He or she is at liberty to begin reading at random, even in Chinese-form, from back to front: and will still find it absorbing.

Some of the stories — 'Waiting For Leila'; 'Noorjehan', 'To Kill A Man's Pride', 'A Different Time'; and 'Forced Landing' have not been published previously. Those which were published are: 'African Trombone', 'The Truth, Mama', 'Dumani', 'Cops', 'Dreams Wither

Slowly' (all in *The Voice*); 'The Moon', 'A Present' (in *Marang*); 'Fling' and 'Darkie' (both in *Drum*); 'Side-step', 'Bad Times', 'Rebecca' and 'Taylor' (all in *The Classic*); 'Thoughts' and 'Point' (both in *Staffrider*). From Zimbabwe comes Charles Rukuni's 'Who Started the War?'

'Nightmarish Fear' is reproduced in full for the first time, while 'Here I Stand' has been published here and there, but not for mass distribution.

I hereby wish to *leboga* all the people who were involved in the production of this anthology: including the typing, proof-reading, graphics and design. A magnificent team effort: especially from my then Botswana-connection, Mbulelo (for the Guma and Nkosi gems); Mafika for his insistence on a collection of prose; the entire Ravan Press staff for its diligence and patience; *Ndifuna ukubulela u*Fikile *no*Nkoana for their breathtaking graphics, which in many ways have revolutionised black literature and art, and therefore establish yet another dimension in *Forced Landing*: the unbeatable combination of prose and art.

Oh, Mother Africa, one day we'll break these chains . . . of oppression and censorship, after which we will not have forever to make a forced landing into our normal lives!

Mothobi Mutloatse
January 23, 1980
Skotaville (officially nicknamed Pimville)

P.S. Why are you so silent, Sisters and Mothers of Africa?

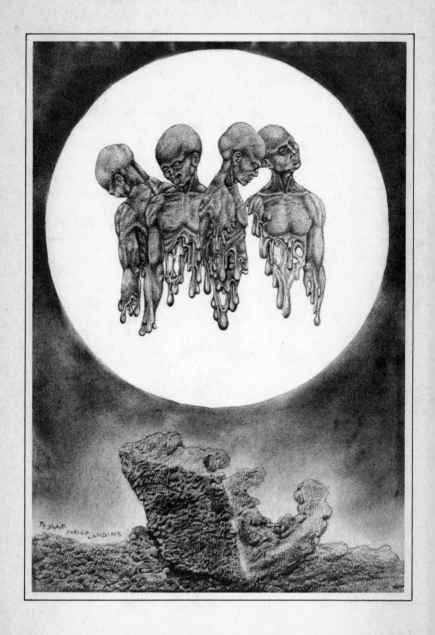

Stories

Chicks Nkosi/A DIFFERENT TIME

Umhlathi owehlula izimolontshisi zama khafula emabhunu, the jaw that defied the force of kaffir knobkerries. Those were his praises.

Whenever one of the old men greeted him with these praises, he would shake his head and say: *'Shiyakhona,* leave it there.'

His jaw was crooked and a big scar ran from ear to chin. He was a kind old soul who always greeted us children with a smile, even though the smile was a bit wry because of his disfigured jaw.

Still, we liked him very much, but wondered what it was that had hurt him so badly.

One evening we were sitting around a fire eating *imbasha. Imbasha* is a word for grains of dry mealies which have been soaked overnight in water. We fried *imbasha* in a *likesi,* the upturned lid of a three-legged iron pot. We had to snatch it off the *likesi* whilst it was still hot and dancing. Once *imbasha* cooled, it became hard again and unchewable.

We were having our *imbasha* when bold Mncina started telling us about what they used to do when they were *umbutho,* the King's regiment.

'You know Nkambule,' he said screwing up his jaw. 'You know whom I mean?' Yes, we knew whom he meant.

'I was in the same regiment with him. Ho, ho, you boys do not know anything. Ask from this one,' he said pointing at his chest.

'You say so Mkhulu?'

'Yes, I say so. What can you tell me? You whose food is cooked for you by women, and yet have the liver to call yourselves men! *Sukani lapha,* get off. You are nothing. You would never survive a single battle. You would die like flies sprayed with sheep dip.'

'What are we supposed to do, Mkhulu?'

'Supposed to do? Listen to them. They ask what they are supposed to do!

'Do you not know that you should defend your king, your women, your children, your country and your cattle? Is that not what a man was made for?

'Do you think that the Gods of Mswati made you to live and work for whitemen and become their kaffirs? You are like women who work for their husbands. You till the fields and do all the odd chores. You work for your white bosses in exchange for money, food and shelter. *Sukani lapha*, get away. You are a disgrace.

'*Thina*, we became regiments of the king. We learnt to live a hard life. Nobody gave us food. We had to fend for ourselves. Who would feed you in the field of battle?'

'You say so, Mkhulu?'

The old man did not answer. He looked into the distance, the distance of time.

The firelight showed the skin of his furrowed forehead. It drew tighter and tighter into wrinkles and his eyes shone brighter and smaller as he looked back into the past.

No one could disturb him then.

'Ya,' he said after a time. 'You cannot understand, children of my children. I lived in a different world. You cannot understand.'

'*Hawu* Mkhulu?'

'I was telling you about the scar on . . .' Mkhulu twisted his jaw to indicate whom he meant.

'Yes, Mkhulu. Please tell us. What happened to him?'

'What happened? He nearly died, that one. But, *hayi*, the man is strong. I tell you, they thought they had finished him. *Ubani yena*, not that one. He got away through the small hole of a rat.'

'*Hawu* Mkhulu?'

'*Lalelani nginitshele*, just listen and let me tell you. You see, it all started a long time ago, this trouble with the white people. It started when the great king Somhlolo prophesied that people with white skins, blue eyes and hair that hangs down like mealie tassles would come from from the sea.

King Somhlolo said we should not fight them. We should not spill even a drop of that foreign blood on this land.

Indeed, long after he of the right hand had gone to join his forefathers, the white people came.

When they came, they asked for, and were given land by the good king Mbandzeni who was reigning at the time.

You see, it was our tradition that strangers to a country should be given land and helped to set up home. It was in that spirit that they were given land to pasture their sheep and cattle.

The white people used to come down to Swaziland in the winter, driving flocks of sheep to eat up the king's green grass.

Unlike other black people who had come to the country, the whites did not join the Swazi nations. They merely used the privileges and rights of the Swazis without the attendant responsibilities, like serving in the regiments, joining in collective community work and so on.

Naturally, we did not like that. We did not like to see those flocks driven down from faraway Transvaal, coming here to devour our grass free of charge. Especially because those animals, the *tiklabu* sheep, were so very tasty to the tongue.

We decided to have our own back for the destruction of our grass by these animals.

The whitemen used to come here with people whom they had dressed up in old torn dirty clothing. These people they called their kaffirs, and that is how we came to call them, *emakhafula emabhunu.*

Usually two of these men would look after a big flock of sheep. They used to drive the sheep in a long line on the road. One chap would lead the flock and the other would be right at the back.

The line would extend as far as from here to that antheap.' Mkhulu pointed into the dark at an antheap that was about two hundred yards away.

'We studied the way they were driven,' said Mkhulu. 'We got the kaffirs to get used to seeing us washing in the rivers near the bridges over which they passed.

The bridges were low and narrow in those days; just wide enough for a wagon to cross.

As the line of sheep went past over the bridge, we quickly snatched a few, and sat on them in the water. Sheep do not cry so they drowned quietly, and the shepherds went on unaware.

At the next bridge the same thing happened. Altogether, we found ourselves with over twenty sheep.

The sheep were normally counted in the mornings to see if any had strayed off or been stolen during the night.

That gave us the whole night to hide our loot. We never regarded ourselves as having stolen the sheep. We felt we were entitled to repossess some of these animals to avenge the loss of our grass, that's all.

Anyway we dug a big hole in the middle of the king's field and buried our sheep in a hole this deep.' Mkhulu raised his hand about four feet from the ground.

'We stacked the animals close, wool and all, and we covered the hole. Then early in the morning when you could only see the horns of the cattle, we were up collecting wood and stacking the wood over our secret.

The Lion of Somhlolo had been pleased to give relish to the regiment, that day we got the sheep. Relish for the regiments meant an ox. It had been slaughtered and hung overnight.

By sunrise the fire was roaring and we were cutting up the beast, ready to roast it.

When the shepherds counted their flock that morning, they found over twenty sheep missing.

The Boer had arrived at the camp with dogs to watch overnight. No dog had barked in the night.

However, the shepherds remembered seeing members of the regiment bathing in the rivers when they were driving the sheep.

The Boer suspected.

Onto his horse, straight to the nearest police post at Bremersdorp.

When the sun was this high, we saw them raising dust in the distance. The metal plates on their mounts glittered in the morning sun. It was them. It was the formidable mounted police, *zona ngempela izimawundeni.*

They came with the Boer and his shepherds in tow.

Yes, the shepherds recognized some of us. We were the ones they had passed as they drove the sheep down the previous day.

Did we see any lost sheep?

No. Which lost sheep?

What are we roasting on the fire?

Meat.

Meat? What kind of meat?

Meat from an ox. There is the skin.

Can we taste a piece of that meat?

Sure. Why not? Any piece you fancy.

After that the Boer and the police held short counsel. They left a few to watch over us and the rest continued to the Great Place. They got permission to search our huts. Nothing.

They searched the surrounding area. Nothing.

They gave up the search and came back to join those they had left to watch us.

We were too busy roasting and feasting on our meat to worry about them and their lost sheep.

After lingering around a bit, asking stupid questions and getting stupid answers, they decided to go.

I do not need to tell you that the sheep were roasting beautifully in the earth below the big fire. The coolness of the earth preserved the meat for days and days. Every evening we dug up a sheep or two.'

'*Kanti* Mkhulu, you used to be naughty when you were young,' somebody said.

'Naughty? Just listen to this one. What do you mean naughty? Can't you see that ours was a mere act of avenging the grass which belonged to the land, grass that was being destroyed by these animals? What are you saying, *kanti bakuthengile*, eh? You have eaten the saliva of the white man.'

We all laughed.

'But Mkhulu you have not told us about the one who is like this.'

'Ssh,' whispered Mkhulu. 'He does not like it. Never talk about it again.'

He looked about him in the dark to see if anyone was snooping.

'You see,' he continued, 'most Boers used to come with their flocks of sheep and go back to the Transvaal in summer.

But there was this one who decided to bring his wife and build a house across the river. He came down with his shepherds, his sheep, cattle, goats, pigs and chickens.

He was clever. He changed his workers frequently so that we never came to know them well enough to get them drunk and help ourselves to the Boer's animals.

However, our hearts did not stop bleeding for the King's grass as the animals multiplied. We decided that enough was enough.

One evening we approached the place about midnight. It was a cloudy and misty night, just the right time and setting for repossession.

Quickly, we collected a few chickens and sheep. Sheep are easy because they never make a noise and, of course, they are the tastiest.'

'What about the chickens Mkhulu? They are so noisy.'

'Boys of today know nothing. We had learnt that when it rains, chickens hide their heads under their wings.

So, we carried a tin of water with us and as we approached the chickens, we scattered the water over the fowls and the fowls put their

14

heads under their wings.

Whilst it was still in that position, we would grab a fowl and wring its neck. Not a sound.

The following day the Boer quarrelled with his workers and sent them away. He brought out a new group but he continued to lose his animals.

But, *lafika ilanga elisilima,* and indeed, when it dawned we did not realise that it was the day that was to make us look stupid with our well-planned designs.

We used to go in turns to pick up something from the Boer's farm. It happened to be Nkambule's turn that night.

He had just got inside the fence when he stumbled over a string.

Maye babo. O fathers. The string was tied to a bell on the Boer's verandah. The bell went *kring, kring, kring.*

The Boer was up, gun in hand. His workers came out carrying lanterns and kerries. They surrounded the whole place. Feet were running and people were shouting; the place was in an uproar.

The chickens clacked and the pigs squealed and grunted, grousing at the untimely disturbance.

The night was so dark you could not see you own hand if you put it out in front of your eyes. The mist was thick and it was drizzling and slippery. The lanterns were closing in around the yard.

He knew he did not dare to try and get out. He was trapped.

The area in which the Boer kept his animals was fenced in and the lanterns were surrounding it. Nkambule decided at that moment to take off the only thing he had on, *emajobo,* the loin skin covering his front and back below the waist.

He put his head between his forearms and joined the pigs, grunting and pushing in the dark.

His shining black body was difficult to detect among the large black pigs, in the dim light of the lanterns. They could not spot him, but they knew he was somewhere in there.

After waiting for some time in the dampness of the night, the Boer left the others with instructions to *vang hom,* you must catch him, and went back into his house to catch some sleep.

By this time, if it had been a clear night, the morning star *inkwen-kwezi* would be rising. Before long it was going to be light. Nkambule realized his time was running out.

Gingerly, he crawled towards the fence. He had his hand out-stretched in an attempt to feel for the string. He touched nothing.

He crawled further and still he touched nothing. He raised his head just that much. His head found the string.

He had no time. He jumped over the fence and dashed. He was just a little slower than the raised knobkerrie in front of him.

It caught him flush on the jaw.

He stumbled and fell. He got up and ran on all fours.

The man behind reached out to catch him. The man's hand glided down the slippery wet naked body.

Nkambule regained his feet and ran. *Nango eshona.* But *suka*, the man behind him was closing in again fast. The thudding steps were directly behind him.

Quickly, he squatted on the ground. The chap came upon him full speed. He tripped over Nkambule's body and fell on his face. He landed on hard gravel which stripped his flesh into strings.

Meantime, Nkambule picked himself up and got on to the man. *"Nangu nyoko,"* he said, bringing his bare foot down hard onto the back of the man's head.

The man's front teeth collided violently with the hard gravel and dislodged.

Gone was Nkambule.'

Xolile Guma/AFRICAN TROMBONE

It was a clear October morning, graced by the warmth of the sun, caressed by a capricious breeze typical of such a morning in sub-equatorial Africa. Towards the arena they came, in all shapes and sizes. Big ones, small ones, tall ones, short ones, fat ones, thin ones, a seething mass of people. Colourfully adorned in costumes of origin as varied as the people who wore them. Africans, independent Africans, proud of their independence and gathered now to celebrate the occasion, commemorating the day on which the colonial flag was brought down and theirs slowly and triumphantly raised to the heavens, there to flutter and sway, symbol of the African dream accomplished; Africans — and known as such, not the 'native hordes' of the old textbook descriptions, descending onto the plains to meet the long-haired gentlemen from across the sea.

Within the arena, festivities had begun. The army, resplendent in their new uniforms, stood in formation in the centre, flanked on the left by the youth league, on the right by the police, while in the background one saw 'Dad's army', veterans of the Second World War. How graphically that arena portrayed history, the old and the new, unable to merge but seemingly capable of peaceful co-existence. The neat, disciplined, modern, rectangular formation of the armed forces framed by the veterans: rugged, too old for discipline, outdated, standing in a rough semi-circle, a formation dating back to the Africa which was being rediscovered.

I sat in the covered area immediately to the left of the seats reserved for 'honourable members of the diplomatic corps'. Further to the left, people were streaming in through all possible gates, filling whatever space there was, losing themselves in that sea of people with amazing ease. To the right, beyond a stately row of red seats enclosed by a green rope threaded through a progression of stainless steel rings, the sea of faces flowed endlessly, reaching the furthest boundaries of the arena, finally merging into the people to my left, thus completing the circle, punctuated only by the red hiatus, reserved for foreign emissaries and 'honourable members of the diplomatic corps'.

Intent as I was on surveying the panorama bedecking that green arena, my attention was arrested by one piercing note. The semi-circle composed of the veterans was now alive with motion, swaying in a manner not unlike a giant millepede unsuccessfully attempting to do the twist: uncoordinated and ragged and yet, in some grotesque way, orderly. Nor did the matter end there, for from that undisciplined writhing mass came sounds, rich sounds of deep voices, tremulously raised in haphazard fashion, accompanied by the honking of an assortment of brassware; bugles, trumpets, French horns, all relics of the Second World War, manfully handled by the veterans. And then I saw him, resplendent in the uniform of a regimental sergeant-major, medals proudly displayed, complemented by a loin-cloth of cowhide, feet encased in brown boots which had long resigned themselves to the inevitability of decay, blowing a trombone. He emerged from the ranks, taking halting, measured steps, veins bulging from the neck upwards, testimony of the magnitude of his exertion, blowing his trombone. Bent double but refusing to be cowed, his face lined by years of insecurity and anguish, hands gnarled by the experience of war and the passage of time, he blew his trombone. His trombone became vehicle of his emotions, emotions aroused by his peers, who like himself had actively fought for the day when their country would be free. The notes emanating from that trombone were not amenable to chromatic definition: they emanated from his guts and seemed to be directed at my guts, like the sound of a cow being slaughtered, blood flowing in viscous rivulets of red, drawing my stomach along for companionship. 'What does all this mean?' he seemed to be saying. 'Is this what I fought for, all those many years ago?' I watched transfixed. I could imagine the scene as it must have been thirty years earlier, in this same arena, when the then young men answered the call to arms. How straight and tall they must have stood then. Fired by the zeal of youth, prepared to die for their country. Now they were bent double.

The British ambassador's daughter, seated in the red hiatus, lisped 'Goth, ithn't that old man wif the trombone thweet?'

18

Intent on discovering the truth about that old man, I made my way through the crowds, pushing and heaving, cursing and pleading as the occasion demanded, until I too emerged through the iron gate leading out of the arena, feeling as I did so, as exalted as I would imagine the biblical camel feels when it manages to negotiate the proverbial eye of the needle. My task seemed almost hopeless. Where amongst that impossible mob, was I going to find an aged man, member of a royal regiment, in the uniform of a regimental sergeant-major, carrying a shiny trombone, whom the British ambassador's daughter had described as 'thweet'? On every side the people thronged, ululating and gesticulating in wild abandon, emerging from that arena as though it was a giant dam, pregnant with people, whose sluice gates had just been opened. I reluctantly decided to drown myself in that sea of people, to be carried along by it like some bottle tossed in desperation by a marooned sailor, he not knowing where it would land, but hopeful that it would.

I 'landed' in town, part of a band of travellers which had boarded a bus whose bonnet bore some resemblance to a pig's snout. Looking about me, I noticed that people were gravitating towards various centres of amusement: pubs and discotheques, with neon lights brazenly announcing their wares. The bus stop was opposite a church whose wares, not being amenable to advertisement by neon lights, were surreptitiously implicit in the mystical darkness which it exuded. I paused a while, reflecting on all that had passed. The green snout coughed as the bus, 'Maphala Special: Never Say Die', jerked into clumsy motion, panting blue smoke through its posterior; low and squat, straddling the road like an overfed pig, obviously intent on returning to the arena, there to swallow more people before returning once again to relieve itself before the church.

The sun setting in the western sky spread the last rays of day with the tenderness of a mother laying her first-born to sleep. In the east, the moon made its coy appearance. Depressed by my inability to locate the trombonist, and yet soothed by the sky's version of the day's aftermath, I stood, pensive.

A woman came walking down the street towards me, with the strange, jerky gait peculiar to one who is two-in-one. I say a woman, in fact she was more of a girl than a woman, with narrow shoulders accentuating the bulge which was the source of her discomfort. As she passed, she seemed to smile ever so slightly, obviously amused by what must have been a look of incredulity on my face. 'Men,' she seemed to be saying, 'can never understand these things. Theirs is only to plant the seed — forgetting that, given a fertile environment, that seed must prosper and grow.' She waddled on, pausing to examine the flow of traffic before crossing to the church, eternal refuge of the desperate. To this day, I still wonder which startled me more, the sound of that piercing trombone, or the frenzied screech of tyres. I jumped, startled, rudely jolted by the reality of life and death. She lay in a pool of blood, which only seconds earlier had given radiance to her coy smile; blood which only seconds earlier had held the promise of life. He came prancing down the street, rejuvenated by heaven-knows-what, trombone in hand. Absent was any of the 'thweetness' which the British ambassador's daughter might have seen. This was a man driven by frustration, like a lion mortally wounded, maddened by pain and seeking revenge. Cognizant of the fact that death was at hand, and yet mindful of the sweetness of life, he pranced down the street, coming towards us.

Meanwhile the crowds had converged on that pitiful spectacle; drawn and yet repelled by the horror of it. Like green flies around a dump of manure they buzzed, none venturing to do anything and none prepared to sacrifice his vantage point. 'Get the police somebody,' I howled, and immediately felt ashamed. Why the hell wouldn't I go and fetch the police? The refrain was picked up by others. 'Get the police, somebody!' — and still she bled.

The cavernous door of the church opened and the priest emerged. We all breathed a sigh of relief. The minister was come, defender of the faith, anointer of God, healer supreme; for who, but the minister, can heal what he cannot see? His appearance was greeted by a frenzied run of notes from the trombonist. Like an angel in mourning, white upon black, the minister floated out of the church.

'Do not touch that woman, old one,' he said, 'she needs medical attention which you are not capable of giving.'

Frightened by the tone of the 'angel', the old man who had been cradling the injured woman, let go. Her head hit the ground with a sickening thud; we all winced simultaneously.

'Fool,' the angel roared, 'now look what you've done.'

The old man picked up his trombone from the congealing blood, shook his head slowly from side to side, and began to walk away.

'Do you know who I am, young man?' he whispered, obviously hurt. I edged a little closer, hopefully.

'Be gone old one,' the minister threatened, 'your filthy loin skin and unwashed hands have already done damage not only to this poor woman but to us all. We who have self-respect and acceptable standards of conduct.'

He left, trombone in hand, disappearing into the night. To this day I have not been able to find him, possessor of the history of this land, without whose efforts we would not today be where we are. What he said to me with that trombone was, 'What is this independence for which I fought, but which now passes me by? Children for whom I selected education and not bribery as a means of salvation now use that education as a means of bribery, and call me a fool. I must stand as a curio for children. But always remember that with my death, your greatest source of information also dies. You will become the curiosity of the international society, a people denying their history.'

If you ever meet an old man carrying a trombone, or as is more likely, blowing his trombone, stop and listen. That African trombone has a great deal to say, and not much time in which to say it.

Mbulelo Vizikhungo Mzamane/A PRESENT FOR MY WIFE

What do you do with a nagging wife? She knows very well that I barely earn enough to enable us to rise above *pap* and *morogo*. Yet she expects me to buy her expensive presents of leather jackets, mink coats and evening dresses — which she'll never wear, anyway, since we can't afford to attend balls and shows. She can't even dance, even if we could. What intensifies her nagging is the fact that our next-door neighbour, Mazibuko, is always bringing his wife nice things. She won't believe me when I tell her that the things Mazibuko brings his wife are all stolen, every single item of them.

'*Keng wena o sa dire je ka banna ba bang?*' she asks.

I tell her I can't steal just because everybody's husband is a thief. It's against my convictions.

'*Empa ga o na conscience dicheleteng tsa batho.*'

She's got me there and she knows it. I don't say tomorrow where money is concerned. I've emptied her purse before and denied it flatly, even though we both knew that it could only have been me. On several occasions she's caught me redhanded, disappearing with her handbag into the toilet.

My problems gather momentum with the arrival of the new fridge Mazibuko brings his wife. We're watching from our stoep.

'I want to branch into private business,' she says as the stolen fridge is being carried next door. I'm convinced it's stolen. Mazibuko later confirms this himself in a little conversation we have across the fence. 'And I need a refrigerator for the business,' she adds. Whoever taught her that word!

I know just what 'private business' she means. Hasn't she been telling me about that, nights on end? I wish I was like the other fellows who have *dinyatsi* to whom they can escape. My problem is that I'm generally shy with women. She was the first and only girl friend I ever had so when she proposed we marry or split, we married, of course. But she's not going to steamroll me now. I just don't like this other proposition. Who wants to get to bed, each night, only after all the others have had their fill? Who wants to live in constant fear of police raids? Who would like to be woken up by fellows demanding drinks at all sorts of unreasonable hours? Her idea of starting a shebeen just doesn't sit too well on my chest.

'It's not as if you were earning a fortune,' she says, as if I'd ever claimed to be Oppenheimer's financial equal. 'The extra cash would come in handy,' she adds.

I must resist that as long as I can. Has she ever gone hungry? Let her name a single day when she's gone to bed without food. Not always decent meals, I must confess. But don't I eat the same meals? I always augment this with fish and chips and half a loaf of brown bread in town, same as she does. Do I ever hide my pay packet from her? She opens it herself, sealed, every Friday. It's true that I sometimes open it with steam before I get home and seal it again. But it isn't as if I did that every Friday.

Mazibuko jumps across the fence and invites me for a drink, to celebrate the arrival of the new fridge.

She dishes him the kind of smile I used to get when we were still courting. I'd like to see that smile on her face again. Directed at me. But I'm not jealous. Mazibuko is a good neighbour. However, I can't be expected to condescend so low as to pick up a dead man's fridge.

She turns and looks at me as though I'd pumped her full of castor oil. 'You won't forget we've some business to settle, will you?' she says as Mazibuko and I skip across the fence.

'What have you done?'

'She wants a fridge. How did you get yours?'

Mazibuko has brought the bottle of our special K.W.V. What I like about this brandy is that it really has no hangover to talk of. I often provide this speciality myself. Surreptitiously, of course. My method is simple. After I've doctored my pay packet, I buy one and give it to Mazibuko before we get home. It's then up to him to come and invite me. The trick almost always works. As far as she's concerned Mazibuko can never err. The perfect gentleman, neighbourly and all that. She's lectured me more than once about men who parasite on others, because

23

she thinks I drink Mazibuko. The lecture goes in through one ear and out through the other. Take the bottle we're going to drink, for instance. Didn't Mazibuko and I *gazaat* when we met during lunch time? Anyway, I'm not too keen to broadcast the fact, especially to her, that I contributed half the amount that went to buying that bottle. What I'm interested in just now is to know how Mazibuko came by his fridge.

'Tell me about the fridge,' I say as soon as I'm sure Meisie, that's Mazibuko's burden, is out of earshot.

Strange thing about Meisie. She's got all the comforts you'd think a woman needs. Bedroom suite, kitchen scheme and now a fridge. She's by far the best-dressed woman in our street, the first to wear an Afro wig and all that. She wants it like that, she likes it that way. But she won't hear of Mazibuko bringing stolen goods to her house. She knows very well that not even Mazibuko's life savings could buy her half the things she has in the house. She'll accept anything as long as you tell her you bought it. But don't make the mistake of telling her you stole it.

Don't I know what I'm talking about? The other day Mazibuko and I returned home — we travel in the same train to work and back — laden with liquor, grocery and meat. It's a whole chicken and we ask her to fry it for us, sharp sharp. She obliges. I cannot forget how we got that chicken so I keep on reminiscing and laughing off the event. She comes in from the kitchen and asks how we got that chicken. I'm in my most communicative mood and so I do not see Mazibuko's forbidding frown until it's too late. So I explain that we snatched it off a crippled white woman. It's only when she spits on the floor and disappears into the kitchen that I realise that something's gone wrong.

'*Uyinyovile*, you've damn well spoilt everything,' Mazibuko says through clenched teeth.

There's a fierce rattling of pots in the kitchen. She storms out through the kitchen door and walks round the house to the front gate. I watch stealthily through the window. She has a pot which she empties into the rubbish bin. This woman!

She comes back and plants herself across the door, arms akimbo. 'Let me tell you one thing straight,' she says. 'I never harbour any stolen goods in this house. Fancy, asking me to cook you stolen meat! Contaminating my pots with white disease! I'm a self-respecting woman, I must tell you, and I mean to keep my home respectable. *Manifun' ukuphekelwa inyam'entshontshiwe, hambani niyoyipheka*

24

kwa-hell.'

We should have tried my wife. Not that I think she's referring to her when she says we should go fry our chicken in hell.

I've been on my guard since that fateful day. That's why I'm careful not to ask Mazibuko about the fridge in Meisie's respectable presence. The conversation that follows is mainly carried on in whispers.

Mazibuko explains the matter of the fridge this way. At Bradlow's furniture shop where he works, he does deliveries and repossessions. That very afternoon he'd been sent to collect the fridge from a house in the townships whose owner was no longer able to honour the terms of the hire purchase agreement. When he got to this house, he found their property piled outside. They were moving. It was explained to him that the owner of the house had died some three months ago, after a long illness. As it was not permissible by law for his family to occupy the house any longer, they were going to stay elsewhere, with the widow's brother.

An idea was running through Mazibuko's mind. With many apologies he explained his business. The widow responded with such resignation and listlessness that Mazibuko was almost tempted to let them take away the fridge. 'After all it's your job, my son,' she said.

That was it. After all, it wasn't really Mazibuko who'd be cheating the widow. It was Bradlow's. By cheating the company Mazibuko would be getting in a blow for the old lady. At any rate, whose house could contain all the widow's property on top of what was already in that house?

He collected the fridge and delivered it at his own house.

'What explanation will you give to the firm?'

'I'll tell them the truth. I'll tell them the occupants of the house have left. Forwarding address unknown. They can verify that for them-selves, if they like.'

'Nihleba ngani nina lapho?' Meisie asks when she comes into the sitting room. 'Why talk in whispers like two eternal conspirators?'

'Aah! *Izindaba zamadoda nje, Sisi,'* I say.

'I didn't know men also gossiped,' she says and then passes into the bedroom.

That terminates our conversation. I immediately rise to leave.

Meisie comes out of the bedroom and sees me already on my feet. *'Hayi!'* she says. *'Bengingakuxoshi.'*

'I know you weren't chasing me away, Sisi,' I say, 'but I was already on my way out.' If I stay longer there is the probability she'll come and fetch me in person. Hasn't she said she has a bone to chew with me?

You can resist some people's requests some of the time, but you cannot resist her requests all the time. I was bound to surrender some day. She knew that and I knew it too. So why not make it tonight? As good a day as any. Thus it was that on that evening I gave my consent to her proposal that we start a shebeen.

We bought a fridge. Mazibuko came to my rescue. I'm not telling how.

She left her job at the C.N.A., where she used to dust books, to look after the business.

Although we haven't exactly prospered — a good deal of the proceeds goes into police bribes and court fines — we've become a very popular spot. The reason for our success lies mainly in her personality. She's very selective about whom she admits into the house, to keep out the township's riff-raff. The result is that our patrons come from the ranks of the township's leading business men, doctors, lawyers and teachers, and their girl-friends. People call us the Fish Pond because we're like an alcoholic stream that never runs dry.

I won't deny it. I live in constant fear of the liquor squad. On some evenings I can't sleep at all. But the business has certain compensations too. I don't just mean sharing liquor with my customers. That doesn't call for much imagination because drunkards are openhanded by temperament. They'll thrust liquor down your throat even when you're least inclined to drink. I'm not talking about that. There's this other area in which I feel I must act soon, for my own peace of mind. She's been nagging again, about presents.

'You've enough capital of your own,' I say. 'Why can't you buy yourself whatever you want.'

'It's not the same thing,' she says. Don't I know that? Using her money and using my own are two different things. She won't part with hers to buy any of the expensive things she's always at me about, precisely because she knows they're worthless. I must find a way of making her contribute, at least in part, towards the realization of her grandiose schemes.

I've devised this method which has been working fine so far. I suppose that's what drives me to make the rash promise I later make. Success sometimes goes to the head. But it's my scheme I'm talking about. In our business it is very difficult to keep an accurate system of accounts. There are ever so many factors involved. For instance, when a chap buys a lot of liquor from your joint, he's entitled to a *gwaqaza*. The extra liquor you offer him as a gift is never accounted for. Then there's what you take yourself, sometimes, to entertain friends and relatives from afar. All of which makes my scheme particularly simple to carry out. Whenever I sell in her absence — she can't always be in the house, can she? — I pocket the money. There's also the occasional slip, when she leaves her purse lying carelessly about. When I combine all these figures, the amount I'm able to raise as a sideline is quite considerable. I could buy her a mink coat, only that's not what she wants.

'Last year you forgot my birthday,' she says. 'This year you may do the same if I don't keep on reminding you.'

'Not likely. When is it?'

'Listen to that. It's on the 28th of this month.'

'I know. I just meant when would you like us to celebrate,'

'You could ask a more pertinent question than that.'

'Alright.'

We both know that she's got me cornered. She's been at me about this etiquette or torniquet business, I can no longer remember which, for so long that I feel I must play the game her way, if only for my peace of mind. There's such a thick atmosphere of expectation in the room you could kick it. I brace myself for the big plunge.

'What do you want for your birthday?'

'You don't ask people what presents they want. It's not only embarrassing but it also removes the element of surprise. Anyway, since you've already asked, I want a leather jacket.'

'What size?'

I wish I hadn't asked her what she wanted. I should really listen to her sometimes, when she lectures me on civilized conduct. I could tear a page or two from her books on conduct, stolen in the days she used to work at the C.N.A., and fling them back at her. About this present, for instance. It would have been so simple to have deposited a pair of stockings at her feet, in just the way she says these things should be done.

'You know what size. 42.'

That's a fat order, but I'll try to meet it.

Despite the fact that she reminds me on the 27th, I forget to buy her present. The first reason why I forget is that in all the shops I've been to, the largest size I could get was a 36. These things are not designed for battleships, but I can't very well tell her that. The second reason is that I still haven't raised enough money. I'd have to empty her purse to do that and to augment the amount with part of my life's savings. These things are frightfully expensive. I've ransacked her pockets before for a few coins. But to steal her whole purse would prove beyond even me. The only way out is to procrastinate.

'You haven't bought me my present,' she says.

'I'll tell you what. I could have bought you a cheaper jacket, but I didn't want to. I didn't have enough money for the one I deposited.'

'How much does it cost?'

'That would spoil the element of surprise.' I'm learning fast.

'When will you pop out the rest of the money?'

'Do not look a gift horse in the mouth.' It's a proverb I once read from one of her books. I'm not sure whether I've used it appropriately. To cover up, I rise and kiss her fully on the mouth — you can't talk when you're being kissed — and disappear into the bedroom.

You can fool some people all the time but you can't fool her always, to adapt that famous saying again. I'm a glib liar, I know. Survival demands it. But she's my stop station, as they say.

A week passes, two, still no leather jacket.

I've not really made any serious effort for the simple reason that it's impossible to get her what she wants. There were days on which I'd seriously put some money aside, but that money is all gone. I can no longer buy her even the cheapest imitation.

'Oho!' she starts ominously. 'Do you think I still don't know you? After all these years. Tomorrow is Saturday. You're not working. You'll take me with you to show me this leather jacket. I don't know what suddenly turned me into such a fool. Where are the receipts that show you paid the deposit?'

'I deposited it backdoor.'

'Oho! Libala mntwan' abantu.'

Mazibuko descends on us like a godsend. On our way from work I gave him a bottle and asked him to do the usual.

Not even Mazibuko's usual charms will soothe her tonight. 'Akayin-dawo lowo,' she says.

Mazibuko is a sensible man. Doesn't he row a similar boat? If she says I'm not going anywhere, that's final. He beats an immediate retreat and leaves me more crestfallen than before.

One of the few blessings of our business is company. I don't mean when it's not desirable. But right now it's needed. You can't run business along sulky lines. You must, at least, smile to your customers. And a smile has the power to relieve tension.

Since it's a Friday evening, the house is soon agog with spirited conversation. She's soon herself again, or so I think. One chap with a whole bottle to himself offers me a few stiff tots. I'm on my third when my glass is unceremoniously snatched from my lips. 'Don't give this one anything,' she says.

I've my tail between my legs. I must do something or say something to restore my dignity. This woman can be green, green, green with rudeness. Does she want everybody to know that she has me by the cock? I could do something terrible. But I must control my anger. My reputation first.

I laugh behind her back and lean forward to whisper to the other chap. 'I've been ordered off the bottle,' I say. 'Doctor's orders. *Maar dit is nie easy nie om te lay off,* especially if you've been raising the elbow for as long as I've been doing.'

My companion nods with sympathetic understanding.

Life is such that good weather must follow long spells of miserable weather. There are days when the ancestors seem to direct our every movement.

My fortunes took a dramatic turn the next Friday after work. We were in the train with Mazibuko. On his lap was a huge parcel.

'*Wat het jy daar in, Fana?*' I asked.

'*My vrou se leather jacket,*' he says. '*Ek koop hom es'godini, B.D.*'

What's going to become of me if she sees Meisie in a leather jacket? I must talk to Mazibuko. Can't he pass the jacket on to me? I'll pay him by and by. He can obtain another the same way he obtained this one. I don't mind how much I pay him.

Mazibuko is adamant. He won't part with it. He could arrange for me through the same channels to get another. Not this one. He's spent too many sleepless nights over this already.

I also tell him I'm living in shit street, too, on account of just such a jacket. He nods and says nothing.

There's something I don't understand about this. Is every housewife now after a leather jacket? I'm really puzzled by this, but not for long. Mazibuko leans across his seat and says there are many things he could tell me. I know that's just a preamble so I keep quiet.

'*Hawu! Jy's nie curious nie?*' he asks and leans closer. '*Ek sal jou een ding vertel. Ngizokutshayela ngoba ngiyabona ukuthi awukeni. Jy ken nix. Jy word 'n moomish. Babbedgile,* your wife and mine, to see who gets a leather jacket first.'

She can never forgive me for this. For the first time I seriously contemplate sleeping out. No use, she'd send the police after me, that one. And what then.

I should have never succumbed to her request to start a shebeen. My problems backdate to that fateful decision. The business has given her definite airs. I've noticed that she always wants to look better dressed than, or at least as well dressed as, any of the women who come to drink at our house. I must buy her such and such because she's seen so and so wearing it. That's why we're not prospering. Only the other day I watched her deliberately spill beer over her dress just because she wanted to change into her new slack suit to compete with some teenagers who'd come to our house dressed in similar outfits. It didn't matter that slacks don't become her very well. She just doesn't mind displaying her excess flesh to better effect. She won't realize she isn't shaped differently from a sausage. Now she wants to compete with Meisie whose husband does business with every private corporation in town that deals in stolen goods. And I'm expected to . . . But what's the point of taking off like that? Meisie has the leather jacket and she hasn't. That's the salient point I must tackle, with Mazibuko's assistance.

I have a wonderful idea in my head but I need his cooperation. I put my plan to him. He eyes me with a mixture of scepticism and distrust, and shakes his head sadly. That drives me to near-desperation. Mazibuko's essentially a man of action and I'm primarily a man of ideas and very smooth-talking too. Very reluctantly he yields to persuasion, but warns repeatedly that nothing should go wrong, otherwise he'll have to break into my house and retrieve it himself.

When we get off the train I'm carrying the leather jacket. We walk home. Mazibuko is still trying to find a flaw in my plan. But I've already stated that ideas are not his province.

We part company at his gate. He promises he'll join me soon. There are several reasons why Mazibuko has to be with me tonight. First, he's got to keep away from Meisie, to whom he'd promised to bring the parcel today. He also wants to make sure I don't bungle anything. Lastly, I'll need him to lend a hand later.

'What have you got in there?' she asks as soon as I set my toes in the house.

'Hayi, yi-drycleaner yami net,' I say and slip into the bedroom

where I shove the parcel under the bed, behind some crates of beer. I can't let her see it now. She'd rush straight away to go and show it off to Meisie.

Mazibuko walks in, as I come out of the bedroom, and joins two men in the sitting room who've already settled down to their beer. I've given him some cash so that he can order himself some beer too.

'That was fast. Did you tell her I'd invited you over for a drink?' I ask when I'm sure the others can't hear.

'*Ja,* but she wants that thing terribly blind,' he says.

'Your ordeal won't last much longer,' I say, 'while mine is only just beginning.'

I play some records on my Hi-Fi set which I also bought with Mazibuko's assistance. Where would I be without this wonderful man?

Soon the place is packed with the usual Friday evening crowd. Some are dancing while others are talking as if their listeners were a little on the deaf side.

I stuff Mazibuko with beer, some of it bought and the rest stolen straight out of the fridge.

Later in the night we both agree it is time for the presentation. We've been going over the plan again to check for loopholes but, as I've said before, there are none.

I move into the kitchen where she is busy knocking a meal together. I'm used to having my supper after ten. Then I speak of indifferent things to her until Mazibuko appears at the door to announce that he just wants to hop across the fence to collect the key so that he won't have to bother Meisie when he returns later. He promises he won't be long and takes off.

This is when I am supposed to tell her.

'I've a surprise for you,' I say with a grin broad enough to harbour a battleship.

'What is it?'

'Come with me to the bedroom and I'll show you.'

We go through to the bedroom. I make a dive for the parcel, tear the wrapping off and hand her the leather jacket.

'Whose is it?'

'Yours. Fit it on.'

She's hardened herself, this woman. Can no longer let go. But there's no doubt about it, she's deeply affected. I look the other way for I can see her eyes becoming moist. That gives her the chance to dry them with a single, swift sweep of the sleeves.

She struggles into it. It's a size or two too small, and that's an under-statement, but I praise her lavishly. My only fear is that she might tear it. Fortunately she doesn't. She looks at herself in the mirror and shakes her head with dissatisfaction. Her discontentment melts when she sees the smile, like headlines to her praise, on my face.

Someone calls for a drink from the sitting room.

I urge her to go and serve them in her new coat, while I remain gig-gling to myself.

Her entrance is greeted with loud applause and prolonged whistling. What do you expect from drunken chaps and their girl-friends? They praise her profusely. I'm afraid some of the praise may go to her head.

'Wu-u-u!' Each syllable is accompanied by a hand-clap. 'I'm sure it must have cost you a fortune.'

'*Bathong!* Some people are lucky.'

'I saw an identical coat the other day, *ha-John Orr's. Ha ke sa hopola hore ene ele bokae. Maar ene ele over R100.*'

'*Wu-u-u! Ke ye galela joang. Ke can't get.*'

'Baby you look smashing.'

'*Hayi! Suka wena lapha, lesidakwa,*' she says and makes her way back to the bedroom.

She gives me a resounding kiss on both sides of the face and then plants a prolonged one in the centre.

'*Awusenzele i-diet, tu,*' I say, helping her out of the jacket. 'Make it two, to include no-Mazibuko. I'm sure he's not had a bite. I invited him over as soon as we got back from work.'

'He's back already,' she says.

Which was as it should have been. He hadn't gone home really. D'you think Meisie would have let him out of her sight again? He'd only given the illusion of going home, for reasons which should soon be clear.

I folded the jacket and placed it on the bed. We steered ourselves back to the kitchen. While she was dishing up I went to call Mazibuko.

'*Uphi uMeisie?*' she asked. 'Can you two attend to the customers while I make a quick dash to her. Here's your food.'

'She's asleep,' Mazibuko said.

'Why so early? I'll go and wake her up. You've got the key, haven't you?'

'Come on, darling, don't be so inconsiderate,' I said.

'She's not feeling very well,' Mazibuko said. 'But what a remarkable coincidence!'

'What coincidence?' she asked.

'Meisie also has an identical jacket. I bought her one today.'

'How come she didn't show it to me?'

'Because I haven't shown it to her yet. Maybe I should go and show it to her now.'

But Mazibuko didn't go. We hadn't quite finished yet.

'You see,' I said, 'Mazibuko and I bought the leather jackets together. That's what we're celebrating tonight.'

Her enthusiasm had ebbed so considerably that she refused to touch her food, pleading an upset tummy. Mazibuko and I divided her plate between us. She certainly looked sick at heart and lame of will. I knew then that we'd deliver the *coup de grace* with ease.

'I think you should retire to bed, darling,' I said. 'Mazibuko and I will attend to the customers.'

Just then someone shouted for a drink. I rushed to serve him. When I returned she was ready to give in.

'Put the plates in the sink when you've finished and cover them with the dish towel,' she said. 'I'll attend to them in the morning. *Ningadakwa kakhulu, tu, ngiyanicela*, please don't drink too much.'

With that she took off. I escorted her to the bedroom. She began to change into her nightie while I sat on the bed, the leather jacket on my lap. Finally she got into bed. I remained seated and chatted to her until summoned to the sitting room, depositing the jacket at the foot of the bed as I walked off.

'Put it in the wardrobe, will you?'

'I'll do that when I come back, darling. Don't worry.' I blew her a kiss.

I didn't go back to the bedroom until much later.

We drank ourselves to a near-stupor with Mazibuko, so that when he left he nearly forgot to take the jacket with him.

He later told me that when he got home he immediately woke up his wife and presented her with the jacket. He didn't forget to tell her that my wife had a similar jacket. She forgave him all his drunkenness and even overlooked the fact that he'd left her alone for the greater part of the night.

The real drama came in the morning when Meisie came to compare coats.

She'd woken up before me. I was about to wake up too, with a king-size hangover, when she walked into the bedroom. I pretended to be

33

fast asleep and even snored for effect.

She ransacked the wardrobe for a while.

Then I heard her say to herself: '*Ngabe uyibebe kuphi?*'

The next thing she was shaking me up, not so gently, to ask where I'd put her leather jacket.

I pointed to the lower part of the bed.

'But I asked you to hang it in the wardrobe,' she said with a tear-choked voice.

That jerked me up.

We began searching the house. Meisie joined us. I was so bent upon making the search look authentic that I momentarily forgot my throbbing head. We delved into every corner of the house. For a whole hour we searched diligently. I'd even begun pulling out empty bottles of beer from their case, just to make absolutely certain, when she called off the search.

I went to sit on the stoep, a bottle of beer in my hand, and listened to their conversation in the house.

The words were never far from my own mouth, but I wanted her to start condemning them herself. That way she'd come to believe in the truth of her own fancies. Never feed ideas to a wife who can arrive at the same conclusions by independent means. Ideas, even if they may be circulating in her mind, become suspect once you mention them first. I didn't want her to think I was trying to find a scapegoat. So I was greatly relieved when I heard her accuse them herself.

'I'll tell you whom I suspect,' she said to Meisie. '*Di-skeberesh tsa maobane,* they must have stolen it. You've no idea how envious those girls sounded last night. One actually said she wished it was hers. They won't get away with it, they'll certainly hear from my lawyers.'

'Shame!' Meisie said.

'And do you know how much it cost?' she asked.

'R175. That's what the price tag read on mine.'

(I wonder from what article in which shop Mazibuko ripped off that tag. I should go and ask him.)

'Listen to that. And to think that once I never even believed him when he told me he'd deposited it. Poor *skepsel!*'

I crept back to the fridge, pinched two more beers, and hopped across the fence to Mazibuko. Wonderful chap!

James Matthews/AZIKWELWA

He did not have to walk. He looked over his shoulder at the hundreds coming along behind him, all walking, and in front of him hundreds more, walking. It was the fifth day of their long walk to Johannesburg and it was his first. He was one of the few Coloureds who walked along with the mass of Africans. They were old and young, big and small, foot-firm and limping; mothers and sons, fathers and daughters, grandparents and schoolchildren; some dressed in neat clothes, with horn-rimmed glasses and attaché cases, and many more in torn overalls and shoes with soles paper-thin, feeling each stone they trod on. They were all walking the long walk to Johannesburg.

Nights before the boycott was due, the location's fast-beating heart increased its pace. Wherever a man raised his voice, a group formed around him, and as the hours passed, there were many such groups, until the location throbbed as one great meeting place. There were the wild ones whose eyes saw only violence, and their cry was, 'Burn the buses!' Then there were those few who whispered, 'Accept the terms.' But there were also the many who defiantly said, 'Azikwelwa! We will not ride!'

When they started their walk the sky was still dark over the pulsating stars. He watched them from the inside of his room, and after a time went back to the warmth of his blankets. Later he had a bus to himself on the ride to the station. There were angry voices when he boarded the bus, but those who shouted loudest were restrained by others with rosettes pinned to their breasts. Then, when the bus passed the long firm line of walkers, he heard their cry again. His return from work found them homeward bound, a song travelling their length. A stone hit the side of the bus and he peered through the rear window. Four men were shaking a youth by the shoulders, and then they all disappeared from view as the bus turned a bend in the road.

As if by a prearranged plan, the location's streets swarmed with people who embraced each other and sang at the tops of their voices. In the backyards of the shebeen queens, skokiaan flowed freely for those who had the money to pay for it. And even those who came with empty pockets were given something for their throats. As they faced one another they cried, 'Azikwelwa! My brother.'

Four days he watched them walk the long walk and four nights he saw them dance and drink their tiredness away, and the spirit of their pride filled him. Their word was as good as that of the white man. They said they would walk the many miles before paying the extra penny the bus company demanded. There were many whites who scoffed at their determination, and there was their answer, in the line of empty buses. On the fifth morning, when the first wave of walkers had passed his door, he joined them. From side streets poured rushes of walkers, and the mass of people flowed through the gates of the location.

On his left walked an old man who used a stick to help him along, and in front of him waddled a fat woman with a bundle of washing balanced on her head. He looked around him. There were many such and some had babies strapped to their backs, heads jogging with the motion of their mother's hips.

It was still early, the first mile was not done, and they were in a holiday mood. Bicycles carried two passengers. The location's ancient cars, which always threatened to fall apart, were loaded to capacity and wheezed their way forward. One man, his boots tied around his neck, joked with his friend and said that it made for easier walking. All joined in the laughter. They were walking the long walk and they were proud.

The miles passed and the road was long and there was less laughter, but still they walked. The old, the sick, the weak dropped behind. The front of the column was wide, but behind it tapered off into a thin line of stragglers.

Then suddenly there were the police and the cars standing in rows and the people inside pulled out and forced to the side of the road. And the owners protested that the cars were not used as taxis, but they were still charged with over-loading. The harsh demands for passes, and the fear swelling as they waited for the vans to take them away. Then the next block of police waiting with outstretched hands and ready batons for those who had not the slips of paper which gave them the right to move. There were many who slipped down side streets to escape the police, for the police wanted them to ride and not walk, so that there should be no strength of will and so that they should be without a voice.

'Pass! Where is it?' he was asked. The owner of the voice was not bothering to look at him, and only when he made no reply, turned his eyes.

'I don't carry a pass,' he replied.

'Then what are you doing here?'

'I am walking!'

'Are you a Kaffir or are you a Communist?'

'I am walking!'

He walked past the policeman, who had already grasped another victim by the shirt front, demanding his pass.

A large car pulled to a halt in front of him, behind the wheel a young white woman. She opened the doors on each side and cried aloud, 'Come on. Women and old people.' No one moved. Then a woman with a child on her back and a suitcase in one hand shyly approached the car and got into the back. Others followed, but the old man shook his head, saying that he was not too old to finish the long walk. More cars stopped and their drivers were white and they took those who wanted to ride.

A car stopped and the driver asked the young policeman by whose orders he was stopping the car and demanding the removal of the passengers. He stood undecided and the car pulled away. He rushed to the nearest man and screamed, 'You Kaffirs think you're smart!'

Messages were relayed from those arrested to those free. Messages to tell a father a son was arrested, to assure an employer that an employee would come back to his job, to tell the children not to worry and to help each other.

And those who walked were still many and their hearts were heavy, but they walked, and soon the long walk was at an end, for below them was the city. On their entry into the city, the people of the city looked at them with disbelief, and their shoulders straightened and their heads lifted and they smiled. They had done the long walk one more day.

It was late when he entered the chemist shop where he worked as a delivery messenger.

'Jonathan. Why are you late?'

'I walked.'

'All the way?' The white man in the white coat looked at him with surprise.

'All the way.'

'But why? You're not one of them.'

He could not tell the white man of the feeling inside him, that when he was with them he knew it was good.

He joined them on the square at midday. They sat with mugs of coffee and still-hot fat cakes bought from the portable coffee stalls of the vendors. Some sat around draught boards, using bottle tops as counters, but most were clustered around those with newspapers. There were pictures on the front page showing the many walkers, and the reports stated that the boycott would soon be over and that the leaders of the boycott had come to an agreement. There were angry murmurs amongst them, and some said aloud that they did not believe it. One man said what they all had on their minds. 'Why is it that we were not approached? Are we not the people who walk? Does the bus company think because it has spoken to a few men, we, like sheep, will now meekly ride instead of walking?'

The last question was directed at one who wore the colours of the boycott organization on his breast at night in the location.

He was a short, wiry man and his eyes blinked behind the thick-lensed glasses he wore. He took them off, wiped the lenses nervously with his handkerchief, and replaced the glasses on the bridge of his wide, flat nose. He cleared his throat before speaking and then, in a surprisingly loud voice, said, 'Do not believe it, my brothers. It is not for our leaders to say we walk or ride before first asking the will of the people of the location. The men of the bus company must think our leaders are mere children to be so easily swayed by their words. Pay no heed to what is written in the newspapers because it is the word of the white man.'

His words reassured them, but there were the few, already tired of the long walk, who said it was a good thing. 'The white man has seen that the black man is also a man of his word.' Now they would ride.

Jonathan was filled with doubt. Always he was with those who suffered without protest. Always he was with those without voice. Always he was with those who had to bear the many pains. Always he was with those unwanted, and always they lost.

He had secretly thought that the boycott would only last the first day, then the people of the location with their tired limbs would once more ride the buses and their purpose would die. But when it entered the second day, the third day, and the day after that, his hopes mount-

ed, hoping that this would be the one time they would prove themselves men. It had become a symbol for him. As long as they walked,
his life would not be altogether meaningless. He would be able to say
with pride that he too was one of those who had walked the long walk,
when they proved to the bus company that they had a will of their own
and were not to be silenced into obedience by words.

During all his deliveries Jonathan was depressed, and when he read
the afternoon paper, his despair swamped him, and he felt cold in the
afternoon sun. He felt betrayed. The paper stated that an agreement
had been reached and that the following morning the buses would be
filled. The boycott would be over.

To forget, he busied himself with his work and was relieved when
he was given a stack of deliveries that would keep him occupied for the
rest of the afternoon.

Work done, he joined the lines of walkers ascending the first incline
out of the icy city. They were a silent lot, and when someone asked
whether it was indeed to be the last day of the long walk, he was
answered with shrugs of the shoulders and the shaking of heads in
bewilderment. The lines merged into one long column of heavy hearts
and dragging feet. There were no jokes, no laughter. Only doubts and
uncertainty, the ringing footsteps now turned into drumbeats of defeat.

The walk was long and the road without end. The cars stopped, and
the walkers looked without interest at those who climbed inside. With
apprehension they passed the first group of grinning policemen, and
when they were not stopped, their betrayal seemed complete.

A youth raised his voice and said loudly: 'Azikwelwa!' And he was
cursed by some around him. But he would not be denied and he
repeated it louder, his voice carrying farther: 'Azikwelwa! My brothers
and sisters!' Those who heard the youth's outburst turned their heads
and stared at him, and they buzzed with curiosity.

'Has news been heard? 'Do we do the long walk tomorrow?' 'What
has happened?' They shouted but there was no answer. Then a voice
cried, 'We will hear tonight in the location,' and it was taken up and
passed along the ranks. And the stride of the walkers increased, and
Jonathan's heart kept pace with their footsteps.

They passed further blocks of policemen, and there were no
stoppings, and there was not the demand for passes. And the cars
loaded with people passed unchallenged. And the miles slipped behind
as they hurried to the location.

His supper ended, Jonathan walked with the others to the football field where the boycott organization held its meetings, and pushed himself to the front. The field filled, and when he turned his head the back of the field was blocked out by the bodies of the many people.

A speaker mounted an upended crate, his hands held aloft. It was the same man who had spoken on the square during the afternoon. His voice roared.

'The bus company has taken it on itself, after speaking to those who could never speak for us, to have it printed in the papers of the white man that the boycott is ended! Is done with! That we have, like little children, agreed to their talks and will board the buses tomorrow. But they are wrong. This is our answer. Azikwelwa! Azikwelwa! . . .' The rest of the speech was lost in the clamour pouring from the open throats, and when other speakers tried to speak they met with the same result. The people of the location needed no further speeches, and the crowd spilled apart.

Again the backyards of the shebeen queens were flooded and skokiaan was to be had for the asking.

Jonathan sat on a bench with his mug of skokiaan untouched, a bemused smile on his face. Opposite, a drinker was slumped against the wall and his wife looked boldly at Jonathan. Looking at her, and with the people swarming around him, Jonathan felt a surge of love sweeping through his body and he raised his mug to the woman.

'Azikwelwa! My sister,' he said.

Moteane Melamu/BAD TIMES, SAD TIMES

They all know in Meyer Street that Georgina rules me with an iron hand. She's an enormous female, and she's only thirty, older than me by four years. I wonder what she'll look like by the time she turns forty! She wasn't this size when I got hitched to her, after a 'forced landing'. But, boy, after that first baby, who mercifully died in infancy (God bless her lovely soul), did Georgina swell up! She now resembles an overstuffed bag of lard. She's bursting at the seams, I tell you. And she's literally pushing me out of our one-room, all purpose arrangement, as if the damn huge old-fashioned steel bed she inherited from her late grandma was not already taking up too much space. As for that bed, me I don't want to talk about it. It's one-hundred percent Georgina's kingdom. My share in it is, you might say, almost nil. Have you ever spent the whole night trying to doge a woman of substance? That's my lot, brother — every blessed night. And when she snores, boy, the china in the joint rattles like there's an earthquake. This Georgina, *hayi!*

I am, by common Meyer Street consent, a hen-pecked husband. Goes to show you how a man's reputation can hit rock bottom in this place. Every Tom, Dick and Harry knows about me and my worldly predicament. Like the other day, my two home-boys, Cy and Biza are making my troubles the bus-stop gossip. They don't spot me standing in the queue some six passengers away. They are talking full-blast, real township style. No inhibitions, *my bla.*

'*Ou* Cy, *lewe is reely bad,*' says Biza. 'For a female to pass water on a guy like that Georgina is doing to *meester! Neh, man, is reely bad,* I'd never take it.'

'*Bra* Biza' Cy retorts, '*die Kofifi cherries is very bad coward* (meaning 'cruel'). I just can't figure out how *meester* ever got himself mixed up with an old rubberneck like that Georgina of his.'

He wipes the sweat from his prematurely balding dome and concludes,

'She's bewitched him, *'strues God. Die arme ou is hinty, ek vertel jou, Bra Biza.'*

Declaring my doom with awful certitude.

I say 'To hell, man' — to myself, of course — 'you can't insult me this way.' But I can't very well belch out all the stinking filth I feel rising inside me when my matrimonial tragedy is so publicly discussed. I just stand there and do fuck-all. My manhood shrivels up badly in the face of such trying situations. So I hide, as usual, in the uneasy security of anonymity there in the eternal bus queue, while Biza and Cy continue cold-bloodedly to lay bare my domestic inadequacies with much shaking of their heads.

I'd met Georgina at a stokvel at Ma-Mthombeni's hideout in Gibson Street. I was then what you might call, in the conventional parlance, an eligible young bachelor. I had just breezed through a B.A. at Fort Hare and was quite a hot thing on the market, brother. My looks were not exactly bad, and boy, did the cherries fall hard for me! I had the whole universe to choose from, but I went for Georgina! Don't ask me why, but I did. Well, I start this lightning affair with Georgina at Ma-Mthombeni's joint. My friends tell me Georgina is an old horse, but me, I tell them to go fry in hell. I fancy the female very bad, and that's all I care for. Only trouble is, she's baled out of school after Form III. The guys put me in the picture about this, but me I tell them it's just too bad, *want ek mnca die cherrie very bad*. As they say, love is mole-blind, so I ignore my friends. Georgina and me have a hell of a good time after this. Our affair is a real tornado, man, and the upshot of it is that Georgina finds herself with a big tummy and me with a wife I hadn't really budgeted for. *Ja, daais die lewe, my bla.*

But that's history. What of now? Georgina has turned out quite different from what she was. Having landed myself in this marriage soup, I sort of resign myself philosophically to what the gods have decreed. 'What I can do? God give . . .' As Abdul says. Me I see the logic of Abdul's argument. Only snag is that Georgina's temper gets worse and worse proportionately as she swells up physically, as if she blames the whole world for this. *Hayi,* she's got the strength of ten bulls, so I can't discipline her. And I should know about it, shouldn't I? After all,

I'm constantly on the receiving end, battered to a complete standstill, I tell you. *Heh,* this woman! She thinks I'm her punch-bag, you know. Every time I gainsay her ladyship, I kiss Mother Earth. *Hayikona,* this female is fierce. She's certainly not the woman I married. *Nix!* I've become the laughing stock of No.16. They call me the teacher who's beaten by his wife, even the children. This thing called marriage! Neh, man!

I tell my friends I'll put Georgina in her place one of these days. But they don't believe me. *Jy ken, die mense vat nie 'n man khandi toe.* They reckon I mean daring the vicious lump to a straight fight. No, siree. *Nie ek nie.* I've got my own methods, me, foolproof. A bit risky, perhaps, but so what! Anything to put this bloody female straight will do. Bra Biza laughs at me, the other day, when I bump into him at Ma-Mthombeni's — that's where I evaporate my sorrows these days. I reckon like this to Bra Biza:

'Bra B, *die Here hoor my,* one of these days I'm going to do a *coward* thing to this female.'

Bra Biza laughs. *Ja, majita, hy lag 'n man cruel uit.* What's wrong with Bra B? He guffaws until his entire anatomy shakes and his eyes swim in tears. When he has finished he says:

'*Jou kop vat nie reg nie, jou moegoe van 'n ticher. Ma-Mthombeni se sqo het jou lankal hinty gemaak.* B.A., B.A. *Sies!* Georgina will turn you and your wretched B.A. into mincemeat if you try any monkey tricks.'

It's useless trying to convince guys like Bra B. They always reckon I mean a face-to-face with Georgina when I say I'll put her in her place. Of course, Bra B. should know what he's talking about. Georgina gave him hell last year when he foolishly decided to take sides with me in one of my confrontations with the tigress. Me, I know what to do at such moments. I take no chances, *my bla.* I do mental arithmetic. I add one and one, and make for the door of the joint and keep mum. If things go bad, as they always do, I give myself the breeze. Yes, brother, I do the vanishing act. No shame. But Bra B. wouldn't listen to me, so Georgina panel-beat him.

Me, I know better. When I say I'll do something really *coward* to Georgina, I know what I'm talking about. I've got a secret weapon. Hope to God this Georgina woman doesn't get to know about it. She'd eat me up alive just like that. Now, let me tell you: Babsy's the secret weapon I'm talking about. Hey, don't breathe a word about it to Georgina. Yes, that same Babsy *wat vir die Jewish lawyer in Macosa*

House julyt. Me and Babsy have been undermining Georgina's interests since August. I've even put the brakes on boozing. This gets Georgina very bad suspicious. Man, this woman must have a twelfth sense or something. I tell her I've quit lifting the elbow on doctor's orders. You know what she says to me? *Hee! Lomfazi!* She says:

'Shit, Joe! You know that's a bloomin' lie.'

She spits it out venomously, while I maintain a quivering silence. She goes on with menace:

'You're lying like the dirty pig you are!'

Hm! Me, I reckon to myself: 'Never heard of a pig that could lie.' Anyway, Georgina tells me she knows I'm running after some filthy *hoermeid.* This woman's language, *hayi!* I shudder at her coarseness. Certainly needs caustic soda to wash her mouth. But the dreadful warning is given: If she ever discovers the slut I'm running around with, she'll show both of us the backside of a snake, as sure as she's Sibanyoni's daughter. Silently I protest that Babsy's no slut. I dare not speak up. Have you ever willingly dived into the jaws of a tiger? Well, why the blazes do you think I would? Me, I'm deadly careful. I zip my mouth shut. I don't say anything, *my bla,* lest it be used in evidence against me.

I'm sure things would have gone all right if it hadn't been for that fuckin' letter from Babsy through the School Box as usual. And boy, it's really hot stuff. I shove it in the inside pocket of my Barathea blazer when I've read it — for later consideration, I tell myself.

The time strikes 8 p.m. Georgina goes next door for a little chit-chat with Ous Tricy. I never can tell who does the listening when these two meet. *Hulle skinder, neh!* Bra Mike, Ous Tricy's husband, does 'country', and is away from home for a week. So it's 'coast clear' for the two women. Apart from this, Ous Tricy is in the nursing profession, you see, and Georgina has been seeing her 'professionally', you may say, lately. Me, I didn't know at first, but there were stories flying around. Then one day she told me that she's *thwa!* No, no, I'm not responsible. No, sir! Haven't touched the fat lump for years now. Not since that first time when I took the plunge. She wouldn't let me, anyway, even if I had the guts to try. And since Babsy materialised, I haven't thought of trying. She told me that Bra Rufus, the big one from Edith Street who drives the huge Buick taxi, has graciously usurped my conjugal responsibilities. Imagine it, dumping me for a taxi-driver! *Sies! Uya delela lomfazi!* But me, I don't give a damn. If Rufus is too bloody daft to see that he's playing with fire why should I bother? *Ek het nie tyd vir moegoes nie.* Anyway the other day Georgina catches me scrutinising her belly, barks at me savagely:

'*Hei, wena! Jou nonsense!* What are you staring at me for?'

I shut up, *my bla.* I'd been caught in the very act. She goes on, this woman. She gives me straight-talk. She says:

'*Ek ken jou chommies zikutshela i-rubbish ngam. Laat ek jou something for nothing vertel.* You are not a man.'

She eyes me as though I'm fit for the rubbish-heap and continues:

'You'll never touch me again, you, never. *Nie ek ou Sibanyoni se kind nie. En as jy wil weet, ngi-thwa mina.* And it's Rufus's child I carry in this belly. Now what do you want to do about it?'

And she slaps her disgustingly fat stomach as she says this. *Sies! Akana nhloni!* I blush on her behalf. But that's how she is, this Georgina. Straight talk and no *lapha-lapha,* as she says.

Hey, I'm digressing. I'm telling you about Babsy's letter. Georgina is next door — this gives me a chance to reply. *Hayi, maar die cherrie skryf really hot stuff, my bla.* I have read the letter five times at school today. No teaching. *Nix.* Silent reading, I tell the kids. So I read and re-read Babsy's letter. Now I have time to reply. I've been at it for about half-an-hour, when the call of nature arrives unexpectedly. I bale out double-quick from the joint and make for the communal loo nearly twenty paces away. Dash it all, someone else has beaten me to it and is loudly performing the major operation. I've no choice but to irrigate the outside of the loo, while the landlord's mongrel, Spotty, playfully tugs at my trouser-pipe. *Ag, man, voetsek!* And the poor wretch decamps quietly with his tail between his hind legs. I finish my wet business in peace.

I get back to the joint to find the door wide open. I put on the brakes, and instead of engaging the reverse gear, I stand transfixed. Georgina, her broad hippo rear to the door, is perusing the unfinished letter. My knees quake, I tell you. *Ek is gemang.* I know, sure case, I'm in a mess. She doesn't spot me doing the mid-winter thing by the door, silently supplicating good Mother Earth to yawn open and hide me from the devils I know are building up in Georgina's huge breast.

Suddenly she turns round and discovers me at the door, my knees still playing the concertina. A quick fart escapes me. I press my buttocks tight to stop a logical successor, but it's useless. Out it comes. This always happens to me every time I have to face this terrible female. She grins at me and talks like this:

45

'Where've you been, wise guy?'

She speaks to me like this when she really means to be nasty. *Ag,* I say to myself, *wise guy jouself, man, wat dink jy?* To her,

'I've been to the small house.'

'Well, why the hell didn't you finish shitting there instead of coming to pollute my house with your stink?'

Oho! I say to myself. Your house indeed. *Dié dladla is myne,* my sister. *Ek slaan die 'skhwama vir die rent.* Just then, I take a desperate chance. I dash in, grab the letter from the table and am back at the door with lightning speed. Hey, adrenalin can do wonders I tell you! The elephant is too bloody slow to catch me.

But Georgina takes her time. Hell man, the bloody female knows she's got me staked and she's deadly calm. If she would only dive into one of her rotten fits and beat the devil out of me, at least she'd save me this fuckin' agony. My thoughts are suddenly interrupted:

'Ek sê, clever, who have you been writing to?'

The instinctive reply is a rapid machine-gun fart interrupted only by Georgina's screaming:

'And stop *daai morsig, jou vark,* before I crack your stupid skull!'

The smelly explosion stops at once. *Heh,* these things! At that time, Ous Tricy, attracted by Georgina's howling, pops an enquiring head from her door:

'Hei, bathong, what's going on now? Georgina, *go diragalang, motho wa Modimo?'*

'Tricy, *mntakwethu,'* answers the buffalo, 'just leave me to deal with this thing. You go back to bed, my dear. *Unga zihluphi. Hy sal die waarheid praat vandag.* Just let me deal with him.'

Ous Tricy, who has got used to our connubial battles, obliges with a resigned:

'Ngwana wa ga Paulus, ya go ithobalela o tswe mo di-nonsensing.' As she withdraws thus from the battle-front, I silently wish Ous Tricy would stay on and save me from the explosion I know is coming. But she rescues herself and leaves me to handle the situation single-handed. *Hell, 'n man is bad luck.* Georgina continues relentlessly:

'En nou, manocha, answer me. Who are you writing to?'

Her eyes flash fire and brimstone, and I know I'm trapped. *Jislaaik,* the woman of the house means business, I tell you. Her cool behaviour amazes me no end. It makes my thinking-apparatus jam stock-still. I dare:

'I'm preparing my lessons.'

46

A puerile, amateurish lie! I could kick myself for it. Where have you ever seen a lesson beginning with 'Sweetie Pie'? Even a kid of yesterday can see I'm a damn miserable liar. Georgina throws me a cold, devilish look that makes my hair stand on end. Then finally she demands:

'Let me read what you were writing before you went to shit.'

Come off it, I wasn't shitting, I say to myself. But why the blazes I had to leave the damn letter on the table when I knew it was highly explosive, I don't know. *Ag,* blast it, she's read the bloody incriminating thing, hasn't she? Now why torture me this way? Rubbing it in I suppose. *Ja! Die brou is very bad coward,* I tell you. I'm sure in shit-street today. I summon what little guts I still have. Remember, I'm still at the door, and I can make a quick exit in the event of an emergency. Meanwhile, I have to answer that crucial question.

'Suka, jy's nie my inspector nie.'

This is sterile cheek and doesn't impress her one little bit. *Sy's very bad cool, my bla.* If ever I knew I was losing a fight, it's today. Do I take the plunge and make a clean breast of it? *Hayikona! Nix!* That would be yielding hands down. No, I'll go down fighting. But Georgina's cold stare unnerves me badly. I shuffle about uneasily at the door where I remain for strategic reasons, looking bloody silly like a naughty school boy.

'Hei, wena clever, I want to see your lessons,' she insists cruelly, with a crushing emphasis on 'lessons'.

Ja, majita, I know I've got to relent. I try to remember whether I've said anything damaging in the letter so far. I crassly decide there isn't anything so explosive yet. I haven't got to the most crucial part of the letter. So, let her read the damn thing to her heart's content. But, *hayi, hayi!* Wait a minute! There's that bit about meeting 'same time, same spot' next Saturday. Boy, that's damning evidence, if ever there was any. Now why the hell did I have to mention that? Then there's that bit about 'a comfy hideout.' Hell, man, I'm in real trouble. Suddenly from Georgina:

'Hei, wena, what are you up to? I'm waiting!'

Majita, when she screams like that and calls me 'Hei wena,' it means the woman of the house is *real* cross.

Damn it all, I decide, I'm caught red-handed and it's *finish en klaar.* I can't do anything about it. So let me see it through. I move cautiously back into the house, in case all this is a trap. I dutifully hand over the letter to her gracious majesty, while my hand keeps doing the winter thing. Meanwhile, Georgina is cool as she reads the letter. I wonder how much of it she understands. But I know this is small comfort to me.

Suddenly she throws the unfinished letter on the table and orders me to finish it. *Ja, my bla,* she commands my shaking self to finish the letter. Hmm! *Uya ganga lomfazi!* How the blazes do I finish a letter when I can't even keep my hands steady? The dread command is sternly repeated. What do I do? I bale out of the joint like a bullet, *my bla.* Yes, I flee like nobody's business and position myself as far from danger as possible. Georgina plants her enormous self at the door and throws her next question with undisguised hate:

'Is this Babsy the slut you've been whoring with?'

Do I answer yes or no? *Hayikona, die wereld is vir 'n man upside-down.* This thing called fear! It emasculates a man and turns him into a eunuch. Especially when you're faced with stinking farts and you dare not answer yes or no to a bitch like Georgina. To say 'no' would be suicidal; to say 'yes' would be equally suicidal. So, what does a man do? Surely, I'm not going to spend the whole bloody night outside the joint facing my big terror! Should I perhaps . . . ? *Hayikona,* the mind boggles. Then rudely my thoughts that are no thoughts at all are interrupted:

'Hey, *wena* wise guy, let me see Babsy's letter,' she demands in a no-more-nonsense voice.

Man, why the hell did I have to keep the damn letter on me? I stall over Babsy's letter. After all, it's *my* letter and she has no blooming right to demand it, but I soon remember that as far as I'm concerned, Georgina's rights are boundless. So I cool down. I want to tell her that it's innocuous and all that shit, but I know she won't believe me until she's actually seen the letter. Instead, I tell her it's at school, and she counters by telling me to stop trying to bullshit her. *Neh, majita, 'n ou is reely-reely in shit-street.* Before I know what is happening, she's got me by the scruff and is lifting me back into the joint like a dirty rag. She deposits me not too gently on a rickety chair. A resounding back-hand almost decapitates me. That's merely to establish a point or two about who's boss. I know this is only preliminary — the shape of things to come if I persist in my stubbornness. Well, *majita,* a man should know when he's beaten. I mean, you can't accuse me of not having tried, but there's a limit to how long one can resist Georgina. So, there's nothing for it but to unload my sins to her. I deliver the goods, *my bla,* and remain glued to the chair, awaiting her ladyship's pleasure.

A generation passes before she completes her laborious plodding through that damnatory missive, and boy, as she eyes me, her eyes are like flaming balls. Another fart comes unbidden and this time I do not even pretend to stop it. It goes on uninterrupted and she glares at me.

'*Hei* rubbish, stop shitting!'

Immediate silence from below; I sit there looking positively martyred. I feel very sorry for myself. Suddenly, from her ladyship:

'*Jou vark, hoe lank jol jy met die bitch?*'

I'm about to protest that Babsy's no bitch, but think better of it. You don't just let yourself into bigger trouble by defending a co-conspirator, do you? No sir. I'm foolish, but not to that extent. So I stay mum, and wait for the worst. She repeats the question with obvious irritation at what seems to her my deliberate defiance, and I try to lie:

'I haven't done anything with . . .'

I don't complete the fib, brother. Thunder lands on my jaw and I kiss the floor and see the milky way. In a semi-daze I hear the question repeated, and there's nothing for it but to own up. A man should know when he's beaten, shouldn't he? So the truth must out:

'Since last August.'

I wait for thunder and lightning to strike once more, but instead I'm brusquely ordered by her ladyship to get up. I lift myself onto the chair. Hell, man, is this some kind of inquisition? Me, I'll run away from this place, '*strues God,* then I'll see who her punch-bag will be. You see, this is a kind of sterile vengeance typical of kids. Perhaps that's what I've become: a child.

She leaves me seated on the rickety chair — to lick my wounds both physical and spiritual. My mind wanders again and I think of the day I met Babsy. Strange how in the middle of a crisis I think of the very cause of my troubles. But, there you are. I day-dream about that beautiful night, and become oblivious of all dangers, past or present.

It all started on the night of Bra Sparks's wedding reception at the Communal Hall in Western. I had to charter a whole taxi to convey my pile to Western because if we'd tried walking, she'd soon have been puffing like an old steam-engine half-way to Western. *My bla,* she's dressed to kill my Georgie girl, *my ma hoor my.* She looks like an over-inflated balloon, her superfluous lard worming its way in her shiny, tight-fitting silken evening dress — a present from Bra Rufus, for services rendered, I suppose. Somehow, I'm glad we're not walking. It would have been bloody awful. Imagine all those eyes staring at me walking my load to Western. So, I'd rather spend five bob on a taxi to avoid the bad publicity. By the time we arrive at the Communal Hall, everybody is settled. Brother, when we get to the door, I take one peep and my courage fails. I put the brakes on and decide I'm not entering the Hall in Georgina's company. *Nix.* I don't want to be laughed at. I tell her I have to answer the call of nature. She walks imperially into the Hall and I can hear peals of derisive laughter. I take a walk to the gate and hang around there for some time — mind you, not too long to start Georgina up on the suspicious trail. I walk back and slip into the Hall. Fortunately, for me, the Harlem Swingsters have just struck up a lively jive number and the floor is teeming with gyrating humanity. Dubaduba, the flatpadded jive champion of Sophiatown, is giving a big demonstration of his agility.

Manne, luck is on my side today, *die here hoor my.* There's Georgina, ensconced in a corner and engrossed in earnest conversation with her man, Rufus. I know when she's organised that way she doesn't want a third party, especially me. So I make myself very scarce from her, and seek a far corner of the hall to hide my shame. Me, I don't interfere with Georgina when she's fixed with Rufus. *Ek is nie 'n bangie nie, maar ek hou timing, my bla.* That drunken fool, Boy-Boy from Edith Street, comes to me in my one-man corner and reckons he's doing me a hell of a big favour telling me Rufus is fiddling with my property, as he puts it. I tell him to lay off those two, because it's definitely ground where the angels fear to stroll. *Die moegoe vat my nie kop toe nie.* He ignores my brotherly advice. He goes and pokes his foolish nose into a bees' nest. Brother, Georgina's wrath lands flush on his jaw and he soils his white tuxedo on the floor as he takes the forced plunge. *Ek het hom mos gesê.* He walks away from the Rufus-Georgina company limited a sadder but wiser man.

I say it's Sparks's hitch reception. But you see, as it turns out, for me that's not the main attraction. I'm not talking about Rufus and Georgina, either. The devil takes care of those two. I'm telling you about me and Babsy, the acquisition from near Odin Bio in Good Street. Brother, she's a rare specimen, I tell you. She's seated a few chairs away from me — one out, *my bla,* wall-flowering the show the way I'm doing. *Ek hou timing.* At that same moment, I notice Rufus and Georgina decamping, and I reckon I'm free to explore new territory. I flash my teeth in a hello-beautiful way, and the kid throws back a snow-white, compliments-returned smile at me. I move up to where she's sitting and ask her for a dance. Boy, she obliges. No conditions laid down. She simply sails into my arms and the Harlem boys waltz us away magically. Brother, suddenly life is nice; yes, life is nice outside the Georgina-dominated world. I feel great. In the middle of the waltz my hand slips accidentally down her buttocks. I jerk it up quickly. She giggles. I reckon she likes it, so I let the accident happen once more, with the same gratifying results.

From then on, I'm glued to her like bubble gum. I guard her jealously. Rufus and Georgina can dabble in their sweaty filth wherever they've gone for all I care. I'm free, brother. And Babsy is real great sport. I soon find out she's situations-vacant. I apply and am duly appointed. *Ons jol same time very bad.*

What more should I say? I've spilled all the beans, hot from the can. Me and Babsy go steady, and we undermine Georgina's authority.

The Christmas school break comes. Georgina is away in Ermelo. Cy explains her visit this way: She's run out of her *muti* stock and has gone home to replenish. Well, I don't know how Cy comes by that bit of know-how. But he's positive, brother. Me, I just keep mum. *Ek is fuck-all ge-worry.* This is just fairy-tale stuff Cy dishes out. In any case, I don't see that I matter so much for Georgina to take the trouble of going to a *nyanga* on my account. If she goes to bone-throwers, that's her own *indaba.* Anyway, she's gone. I wish she'd go for keeps. Me, I don't give a damn.

Hey, I can never forget the day we decide to take a fling at Magaliesburg. It's 'Sheila's Day' and Babsy gets a special dispensation from her lawyer boss to share the privilege of a day off with the Jo'burg domestics. It's not easy, of course, to ask Goldberg simply to let her off for the day. What do we do? Boy, *ons hou timing.* We 'kill' Babsy's 'brother' in Rustenburg. In fact, Babsy is an only child and comes from East London. But you can bluff these white people with the greatest ease in the world, if you know what to say. So, as I say, we 'kill' the unfortunate fictitious brother and arrange for his 'burial' on Thursday. Lawyer Goldberg proves very gullible indeed. Not only does he let Babsy off but he also gives her a nice crisp fiver to help cover the 'funeral' expenses. I nearly laugh, but Babsy steps on my toes . So I put on my best Sunday manners to suit the 'solemn' occasion.

The long and the short of it is that on Wednesday evening we arrange with Mthembu, who owns a '48 Chev, to convey us to Magalies. We decide to be a foursome. Mthembu brings his girl Mavis along. We pay Mthembu six pounds in advance. Goldberg's fiver comes in handy, it turns out. The girls get the provisions ready for early next morning. Brother, I don't get half a wink, so great is my excitement.

Thursday 5.30 a.m. I'm up and about. Hey brother, don't tell

Georgina, but Babsy had to move into the cabin for the night. I only hope the landlord's hunchback daughter doesn't wag her tongue when Georgina comes back. She's the only one who saw Babsy. Man, that would be like igniting a powderkeg. If she talks, I'm done for. I keep my fingers crossed.

7.30, Mthembu's horn blows outside and we take our seats. The morning is cool. There had been a threat of rain the previous night, but now the sky is clear, except for a speck of cloud here and there. Mthembu's car isn't the most comfortable machine in the world. I'm pressing down a jutting coil-spring that insists on pinching my buttocks. The back-seat keeps sliding forward every time Mthembu applies the brakes. I pity the two girls at the back. *Sies!* Imagine paying six pounds for the agony of riding in this bloody crock. I tell Mthembu my mind. He laughs and tells me to buy my own car if I want to travel like the King of England. The bastard. Of course I'll buy a car, but never this fuckin' old rubbish he calls a car. He keeps laughing and makes me feel an ass. The girls join him.

Then suddenly it happens. Just outside Maraisburg, one of the tyres goes flat. Mthembu and me work hard to change the thing. The spare tyre is as smooth as a baby's arse. How the hell he slips through the traffic police net, this Mthembu guy, is a miracle, but he does. We change the wheel and are off again. We stop at a nearby service station to have the flat tyre mended. Dammit, the tube is full of patches. It's positively rotten. These taximen! *Hayi.* Originally black, the tube is now full of red patches where it's been mended. However, the garage boys manage somehow to mend it and we're soon on our way again. It's now 9 a.m. The old crock doesn't seem to be able to do more than 40 m.p.h. Man, we crawl on and get to Krugersdorp at 10.30. We have to stop at a garage because the girls want to relieve themselves. Brother, believe me, as soon as we stop, *psst* goes the very spare we'd fitted in Maraisburg.

We're out again to change the damn wheel. We have the spare patched. By the time we're through, it's 11.30. Well, the best part of the day has been wasted on Mthembu's crazy car. Anyway, we're now heading for Magaliesburg at last. I think of all the fun lying ahead, when suddenly Mthembu exclaims:

'Ye-e-e-ses!'

And the old chariot comes to a jolting halt. It's smoking from the bonnet like twenty devils out of hell. The thing's boiling mad. We open the bonnet. Guess what? The fuckin' fanbelt's gone and got snapped.

Boy, what a mix-up. And the girls are not wearing stockings. And this, in the middle of nowhere. *Neh, my bla, goede is bad.*

Magaliesburg is still some twelve miles off. Well, a decision is made. Mthembu and me are to trudge those twelve miles to get a new fanbelt, while the two girls watch the crock — as if any self-respecting thief would want to steal that rubbish! Me, I say *Nix!* I've forked out six pounds (it does not matter if five came from Goldberg), and all that's happened is that I've been forced to mess around with Mthembu's fuckin' rotten tin-can the whole morning. I say I'd sooner eat my elbow than walk to Magalies. Never! What happens? Mthembu and Mavis make it a two-some sentimental walk to buy a fanbelt, and Babsy and me keep silent vigil over this bloody apology for a car.

Man, do we wait? It's 2.30 p.m. when they return, completely fagged. All the enthusiasm for the picnic dissipates. The fanbelt is replaced, we eat a sad lunch and drive back to Sophiatown very disappointed. I'm sure it's that malicious Georgina woman. She's always holding me by the heart. The day I . . .

Georgina's voice jolts me back to the 20th Century. In fact, it's more the hell she unleashes on me that does the trick. *My bla,* I feel I'm being attacked by a hundred bulls.

Bathong, that unfinished letter put me in real shit-street, I tell you. I decide I'm going to quit this joint once and for all before this woman murders me. *'Strues God,* she'll know me this time. She'll know that I'm no fuckin' fat woman's plaything, me. I'm going to vanish just like that, and she won't know who to toss around. I know you don't believe me, *maar ek vertel jou, my bla,* this time it's real. You'll see . . .

Kaizer Ngwenya/DREAMS WITHER SLOWLY

Benny Mosolodi was one of those enigmas that occur in any music circle — a musician who had agonised for twenty years or more to perfect his technique, and who had in the past two years suddenly become a highly popular tenor saxophonist.

He had sold more through his efforts in those two years since he had known David Goldstein, who shrewdly produced and engineered his records, than he had done in the past two decades. Goldstein, who knew everything about the business but nothing about a musician's inner feelings, could not understand Benny's increasing reluctance to churn out endless albums and seven singles.

The problem lay in the fact that there was a great musical gulf between Benny and Goldstein. The latter wanted Benny, who played and sounded like Coleman Hawkins, to change his sound and play the funky, *mbaqanga* stuff that was often heard blaring from stereos in the townships.

But the musician was aiming more at an audacious bop approach than at commercial stuff. He wanted to be as jazzy as Charlie Parker. He also knew that David Goldstein's Midas touch was guiding him to fame and riches. But he was tired of recording rubbish — fool's gold.

His dissatisfaction was heightened by the feeling that, although not so old (he was 42), he had only another year or so in which to deliver the unique sound which lay boiling like lava inside him.

He did not want to be like other black musicians who disappeared into oblivion because they did not play to expose what was inside them but to get rich quick. He felt that any musician who deviated from the established black music formula was not likely to fire enthusiasm in the youngsters who rehearsed in the backyards of the townships.

Music was part of Benny's life and he knew that his marriage might not have foundered had he not taken music so seriously all those years.

His responsibilities might not have been so heavy if he had decided on some other profession that would have had him earning far better money. But there was no going back, no variation he could play on time past and things done.

Sometimes Benny would stop playing during rehearsals when he remembered how his ex-wife shouted at him when he came back from a concert with chicken feed in his pocket. He would also remember how Montso, his daughter, shook her head contemptuously and passed silly remarks whenever one of his records was playing on the radio.

And there was his son Raymond who was a laggard at home and at school but a tough guy in the township streets. It was he who always assaulted him when he was quarrelling with his wife. Tears fell down his cheeks after every retrospection. The worst part of it was that his garrulous wife and incorrigible children deserted him because of his love of music.

These ugly experiences accumulated and coalesced to form a dreadful incubus. They haunted him and he could not dismiss them from his mind. He became hostile to everybody who challenged his ideas or criticised his revolutionary spirit in music. Goldstein and the musicians in the band kept out of his way when he was blowing or composing.

Things fell apart one day in the studio during a recording session. According to the score, Benny and the drummer were supposed to answer submissively the joint demands of the bassist and pianist.

The musicians were playing superlatively and the recording producer and engineers were busy balancing the sound. Suddenly, Benny started to blow powerfully and fingered the keys of the sax deftly. Everybody in the studio was perplexed since the musicians had stopped playing and looked at one another with popping eyes. The engineers swore indistinctly at Benny.

Everything was ruined!

'You fool!' David Goldstein shrieked and rushed at Benny like an enraged bull. 'You've ruined everything and we must start from square one.'

Benny smiled. But there was nothing like a smile in his eyes.

'What's wrong with you, Benny?' Goldstein asked, shaking with anger.

'I want to play the way I feel,' Benny said bluntly.

'But you're playing perfectly,' Goldstein said, near tears.

'I'm not beholden to you!' Benny told him acidly. 'You're making more from my music than I am!'

'Look here Benny, since you met me you've become the best-known musician in South Africa,' Goldstein pointed out wildly.

'I'm damned if I'll go on sacrificing my talent to this inferior type of music!' Benny yelled, his baritone voice booming in the studio. 'I've already lost so much for so little.'

'If you don't want to do as you are told,' Goldstein said and pointed at the door, 'get out and stay out.'

Benny looked at Goldstein and spat on the floor.

'There is no man living who can tell me what I can do and what I can't do,' Benny said, jabbing an emphasizing finger in the air.

'If you can't take orders,' Goldstein said irately, 'get out before I punch you in the face!'

Benny put his saxophone in its case and walked to the door slowly like a man who was lost in the concrete jungle.

It was four days since Benny had walked out of the studio when Goldstein went to Pimville to look for him. He wanted to tell Benny how sorry he was and that he would be happy if they buried the hatchet. After knocking on the door and getting no response he pushed open the door of the backyard shack and stepped in.

Goldstein nearly vomited when he saw the appalling conditions under which Benny was living. The place looked as if it had been hit by a cyclone — there were dilapidated paperbacks, newspapers, three ash-trays overflowing with cigarette butts and empty bottles of fortified wine on the floor. In the middle of the shack stood a sink full of unwashed dishes and a swarm of flies enjoying themselves.

But it was the putrid smell that hung in the shack that increased Goldstein's nausea.

'Benny,' Goldstein said softly. 'It's me. I've come to apologise. We need you at the studio. Benny, do you hear me? I'm sorry Benny.'

Benny lay on his back in the tiny iron bed. His eyes were staring at the roof and his mouth was open in an animal-like sneering grin. On the rickety bedside table stood an empty bottle of vodka, a crumpled pack of Venus, an ash-tray full of butts and an empty bottle of sleeping tablets.

The tearful Goldstein found a note on the floor and he recognised

Benny's scrawled handwriting. Choking back tears he read the note:

'I tried to offer to the people my music and happiness. But everybody scorned and ridiculed me. Now I have taken a one-way ticket to the unknown world. Maybe there I will be permitted to play the way I feel.'

Bereng Setuke/DUMANI

It is any time during the day on any day of the week. The 'non-white' concourse of Johannesburg Station ('Parkie' to the people of Soweto) is trampled to the edges by people of the ghettoes waiting impatiently for the uncertain arrival of the much-resented Soweto-bound train.

These people are watching the whites on the 'whites-only' concourse as they step with enormous dignity into their trains which arrive and depart so regularly according to schedule; very unlike the 'non-white' train, which comes and goes only when the white trains have had their way.

The same expression is on all their faces. They do not know whether the train is going to come today or not, and if it arrives they are not sure whether they will reach their destination in one piece travelling in this train, because survival is the lot of the fittest and even the fittest do not survive so often in a train infested by the notorious Soweto gangs and dominated by their 'might-is-right' rule.

More people are pouring into the station through the barriers which are attended by a number of black-uniformed Africans, demanding tickets from all and sundry, though not from certain commuters who just walk through the barriers with their hands deep down in their pockets.

These are the amateur gangsters who pay their way to and from the ghetto by bribing the barrier-attendants with a nip or 'ha-ja' of mahog as they pick the pockets of innocent passengers throughout the day in each and every train on the railway-line. They are followed by the 'big-shots' who pay their 'fare' with a fixed stare at the frightened barrier-attendant, who knows what to anticipate if he does not compromise:

he can be waited for after his shift, when there will be no 'arrest' to come to his rescue.

As soon as they are in the station they scatter, each one aligning himself so as to be abreast of a coach when the long-awaited train arrives. Some of them will be marking their would-be victims by 'following their noses', that is, standing next to the person that they suspect is loaded with money and never losing sight of him or her until the arrival of the train. It is a very easy game for these surgeons of the pocket to perform their diagnosis, their eyes slily measuring the prey, scanning the face, able to calculate from each reaction a precise estimate. They find the game much easier with the weaker sex. One simple way of picking a victim is by checking passengers with parcels in their hands. They could be the ones who have pay-packets today.

Now and again there will be a small boy walking up and down the platform, selling apples after school to augment the budget for his schooling requirements. His stock is usually peanuts or sweets. These gangsters will just help themselves and not pay the poor boy. It is already a way of life to him.

Comes the train at long, long last. Those who have, time and again, been craning their necks curiously to see if the train is coming are sighing with relief and preparing themselves for the 'hotrod' scramble for seats in the third-class coaches.

It goes without saying that the first people to board the train will be the 'staffriders', as they have come to be known all over the country. These guys jump into the train while it is still in motion to secure themselves a place before anybody else ever sets his foot on the train. Their object is to be stationed, according to their bosses' instructions, in a place where they will be able to perform their tricky-finger game on distracted passengers during the strenuous battle for seats.

Meanwhile another group of hooligans is 'booking' seats for the 'big-shots' and their mistresses. Booking is done by throwing any object on the seat, such as a jacket, jersey, shoe, belt, hat or a parcel of dry-cleaning; the people of Soweto know what to expect if they ever remove any of these items from unoccupied seats. The person seated next to a 'reserved' place does not feel too easy, anticipating the kind of character he is going to share a seat with on his journey home.

Walking down the 'non-white' stairs on the platform where trains leave for the ghettoes one sees a sea of black faces which then swirls into just one face as the stampede gets under way. Some battle for the door while others jump through the window, others again leap onto the linkages between the coaches. This is when some of the commuters fall on the platform and are stampeded by the raging crowd, while others are pushed under the platform. The screams are so wild that one cannot tell whether they express jubilation at the arrival of the train or pain as the mighty crush the weak in the 'hotrod' for seats. Some of the screams are laid on by the hooligans to add to the confusion while they are busy as bees 'pulling their job'. The noise is so deafening that it supersedes the voice of the official on the loud-hailers as he announces the destination of the train.

As the hailing and the wailing goes on the cunning hand of the pickpocket ('ma-liner' is the word in underground circles) will be doing its thing in the pockets and handbags of the unsuspecting passengers; the hooligans will be throwing their weight about, deliberately staggering in a false, drunken stupor to throw a victim off balance so as to get access to his pockets. These 'doorkeepers', as one may call them, are still newcomers to the world of gangsterism and as such, must prove their bravery to their bosses by picking the pockets of those who are boarding and alighting from the train at every station.

The hand of the pickpocket does not probe and pluck so expertly as to be unnoticed by most of the people in the commotion, but even though they are aware of what is going on in their pockets they will keep mum for fear of the worst should they try to object to this humiliation. The victim will stand stiff and straight until the thugs are through with him, whilst others will watch the episode frozen by the knowledge that their turn is either just past or still coming. The victims look one another in the face with dumb disgust. Sometimes one scans the face of the other as if to ask him, 'When will we unite and fight this crime?' and the other retorts with a stare that seems to say, 'You expect me to object — why didn't you?' whilst yet another seems to be saying, 'You reckon I'll risk my life for you, when I don't even know who you are? . . . Go and jump in the lake!'

Unlike the newcomers to the train, who jump into any coach with their eyes shut, there are the passengers who never involve themselves in this fruitless struggle because of past experience. They always check the coaches they board, and they avoid some coaches in particular. They know the positions of these coaches like they know their own palms. And they know that in one of these coaches they would encounter iniquity and corruption on a scale that would leave Sodom and Gomorrha dumb with shame. This is the dangerous 'Dumani'.

'Dumani', in the third-class section, is the first coach in the train, and the last when the train is travelling in the opposite direction. It is not the only coach which bears this nickname. There is another 'Dumani' in the middle of the train — fourth from the front and eighth from the end. These coaches are not to be confused with the first coach in the first-class section, which is occupied by the well-to-do middle-class passengers and is always guarded by a ticket-examiner, who can call on the assistance of the railway police in the event of unwarranted occupation by hooligans without first-class tickets.

'Dumani' derives its feared name from the sound it makes when the train is in motion, especially at high speed — *'ukuduma'* in Zulu, 'the buzzer'. It carries all the main power switches, and is furnished with a driver's seat and a fully-equipped dashboard. This is where the hooligans meet to 'learn' the husbandry of electrical technology. Teachers are the older members of the various train-gangs. They fiddle with anything they can put their dirty hands on, from the interior of the coach outwards.

The favoured 'lecture-room' is the 'Dumani' in the middle of the train. They always choose this coach because there will be no authoritarian intervention from the train-driver or the guard. They are free to do what they want to victimise the 'blind-deaf-and-dumb' passengers anytime, anywhere, just for sweet pleasure. These boys know the control of the light-switches from the coach-lights to the main beam-light of this coach — in case they want to do dirty work in the dark. Dirty work could mean anything from the picking of a pocket to the stripping of a 'customer' stark naked if he is wearing elegant clothing which is too good for him, or even a brutal rape in the toilet — but of that a little later.

They know how to 'lock' a moving train, so that no one can alight at his destination before they are through with his persecution.

They know how to sound the siren of the train when they are molesting the people and want to drown their frightened screams. Sometimes they undo the screws on the joints of the train, while the train is in motion, to scare the poor commuters.

Or they raise the shout that the train is burning so that they can pick the pockets of those who have been seated and therefore inaccessible to them.

Sometimes they start a false squabble in which knives are drawn and apparently wielded in blind terror, thus panicking the passengers who do not know that this hoax furthers the aims and activities of the pocket-bugs.

The train is now packed to capacity with the seated and the standing; the robbers and the robbed, the assailants and the victims; the jubilant and the disgusted; the confident and the confused; the residents and the non-residents — *abaQhashi* as they are dubbed by these high-handed mongrels.

It is only when all is calm that the experienced third-class commuters will bother to get into the train; always the last to board and alight.

Those of them who board Dumani will do so only because they already know everything that is practised in it, and have taken the necessary precautions — hiding their money deep in their shoes, or tying it securely in a handkerchief round their calves. Some women hide their money in their corsets — the old trick of the bra is now known and this 'bank' is easily accessible to the thugs. They get all the necessary information from their mistresses, who are always rewarded at the nearest shebeen after a catch is made.

It is also only at this time that the 'big-shots' start to walk in, after they have watched all the performances of subordinates executing their amateurish skills in the quest to qualify for 'apprenticeship' in the underworld. They drag their feet in cowboy-style, kicking at innocent passengers' legs as they stagger about, swollen with their own importance, on the way to their already 'booked' seats. At the entrance of these thugs, one is accosted by a terrible, intoxicating stench of dagga-smoke from their self-made 'zols'. They come in laughing so barbarically that even the ancient pagans would be ashamed.

The 'big-shots' then take their seats from the junior members in leisurely fashion, ready to settle for some cool cans of liquor which they have brought along from the bottle-store in the city, and which they slug with their mistresses while the juniors go out in different directions to join the others in the racket of the 'two fingers'.

Some old women — some of them widows in mourning garb — are standing on their feet in this very same coach, but instead of offering them a seat to rest on after a hard day's work, these young men would rather offer that seat to a selfish young girl standing right next to an old lady; selfish yes, because instead of thanking them for their 'kindness' and correctively offering that seat to the old lady, she reckons she should rather take it herself. Offering a seat to a prospective 'catch' is done by sitting with legs wide apart, waiting for fancied girls to be squeezed between you and your companion. Before long the 'good Samaritan' who has just offered a seat to a fit and healthy young lady in the presence of an ailing old widow will want to know the girl better, and she knows what to anticipate if she does not compromise with the proposition that she be added at the bottom of the list of 'dakotas'.

One of the boys spreads a newspaper on the floor of the coach for a game of cards to commence, while another is spread for a game of dice. The standing passengers are expected to cram themselves like a flock of sheep at one corner of the coach to allow them to play their game unhindered.

Nobody takes exception to this, as they well know the consequences of such an 'error'. The drinking and the games must never be disturbed. One must just stay put, even when one is pressed and compelled to answer a call of nature. In fact those who have a good knowledge of these trains will always tell one never to patronise any of the toilets in the third-class section of the train, as they are the ideal habitat of rapists.

An old man comes, unsteady and limping, in a hurry to jump in just before the train departs, but then realises that he does not know where this train is heading. So he approaches an open window to enquire from one of the *tsotsis*, as they are always the ones that are seated, but the answer he will get will be the usual one: 'You can see the direction in which the train is facing, but you still want to bother us with your old man's stupidity.' This, from the lips of the one he was not even addressing, whereupon they all laugh and another shouts, 'There is no fool like an old fool!' The final whistle blows for the train to depart, leaving the poor old man gasping on the platform.

There is one seat which is vacant in the coach, with a shoe on it which was put there during the 'booking' process. One unfortunate male passenger — probably a new-comer to the Soweto-train fraternity — removes the shoe and puts it on the floor to offer his lady this seat.

Suddenly a man emerges from the gambling 'school', pretending to be drunk, and asks this gentleman what under the sun he reckons he is to remove the shoe for his woman to sit there. The gentleman retorts that even at home shoes do not belong on chairs. An argument ensues and the man is manhandled by the mob, who push him out of the moving train. Fortunately the train's wheels screech to a protesting halt as it stops to wait for a signal. One shudders to imagine what would have happened to the man if the train had not been slowing. Or worse still, to the distressed lady who was under the protection of this gentleman, had she not reacted swiftly by following her man out immediately.

Passengers begin to filter through to the next coach in an unsuccessful bid to ward off trouble; unsuccessful in that the more one manoevres in these coaches, the worse one is exposed to pickpocketing. These boys block all the side doors on both sides of the coaches, as well as the doors into the linkages from one coach to the other.

The only people, other than the train-gang, who have free passage between one coach and the next, are the smouses, who, unlike the small boys who sell on the various stations under continual bullying, have a gang of their own and are a force to be reckoned with — they have been known to wage a fierce war against the train-gang. There have been wars, too, between one gang of smouses and another, and a newcomer who is a stranger to the fraternity must expect the worst. These smouses are indeed the most breath-taking 'staffriders' of them all.

When the old teakwood coaches were replaced by the new steel-blue variety known to Sowetonians as 'kitchen-schemes', the people thought it was time to heave a sigh of relief: because unlike the former, which had hinged doors, the latter type have sliding doors which are electrically controlled by the guard. They thought this would reduce the number of train deaths caused by 'staffriding', but to their shock, what they see nowadays is more horrible than even before. These boys stand in the doors of the train every day to hold the doors open for their friends as they flee from one train to another. Some, indeed most of the doors no longer function, and if a door takes too long to open, they know how to disconnect it permanently for their convenience.

A preacherman is singing a hymn to commence his daily chore of delivering the message of repentance from the Good Book, but he is silenced by another song from the train-gang, to the tune of a hymn but in such vulgar wording as would leave the devil himself swimming in a pond of shame. The poor preacherman then has no alternative but to change coaches so as to preach his gospel to people who will at least appreciate it. The train-commuters who join in the singing with the preacher do so, one may assume, to console themselves for the humiliation they are subjected to from these hooligans. But they too have to 'shut up' when the *mfundisi* is silenced and has to quit the coach.

The train has to stop at all stations as announced. There is a tug-of-war at every station: a part of the technique of these mobsters who usurp people's pockets. The gang is divided into groups which alight at each and every station, and change to another coach for a new 'catch'. The groups, alighting and boarding, cross ways with each other at the door of each and every coach. In this way, they are able to collect the 'contents' of any new boarder in such a way that the victim does not know whether the boarding or the alighting group has just deprived him of his money.

This is where one hears the popular rhetorics of *ngena-naye* and *phuma-naye*. The boarding group will always say *'ngena-naye'* (hijack), pushing with all their might to make sure that nobody gets off the train before they get what they want out of them. The sad thing is that the poor hijacked passengers are expected to pay a railway fine for alighting at a station further on than their destination, only to find that at the time they approach the barrier-attendants they have neither their tickets nor the money to pay the fine. So they must now pay a fine equivalent to the full fare of the journey — with the help of donations from sympathisers. The alighting group, meanwhile, answers with the *phuma-naye* (kidnap) song, pushing passengers off balance and out of the coach in a hurry so as to get to the next coach to complete their assignment. People forced off the train in this way find themselves marooned as they are not 'staffriders' and, unable to board again in a hurry, have to remain behind.

Passengers are often pushed out of the train by hooligans such as these while their parcels are on the parcel-racks inside the train, and they lose their luggage to the train-gangs. Those who forget parcels on the luggage-shelves never even bother to inform the station-commander, as they know very well that some of the gang remain behind when passengers alight to pick up the forgotten parcels and sell them in the shebeens.

There are passengers who never put their parcels on the shelves as the thugs grab them from there. Some passengers will never put parcels on the floor of the coach either, as these gangs have a way of dragging a parcel with their feet until it is brought to their accomplices near the doors, who will jump out of the train with their booty before it stops.

Passengers travelling for the first time in Soweto trains with very bulky parcels have lost them to *tsotsis* who pretend to be helping in the hoisting of a parcel to the door, urging the owner of the parcel to alight first so that they can hand the parcel over to him, only for him to find that they are going to hold on to it. They prevent him from boarding again during the *'ngenanaye-phumanaye'* tug-of-war until the train pulls away, leaving the poor passenger behind.

Then there is the question of ventilation. All windows are to stay open no matter what the weather may be. This is laid down as an absolute rule by these brutes so that they can jump in and out of any coach at any station if the doors are jammed with people. But those who know their tactics well will tell you that the most important reason for the open windows is to enable the staffriders to grab people's hats off their heads. Most of the ladies who travel by train have had their wigs, turbans, chiffons and other types of head-gear snatched. They call passengers who wear head-gear 'hat-trees'.

The train now approaches Soweto and the tsotsis are working to a deadline: they have to pounce on last-minute loot of whatever kind they can lay their hands on. A young lady alights from the train minus her 'wrap-over' skirt; fortunately she is offered a blanket by a sympathetic old woman to cover her semi-naked body with.

As the passengers finally alight, those who remain miraculously unscathed by the 'blade-of-fate' begin to count themselves fortunate and thank their ancestors, praying for the same protection in another 'hell-bound' trip the following day. Those who are persuaded by friends to lay charges against the thugs are reluctant to do so. Even those who at first have the nerve to report being molested and robbed to the police are later too scared to point them out in a suspect-parade, for fear of reprisals from the gangs in future. Cases that reach the courts are often withdrawn as there is insufficient evidence to convict the accused, or, as in most cases, because the complainants do not appear in the courts to give evidence.

There are days when delays involving trains on their way to the ghettoes in the evenings are attributable to the *tsotsis'* fiddling with the mechanical equipment. Passengers have no alternative but to alight between stations and search for buses or taxis to take them home. These hooligans see this as a golden opportunity for them to drag women and girls at knife-point into the open veld. They rape expectant mothers-to-be. They even rape old women of their grannies' age on their way from their piece-jobs where they eke out a living as washer-women. *Sies!* They rape little schoolgirls who travel by train to various schools in the area.

The men in the company of these unfortunate women often take to their heels for fear of being butchered, for the pickpockets now no longer only steal in the trains, but rob at knife-point under cover of darkness. Wives are taken from their husbands by these criminals and driven to shebeens and gambling-dens for a whole night's 'train-pulling'. 'Pulling-the-train' means a woman being raped by a gang of hooligans, all in a row, taking turns on her. For her dear life, yes.

The following day they boast about the episode in the train, in the presence of all and sundry, very well aware of the fact that even if the husband reports this premeditated rape to the police, the law requires that the victim must show up herself to give a full statement at the charge-office. And of course eighty times out of a hundred she does not even want her identity to be revealed, even if one of the thugs should shout right into her face, 'Did you reach climax, cherrie? How many times?'

The other dangerous trains to commute in are those that carry night-shift workers to town in the evenings, as these are always empty and are used by these hooligans on their way back to town where they start their racket all over again. In the toilets they molest and rape the women who work on the train at night, as it travels non-stop to town.

There are also the early trains which commence their schedules in the small hours of the morning. Women who do night-shift work, some of them as office-cleaners, do not dare to commute on these trains. They will tell you that these *tsotsis* wait up the whole night just to drag them off the train and rape them under the subways, at a time when there is not a single soul to come to the rescue of the poor women.

Whatever these boys do, they do under the supervision of what may be concisely defined as overseers, and with the aid of 'baboon-shepherds', who give them a tip when the police are approaching, whereupon they disappear into thin air.

These overseers are men fit and healthy and old enough to be settling down to their responsibilities as married men, but instead they impart their bad influence to innocent young men, who might otherwise have grown up to become prominent leaders in various fields of service to their own community.

It is as a result of this that one finds many a good athletic talent, for instance, vanishing down the drain, all because the young man was trying to win admiration as a hero of some calibre, not realising that he was hitting the limelight on the wrong stage.

Who then is to blame for this state of affairs? Surely the parents can do something about it, if they wouldn't mind spoiling the precious rod. These criminals are children who are brought up in homes. Since charity begins at home, is it not a parental duty to give children a primary socialization, right in the home? Every day of our lives? Things may turn out for the better if parents do not leave everything to the nannies at the kindergarten to bring up our children for us, all because they are being paid salaries for it; if we do not leave it up to the teachers at school to educate our children for us just because they have acquired formal training in that profession; if we do not leave it to the minister of the parish to whom we usher our children, while we pass on to the shebeen — to preach the message of repentance from the good book into the hearts of our children on the assumption that he is a servant of God; and if we do not leave it to blind chance that a miracle will change the lives of our children when we as parents have failed to do so, and the juvenile courts have also failed. Because there is one thing that we should never allow to happen to the lives of our dear children, and that is to wait for the supreme court to impose the penalty of capital punishment on their heads.

Then we shall be running from pillar to post, paying for the professional services of legal practitioners of the highest esteem to save the dear lives of our 'beloved', vicious criminals whom we are rearing with an exceptional husbandry never to be equalled anywhere in the world, as if their lives are in any way better or more valuable than the lives they have ended cold-bloodedly, at the wink of an eye.

We shall forever pretend that we do not know that we are harbouring and feeding notorious criminals of no concise definition, who molest, steal, rob, kill and rape at knife-point; who later grow up into guntoting, cold-blooded murderers; who hide themselves from the long arm of the law right under our own cassocks.

'Dumani' is not the only coach in our train where all these iniquities are carried out. This crime is spreading itself, and reaching out a hand to younger boys who will grow up and catch a ride with it. There are so many trains carrying passengers to and from various parts of our beloved, sunny South Africa, which are infested with young criminals molesting millions of helpless people. Unless something is done to check it, if not to bring it to an end, there will, no doubt, forever be at the heart of our lives the recurring cycle that we call 'DUMANI'.

Mathatha Tsedu/FORCED LANDING

It was in the year 2561 that a cruising missile from Mars on its way to Saturnus was forced to make an emergency landing on Jupiter because of food shortages aboard. Contrary to popular belief that the Martians are intelligent, on that specific journey — which was their first on that route — they had made a fatal mistake.

Immediately after the space craft landed, it was surrounded by mounted police of the Anazia Mobile Unit. The captain of the craft, Mr Teargas Ours, climbed out and went down on his knees in front of the commanding officer to plead for *uxolo*. Mr Zwidofhelangani — the commanding officer — replied that as a peace-keeping officer he had no authority to *xolela* them and suggested they went together to the offices of the chairperson of the National Congress.

Mr Zwelethu, the chairperson, was naturally surprised to see the commanding officer with two aliens. He ushered them in, however, and the commanding officer briefed him about the encounter. Mr Zwelethu introduced himself in this fashion: 'Mr Afrika Zwelethu, Minister of Propaganda of the People's Republic of Anazia and chairman of the local branch of the National Congress.'

'Captain Teagas Ours and Deputy Captain Hippo Ours from the Capitalist Republic of Hollyland.' 'Oh! I wonder how you are coping with that exploitative economic system of yours? Anyway, let's leave that. What brings you here?' Mr Zwelethu asked.

'We are here due to food shortages on board. We are Martians on our way to Saturnus. Our supplies of food are exhausted. We have been living for the past two weeks on biscuits only. Everybody in that stinking thing is suffering from dehydration as a result of overexposure. We saw your coastline from high up and decided to land and plead our case, hoping that you would understand. I want to take this opportunity to apologise on behalf of my men and myself for violating the sovereignty and territorial integrity of the Anazian State. We are fully aware of the seriousness of our actions, but we believe, nevertheless, that your sense of humanity will prevail and that you will understand. We were in danger. It was a choice between starvation and survival. We chose the latter. We are appealing to you to allow us to stay until such time as we have collected enough fresh water, vegetables and fruit. I want to assure you that we have no subversive motive in landing here.'

'Well, I really don't know,' the commanding officer sighed. 'Things have changed so much this year, after the publication of that book they found on the moon. Years back it would have been no problem. I would simply tell you, "You are welcome," and the people would agree with me. But right now we are very suspicious about strangers of colour. I can't risk giving you a firm answer: the people will have to decide. The best I can do at the moment is to get you temporary permits and accommodation. You will have to surrender any weapon that you have. You will hand over your papers for safe-keeping. The spacecraft will remain under police guard until further notice. You are to take nothing whatsoever from that craft. I can only warn you that the people are very sensitive, and you should not abuse the hospitality that I am extending on their behalf. Dr Nnathe Mudzimba, the district surgeon, will come and attend to you in your camp.'

'Thank you very much Mr Zwelethu, we won't be a nuisance to your people,' the Martians said.

Teargas and Hippo were taken to the administration block where they were joined by their friends. After completing all the formalities they went to the camp where Dr Mudzimba vaccinated them against various diseases.

Teargas was however very curious about this book that had changed the people's attitude towards strangers. He could not hide his curiosity, and asked C.O. Zwidofhelangani about the book.

Zwidofhelangani told him that the book was brought back by astronauts who had gone to the moon in 2560. 'The book deals with the histories of countries on the planet Earth. In one of the continents called Afrika there is a country called Safrika. The natives of that country were going through sheer hell at the hands of a handful of settlers.

70

'These settlers had conned the local population into allowing them to settle for a time to plant vegetables and fruit. The settlers, however, on realising that Azania — as it was then called — was very fertile, annexed the land by using sophisticated weapons combined with subtle diplomacy and religion. The settlers then declared themselves rulers over the local population and outlawed their culture as barbaric. They passed legislation curbing the natives' movement and their political aspirations, and also exploiting their labour. The next generation in that country cursed the older generation for selling their birthrights. They resolved to win their country back — come what may.'

C.O. Zwidofhelangani explained that this section of the encyclopaedia was particularly popular in Anazia. He also said that the Anazian people believed the book was a warning to them not to extend their hospitality unreservedly to strangers of colour.

In the middle of the night, Captain Teargas summoned his men to a hush-hush meeting of whispers.

'Gentlemen, it seems the game is up. I talked to this senior guard in the afternoon. They know all about that Jan van Riebeeck story that we intended to repeat here. These kaffirs seem to be more advanced than we thought. I really don't think they will allow us to stay. If only they were not guarding that damn craft we would destroy them with those bazookas. I think the best we can do is to wait and see. That minister told me he would tell us their decision in a day or two.' After the meeting they all went back to sleep.

The following morning Captain Teargas was summoned to Mr Zwelethu's office. After the formal greetings, Mr Zwelethu played Captain Teargas a tape recording of his hush-hush message to his people. Unknown to him, the room in which he and his men slept had been bugged.

Mr Zwelethu told Teargas that he was very disappointed in him.

'You are under arrest now. All the weapons in your craft have been confiscated. You are to be formally charged with aggression against an independent sovereign state, alternatively with conspiring to colonise the whole country and subject it to the unjust philosophy of capitalism. The minimum sentence in each case is death by hanging and the maximum is death by firing squad.'

Teargas was so shocked he fainted in the office. They carried him out and he was dumped at the back of a Land Rover, and later joined by his confused men.

They were taken to the Tatamu Prison where they found Bese,

Phuphe, Libuthebuthe, Mansi, Gopi and others who were charged with collaborating with the oppressors against the people. Also in the same prison, though in another block were the big guns in the conspiracy. They included among others, Professor Andries Trinity, Jimmy Thomas and Booi Wosita.

The trial of the invaders was very short, seeing that the prosecution had material evidence. They were found guilty as charged and sentenced to death by firing squad.

There would be no mercy shown to the marauding Zwingwashuntasses who had plotted to make another conquest of Jupiter just like the one they had brought off exactly 909 years ago. The people would turn out in full force at the Petersen Hector National Stadium, two weeks later, to witness the moment of truth for the invaders. The people would also sing praises to the People's Militia and to Minister Afrika Zwelethu, for his cat-like alertness in saving his country from being clawed by the mercenaries of capitalism and cosmic neo-colonialism. The people would also chant slogans like Down With The Invaders and A Luta Continua.

They would rejoice because their atmosphere had been cleared of pollutants from the planet Mars.

Bessie Head/HEAVEN IS NOT CLOSED

All her life Galethebege earnestly believed that her whole heart ought to be devoted to God, yet one catastrophe after another occurred to swerve her from this path.

It was only in the last five years of her life, after her husband Ralokae had died, that she was able to devote her whole mind to her calling. Then, all her pent-up and suppressed love for God burst forth and she talked only of Him day and night — so her grandchildren, solemnly and with deep awe, informed the mourners at her funeral. And all the mourners present at her hour of passing were utterly convinced that they had watched a profound and holy event.

They talked about it for days afterwards.

Galethebege was well over ninety when she died and not at all afflicted by crippling ailments like most of the aged. In fact, only two days before her death she had complained to her grandchildren of a sudden fever and a lameness in her legs and she had remained in bed.

A quiet and thoughtful mood fell upon her. On the morning of the second day she had abruptly demanded that all the relatives be summoned.

'My hour has come,' she said, with lofty dignity.

No one quite believed it, because that whole morning she sat bolt upright in bed and talked to all who had gathered about God, whom she loved with her whole heart.

Then, exactly at noon, she announced once more that her hour had indeed come and lay down peacefully like one about to take a short nap. Her last words were:

'I shall rest now because I believe in God.'

Then, a terrible silence filled the hut and seemed to paralyze the mourners because they all remained immobile for some time; each person present cried quietly, as not one of them had witnessed such a magnificent death before.

They only stirred when the old man, Modise, suddenly observed, with great practicality, that Galethebege was not in the correct position for death. She lay on her side with her right arm thrust out above her head.

She ought to be turned over on her back, with her hands crossed over her chest, he said. A smile flickered over the old man's face as he said this, as though it was just like Galethebege to make a miscalculation.

Why, she knew the hour of her death and everything, then forgot at the last minute the correct sleeping posture for the coffin. And later that evening, as he sat with his children near the out-door fire for the evening meal, a smile again flickered over his face.

I am of a mind to think that Galethebege was praying for forgiveness for her sins this morning,' he said slowly. 'It must have been a sin for her to marry Ralokae. He was an unbeliever to the day of his death . . .'

A gust of astonished laughter shook his family out of the solemn mood of mourning that had fallen upon them and they all turned eagerly towards their grandfather, sensing that he had a story to tell.

'As you all know,' the old man said, wisely, 'Ralokae was my brother. But none of you present knows the story of Galethebege's life, as I know it . . .'

And as the flickering firelight lit up their faces, he told the following story: 'I was never like Ralokae, an unbeliever. But that man, my brother, draws out my heart. He liked to say that we as a tribe would fall into great difficulties if we forgot our own customs and laws. Today, his words seem true. There is thieving and adultery going on such as was not possible under Setswana law.'

In those days when they were young, said the old man, Modise, it had become the fashion for all Black people to embrace the Gospel. For some it was the mark of whether they were 'civilized' or not. For some, like Galethebege, it was their whole life.

Anyone with eyes to see would have known that Galethebege had been born good and under any custom, whether Setswana or Christian, she would still have been good. It was this natural goodness of heart that made her so eagerly pursue the word of the Gospel. There was a look on her face, absent, abstracted, as though she needed to share the final secret of life with God, who would understand all things. So she was always on her way to church, and in hours of leisure in life would have gone on in this quiet and worshipful way, had not a sudden catastrophe occurred in the yard of Ralokae.

Ralokae had been married for nearly a year when his young wife died in childbirth. She died when the crops of the season were being harvested, and for a year Ralokae imposed on himself the traditional restraints and disciplines of *boswagadi* or mourning for the deceased.

A year later, again at the harvest time, he underwent the cleansing ceremony demanded by custom and could once more resume the normal life of a man. It was the unexpectedness of the tragic event and the discipline it imposed on him that made Ralokae take note of the life of Galethebege.

She lived just three yards away from his own yard and formerly he had barely taken note of her existence; it was too quiet and orderly. But during that year of mourning it delighted him to hear that gentle and earnest voice of Gelethebege inform him that such tragedies 'were the will of God.'

As soon as he could, he began courting her. He was young and impatient to be married again and no one could bring back the dead. So a few days after the cleansing ceremony, he made his intentions very clear to her.

'Let us two get together,' he said. 'I am pleased by all your ways.'

Galethebege was all at the same time startled, pleased and hesitant. She was hesitant because it was well known that Ralokae was an unbeliever; he had not once set foot in church. So she looked at him, begging an apology, and mentioned the matter which was foremost in her mind.

'Ralokae,' she said, uncertainly, 'I have set God always before me,' implying by that statement that perhaps he was seeking a Christian life too, like her own. But he only looked at her in a strange way and said nothing. This matter was to stand like a fearful sword between them but he had set his mind on winning Galethebege as his wife. That was all he was certain of. He would turn up in her yard day after day.

'Hello, girl friend,' he'd greet her, enchantingly.

He always wore a black beret perched at a jaunty angle on his head, and his walk and manner were gay and jaunty too. He was so exciting as a man that he threw her whole life into a turmoil. It was the first time love had come her way and it made the blood pound fiercely through her whole body till she could feel its very throbbing at the tips of her fingers.

It turned her thoughts from God a bit to this new magic life was offering her. The day she agreed to be his wife, that sword quivered like a fearful thing between them. Ralokae said quietly and finally: 'I took my first wife according to the old customs. I am going to take my second wife according to the old customs too.'

He could see the protest on her face. She wanted to be married in church according to the Christian custom, but he also had his own protest to make. The God might be all right, he explained. But there was something wrong with the people who had brought the word of the Gospel to the land. Their love was enslaving Black people and he could not stand it.

That was why he was without belief. It was the people he did not trust. They were full of tricks. They were a people who, at the sight of a Black man, pointed a finger in the air, looked away into the distance and said, impatiently: 'Boy! Will you carry this! Boy! Will you fetch this!'

They had brought a new order of things into the land and they made the people cry for love. One never had to cry for love in the customary way of life. Respect was just there for the people all the time. That was why he rejected all things foreign.

What did a woman do with a man like that who knew his own mind? She either loved him or she was mad. From that day on Galethebege knew what she would do. She would do all that Ralokae commanded, as a good wife should.

But her former life was like a drug. Her footsteps were too accustomed to wearing down the foot-path to the church, so they carried her to the home of the missionary which stood just under its shadow.

The missionary was a short, anonymous-looking man who wore glasses. He had been the resident missionary for some time and, like all his fellows, he did not particularly like the people. He always complained to his kind that they were terrible beggars and rather stupid. So when he opened the door and saw Galethebege there his expression with its raised eyebrows clearly said: 'Well what do you want now?'

'I am to be married, sir,' Galethebege said, politely, after the exchange of greetings.

The missionary smiled: 'Well come in, my dear. Let us talk about the arrangements.'

He stared at her with polite, professional interest. She was a complete nonentity, a part of the vague black blur which was his congregation — oh, they noticed chiefs and people like that, but not the silent mass of the humble and lowly who had an almost weird capacity to creep quietly through life. Her next words brought her sharply into focus.

'The man I am to marry, sir, does not wish to be married in the Christian way. He will only marry under Setswana custom,' she said softly.

They always knew the superficial stories about 'heathen customs'; an expression of disgust crept into his face — sexual malpractices had been associated with the traditional marriage ceremony and (shudder!) they draped the stinking intestinal bag of the ox around the necks.

'That we cannot allow!' he said sharply. 'Tell him to come and marry in the Christian way.'

Galethebege started trembling all over. She looked at the missionary in alarm. Ralokae would never agree to this. Her intention in approaching the missionary was to acquire his blessing for the marriage, as though a compromise of tenderness could be made between two traditions opposed to each other.

She trembled because it was beyond her station in life to be involved in controversy and protest. The missionary noted the trembling and alarm and his tone softened a bit, but his next words were devastating.

'My dear,' he said, persuasively, 'Heaven is closed to the unbeliever . . .'

Galethebege stumbled home on faint legs. It never occurred to her to question such a miserable religion which terrified people with the fate of eternal damnation in hell-fire if they were 'heathens' or sinners. Only Ralokae seemed quite unperturbed by the fate that awaited him. He smiled when Galethebege relayed the words of the missionary to him.

'Girl friend,' he said, carelessly. 'You can choose what you like, Setswana custom or Christian custom. I have chosen to live my life by Setswana custom.'

Never once in her life had Galethebege's integrity been called into question. She wanted to make the point clear.

'What you mean, Ralokae,' she said firmly, 'is that I must choose you over my life with the church. I have a great love in my heart for you so I choose you. I shall tell the priest about this matter because his command is that I marry in church.'

Even Galethebege was astounded by the harshness of the missionary's attitude. The catastrophe she never anticipated was that he abruptly excommunicated her from the church. She could no longer enter the church if she married under Setswana custom.

It was beyond her to reason that the missionary was the representative of both God and something evil, the mark of 'civilization.' It was unthinkable that an illiterate and ignorant man could display such contempt for the missionary's civilization. His rage and hatred were directed at Ralokae, but the only way in which he could inflict punishment was to banish Galethebege from the church. If it hurt anyone at all, it was only Galethebege.

The austere rituals of the church, the mass, the sermons, the intimate communication in prayer with God — all this had thrilled her heart deeply. But Ralokae was also representative of an ancient stream of holiness that people had lived with before any white man had set foot on the land, and it only needed a small protest to stir up loyalty for the old customs.

The old man, Modise, paused at this point in the telling of his tale, but his young listeners remained breathless and silent, eager for the conclusion.

'Today,' he continued, 'it is not a matter of debate because the young care neither way about religion. But in that day, the expulsion of Galethebege from the church was a matter of debate. It made the people of our village ward think.

'There was great indignation because both Galethebege and Ralokae were much respected in the community. People then wanted to know how it was that Ralokae, who was an unbeliever, could have heaven closed to him.

'A number of people, all the relatives who officiated at the wedding ceremony, then decided that if heaven was closed to Galethebege and Ralokae, it might as well be closed to them too, so they all no longer attended church.

'On the day of the wedding, we had all our own things. Everyone knows the extent to which the cow was a part of the people's life and customs.

'We took our clothes from the cow and our food from the cow and it was the symbol of our wealth. So the cow was a holy thing in our lives. The elders then cut the intestinal bag of the cow in two, and one portion was placed around the neck of Galethebege and one portion around the neck of Ralokae to indicate the wealth and good luck they would find together in married life.

'Then the porridge and meat were dished up in our *mogopo* bowls which we had used from old times. There was much capering and ululating that day because Ralokae had honoured the old customs . . .'

A tender smile once more flickered over the old man's face.

'Galethebege could never forsake the custom in which she had been brought up. All through her married life she would find a corner in which to pray. Sometimes Ralokae would find her so and ask: 'What are you doing, Mother?' And she would reply: 'I am praying to the Christian God.'

The old man leaned forward and stirred the dying fire with a partially burnt-out log of wood. His listeners sighed, the way people do when they have heard a particularly good story. As they stared at the fire they found themselves debating the matter in their minds, as their elders had done forty or fifty years ago. Was heaven really closed to the unbeliever, Ralokoe?

Or had Christian custom been so intolerant of Setswana custom that it could not bear the holiness of Setswana custom? Wasn't there a place in heaven too for Setswana custom? Then that gust of astonished laughter shook them again. Galethebege had been very well known in the village ward over the past five years for the supreme authority with which she talked about God. Perhaps her simple and good heart had been terrified that the doors of heaven were indeed closed on Ralokae and she had been trying to open them.

Sipho Sepamla/KING TAYLOR

Take a ride into Stirtonville any day. You enter the place facing due South. At the entrance, overlooking you as you drive in, is an old building looking God-forsaken. Few people seem to know why it stands there or why it ever came into being. A little down the road on the left is a row of shops. Quite a sight they are. The number of shops seems to be below the demands of the area.

One can't miss the slanting pillars of the shops. And the fact that the verandahs just manage to hang there. It is amazing, that hanging on of rusted corrugated-iron sheets. One gets the feeling of looking at a Christian, hands thrust out as if to say: There! Lord, see how useful, yet misused I am.

But then the aged appearance of these shops is deceptive. It belies their vitality and the buzz of business revealed to a more discerning eye. For one thing, the eye catches the inevitable sign: SALE NOW ON! And one learns that the signs read thus all year round.

The fruits displayed to tantalize passers-by are neither cheap nor expensive because they are neither fresh nor too stale. If they look somewhat wrinkled or over-ripe, it is said this is the sign of the times: money is tight.

This is the Stirtonville of Meneer Taylor.

To get to Mnr Taylor's place, one has to turn right at the very first street leading due west, past two streets running across it. These are Mgijima and Ntloko. And then turn right on the third street which local residents are likely to give as Kuma — Xuma to be exact! And not surprisingly. For ask anyone what Xuma or Mgijima has to do with the welfare of Mnr Taylor, a 'coloured' of Stirtonville, and the answer never

80

goes beyond the shrugging of shoulders.

Try to visualize Mnr Taylor of Xuma Street, Stirtonville. Outstanding is his look of a temporary sojourner. For this is how the 'coloured' Mnr Taylor would strike one. He has lived here for ten years or near-so. In his God-given humbleness (he won't be shy to say so himself) in all that time he is likely to have struggled to reach the stage of saying Kuma for Xuma — no mean feat that! No doubt he must have been told either he or the Xumas are temporary!

Taylor's place is fairly easy to find, thanks to a moody gumtree towering over the house. And of course the *kaffir-musiek* blaring out of the ever-open front door.

The house itself stands on a defiant piece of ground. Mnr Taylor explains that for years he has been trying to grow a hedge. Why, he even thought of a bed of roses, just to show he too had some love. And also as proof that he was, after all was said and done, apart from the ordinary person. But the greyness of the soil tells of its hardness. Quite likely Amakhafula, who lived here sometime back, in their effort to reduce the dust which rose from the yard or came flying like sheets of snow from the nearby mine-dump, must have poured down ash and water to lay it to sleep over the years. In desperation Taylor stopped trying. He didn't care two hoots what grew or what died in the yard; didn't bother to repair the fence. In any case it had been tottering for a long time. Taylor didn't even care to have a gate. And it so happened that the turn of events in his life convinced him of the wisdom of no-fence and no-gate.

When one runs a shebeen, like Taylor did, certain considerations are important. These need a person with foresight. For instance, one will be told, a gate could be a nuisance to customers driven by an impatient thirst. They might look askance at a place fortified by a fence and gate. The need to scramble to safety during a raid throws any decency to the winds.

Inside the house itself Taylor showed the same type of resourcefulness. The lounge was arranged for the moneyed and the more-moneyed. For the K.B. drinker in the lounge, there were wooden benches leaning on the walls. He too seemed to have heard that Africans are fond of leaning — they had leaned on mountain-sides for a start! For 'coloureds' and better-Africans who came in for bottled liquor, there was a table at the centre of the room. Upright, cushioned chairs went with the table.

As a man succumbed to the influence of what he had taken by his own hand and the force of gravity began to play havoc on him, there were a few options at hand: the man could simply lean on the wall, eyes closed; he could crumple into his own lap like a ready-to-be-ironed garment; he could hide the shame of his condition by supporting his head in his hands, elbows on the table, or he could simply face up, head dangling from the upright chair. The snores he generated would be enough to summon all the help he needed.

At this stage of his life Mnr Taylor lived with a woman many people called Mrs Taylor, when moved by one mood, and maDlamini, when moved by another. The woman seemed to be stimulated into greater activity by those who called her simply, maDlamini.

One will find Mnr Taylor seated on a bench if business is brisk, and at the table during fairly quiet spells like daytime. Next to him there'll be a record player and all around it littered gramophone records. One he likes most is a catchy tune called: *Majuba! Jika Sibhekane!* It can play for ten times at a go. In fact he seems to use it as background music to his story. And is he fond of telling his story? Wow! What a man for business. Knows how to choose his audience, specializing in those who are likely to swell sales under his spell.

Aaa! Majuba . . . he begins. At this moment one notes a bushy moustache dancing merrily with each word uttered; aggressively protruding stomach, legs stretched out, anchored somewhat firmly on the floor; feet bare, toes marching or resting for a while. And a pipe tilted on an ashtray, smouldering.

'I was born at the foot of Majuba Hill,' he says. 'Go there any day, you'll find a handful of huts at the bottom of the Hill. One of them is my birthplace. All right, I've been away from there ten, twenty years now, but that has not been long enough to erase from my head a place that has been seen in it every day . . . I came here to work. I was then a young man full of life, full of strength.' (Here he pushes up the sleeve of his khaki shirt and bends his arm: a bicep stands out angrily to witness to this strength which was once aplenty.) 'I could have worked on the mines but who has heard of a man in his right senses choosing to work in the belly of a snake? *Hawu! Hungh!* Think I would dig my own grave? Ha! Am I mad? M'm? . . . Not me! Not me!

'I worked in one of those tall buildings called flats in Hillbrow. I lived at the top of the building . . . Couldn't believe it at first . . . *Hawu!* Mandlenkosi Thela living on top of white people! Every night I stood in the yard up there to gaze at the stars. Sometimes I felt like plucking off one of the stars to give it to Thembekile, the mother of my children back home at Majuba . . . But do you know what used to make me laugh? *Yebo!* I would laugh until my stomach began to grouse!'

Taylor suddenly folds up at this point, the result of a joyous recollection. And then as the laughter tapers off breathlessly, he begins playing his tongue around the mouth, seeking stray particles of food. He ends up by producing a suction-like sound. Those tiny, structural gaps between the teeth do it. It's a process that reveals the multi-coloured nature of his teeth: brownish-white . . . black-grey . . . off-white with greenish lines of decay and what have you. Ah, Taylor . . .

'Every morning and every night I was going into our toilets up there and doing it. Guess what? Peeing on white people! . . . Just like that. And I did it within the law. *Yebo!* Me and my Zulu brothers, we had the right to be up there in the sky and wee-wee on the heads of white people. *Hawu! iGoli!* . . . I'm not surprised to hear the law now wants to bring down all those Zulus from the sky.

'After a time I got tired of the loneliness up there. Found myself a room in Sophiatown . . . A man can't live like a bachelor all the time. The blood will soon tell something is wrong.

'*Hayi-yaya!* I used to run for the bus in Sophiatown, in the mornings. And I thought everybody was mad. Running, running every blessed day like each was trying to catch a rabbit . . . But come Saturday and Sunday . . . One person goes this way. Another one, that way . . . In street corners it is "tickey-I-do", you know the game of dice . . . In the backyards *"ugologo"*, the drinking of kaffir-beer . . . From the front door the excuse-me-people play music called jazz . . . That was Sophiatown.

'One day we heard we would be moved. *Hawu!* That was a shock to us. We thought someone might have had a terrible dream. Some said: *akubanjwa*, we are not going. Others: God is kind. He heard our prayers. Let's go! Rents are high! Rooms are crowded!

'Joe Pamla came to see me . . . Joe! . . . I can see him in my mind's eye: a very thin man. He looked like he didn't eat enough. But I tell you he had money. From every pocket he could take out any minute, wads of paper-money. Even here, man (shirt pocket). He was fond of those thin trousers of the time — the *tsotsis*. When people speak of *tsotsis* they really mean the trousers, stovepipe-like. He had a silver chain dangling from the small pocket of the trousers. His ties were broad and multi-coloured. Shirts, pure white. Never used a jacket. Not Joe. His cuff-links, pure gold or silver. Very expensive, in other words. Not these things they spray-paint in the backyards of Doornfontein and then write on them: Made in England! ... *Hawu!* ... Sophiatown, I tell you, died with all those beautiful people like Joe ... *Ya!*

'Joe comes to see me. He says: "Mandlenkosi, you mustn't sleep forever. Today they want to move Sophiatown. God knows how life will be in that new place, but I tell you it can't beat Sophiatown, *my ma hoor my,*" says Joe.

"Tomorrow, who knows, they'll be moving the place where Sophiatown is going to now. Be smart! See what they are doing. They move the people, not the place. Are you going to be a stone rolling every now and again? Do as I do: live where you like. Be a spirit, man." I said: "How Joe?" Think he said anything? Never! Nothing. Took out a new green card with his picture. Only then did he say: "*Kyk hier,*" (he was fond of that one) "*kyk hier,* this is my 'IDENTITY'. Read it for yourself." I read: Joseph Palmer ... 007 — can't remember the rest of the number ... I was surprised. Joe remained calm. And serious, you don't know Joe. The boy had a quick mind. He saw I was hesitating. "*Kyk hier,* you know very well everybody in Sophiatown wants to be a 'coloured'. Ever thought why?" I replied: "But Joe, I am a Zulu. It is in my veins, flows to all the tips of my body, this Zulu blood. It is the blood of my ancestors. The blood of my unborn children. How can I give it up, just like that?"

"*Kyk hier,* you must understand why you are in *iGoli* ... "

"Work!"

"That's right!"

"So?"

"But can you work where you like? ... What if they say all Zulus must not work in Johannesburg, can your blood help you?"

"I'll till the soil."

"Till the soil," he sneered. "Till the soil mixing your blood for manure, I suppose."

'I laughed. I did. And I don't know why.

"*Kyk hier,* you are strong not because of your Zulu blood. You are just bloody strong because you are a man with good blood. You have a pair of good stock-hands. Everybody wants to use such hands. Anywhere! Every time! Not because they are Zulu hands or of Zulu blood. Forget that shit about Zulu blood, it's got little to do with the sun above your head, the roof above you, the beer in your stomach. Think big! Think of yourself as a man first — and all the other bullshit will take its place in the queue. Use your hands well. Don't allow any bullshit to stand in your way."

'That was Joe for you.

"All right, all right, stop the preaching. Tell me what you want me to do?"

"*Kyk hier,* for only five pounds you can get one of these. Be a spirit, man."

'Just then I saw myself as a businessman. A very successful one, with all the good things of the world. Joe cut into my thoughts: "Think of it, I'm making you a man among men for only five pounds . . . I don't do this sort of thing for everybody." "Do you mean it?" I asked . . . "*Kyk hier,* get this card and walk into town, any time, you'll see what happens."

'The silence that followed was crowded for me. I looked at Joe. I looked at Joseph Palmer. I heard Joe tell me I would be a spirit: walk, work, anywhere.

"You like the idea?" he asked.

'A thought struck me. A fear lodged somewhere in my make-up thrust itself into my stomach. I asked, "What about my pass-book?"

'Joe shook his head as if he really pitied me. "What is a 'pass'? Your penis? Don't be foolish, man. Guts! There's so much of the yesbaas in you that you can hardly see the difference between the paper you carry and the penis which is part of your body . . . *Kyk hier,* throw the damn thing in the fire. Watch it being scorched, turn colour, crumple and become ash. You can pick up its ghost and hold it to the wind just to satisfy yourself of its whereabouts later on."

'I ordered the IDENTITY. I saw the successful businessman, saw the improved condition of Thembekile and my children. For didn't I come here to improve myself?

'Oh yes, at the time I was keeping myself busy with Meisie. I didn't want to tell her about Joe's idea. You know women, they never want to try what they didn't conceive, especially if it is something to do with the law. *Yebo!* . . . Ah, yes, I didn't know as we were talking with Joe, Meisie was like this (here the hand is held out, the arm half-moon-like, to indicate the pregnant condition of a woman) . . . Not long after that talk with Joe, Meisie gave birth to Fanyana, my son.

'After a couple of months' waiting I received the IDENTITY. It bore the name KING TAYLOR. That was Joe's idea for Mandlenkosi Thela!

'I thought of a place I could start a business with the little money I had been saving. My mind fixed on Stirtonville. I couldn't go to Majuba. Imagine King Taylor meeting Chief Nkosana! No! It wouldn't have worked out well for me out there. But it bore heavily on me. It meant my children and my place had gone up in the smoke of my old "pass".

'When I left my flat-job I thought I was leaving all my troubles behind, you know that business of wee-wee on other people's heads. But then there's no such thing as a man leaving headaches and things behind. Instead he carries these in his pocket like the tobacco and the pipe. Now and then, he's got to drag them out into the sun as if to make sure they are still with him.

'When I entered Stirtonville I gave up the idea of a shop. The aged-ness and the cramped condition of those shops at the entrance knocked out the businessman in me. Still, there was something about Stirtonville I liked a lot. It was at that time one of those few places where Africans and 'coloureds' lived together . . . All right, now and again, somebody pisses on somebody else's head. Oh yes that happens everywhere. But then the people were people. They lived together, man.

'In time I came across maDlamini. Lived in her room for a while. Things were not altogether bad.

'You know women . . . Meisie had refused to leave Johannesburg. She had actually counted on her fingers and toes what we would miss leaving Jo'burg. But then one day she came to look me up, as she said. Found me in this set-up with MaDlamini. What can a man do alone? Nothing, as you know. Meisie never forgave me. I heard she had taken to heavy drinking after that visit. Not long after that she was at a T.B. Hospital. I went to see her . . . *Ou liefde roes nie*, they say . . . She had fallen in, completely.' (The idea shows itself to be heavy for Taylor. The man's sorrow grates on the throat. He clears his throat in order to continue). 'She looked like one about to die. I think in her heart she felt this death. She faced me then as she must have faced death at that moment. I could get it in her faint voice as she said: "Thela!" (she never called me otherwise). "Look after our son. But please don't take him away from ma."

'She died soon after that visit. I buried her. MaDlamini can bear me out, I buried her with my own money. When I spoke to the ol' lady about the boy, Fanyana, she said it very clearly to me. "I'll keep the boy. That is what the deceased wished for."

'Oh yes, by this time my knees had begun to give trouble.' The thought of this makes Taylor change the stretched-out position of his legs. It's an effort. As he draws up his knees there is no doubt about the pain he's going through. With each hand grasping the knee from beneath, he pulls up each leg in turn, emitting a pained: *A-a-ah!*

'I'm no longer the person I was when I came to Johannesburg.'

That statement is made in dead silence. For the music which seems to have been screeching all the time has stopped. The player stands unattended. One gets the impression during this silence that Mnr Taylor has before him a mirror of life. He is looking into it . . .

'When I heard Africans were going to be moved from Stirtonville, I fell on one knee. 'Strue's living God, I did. My first words were *"Nkulunkulu!* Here! You don't do it over the dead body of Fanyana? It is still over my living carcass? *Hawu!"* . . . Then it occurred to me to give thanks to Joe . . . Saved me from another removal. Those bus fares. That sleep. But I hardly knew where Joe was to be found. The man was a spirit indeed . . . It was a battle going down. The pain! I had to. Think what would have happened to me, Mandlenkosi Thela. Who cares for such a name? . . . I would be known by one thing only — a numbered file. Dammit! . . .

'But like I say, I am no longer that man I used to be. I can do nothing more than pick up a record and switch on the turntable. D'you think that's a man's job? A monkey can do more than that . . . And after what they have done to me, with my own blood, what's there for me to stay here for? I might as well crawl back to Majuba even if I have to do it on my belly. That I shall yet do!'

Some brooding silence follows this out-pouring. The furtive smile that has been stealing over his face disappears. Instead a dark cloud snakes over his face. The bushy moustache stands still like an alert sentinel. There is a glimmer of froth around his mouth. No doubt his feelings are a twist of bitterness round some invisible point. Now he plods through to the poisoned end of his story. The man is heavy at heart.

'Fanyana is my son. That truth lives underneath his skin. Nobody can take that away from me or him. *Hawu! . . . Ya! . . .* Here! Some people! . . . I was seated just here where I am. A policeman walks in to say I am wanted at Baragwanath Hospital. Fanyana has been taken there. Not much. Only that. I tried to ask some questions. The man says he knows nothing. If I want to know more I must go to Baragwanath. Oh yes, he did say something like, there's an accident. But then you know the word can mean anything.

'I got there all right. The little boy was in bad shape. Some bloody bastard of a driver had knocked him down. The boy had been playing in the street. Where else could he have played? Nowhere. He had the right to be there like anyone. Dammit!'

The narration is here interrupted by MaDlamini shuffling in. Touching here and there, puffing and heaving as if she is a creature from a story-book, she comes to sit beside her husband. The bench groans painfully as she sits so that one notices a silence after she's settled down. And of course she ends it all with a huge sigh of relief.

'The heat! . . . ' As she says this she stretches out her huge legs and then her toes do a bit of marching as if jostling for a position of rest. Her huge arms share the duty of supporting her on the bench, one doing so as the other rests on her knees. There's something fascinating about her. Being so huge, her body gives the impression that it is always reluctant to move to its destination. She has to propel herself as she goes forward, to lend a hand to her own movement. For this she has to hold onto the table, the chairs, the benches, the walls, oh everything useful to the desired result. If one is to believe the books, her type is built from the stock remaining of Tshaka's impi. Now she is seated next to Taylor as if waiting to be brought abreast on current affairs. Taylor turns to her . . .

'You came in just as I was saying something about Fanyana . . . '

'I spent my money on that boy. Don't see me seated here and think I'm worth nothing! I had to go to hospital and to court many times.'

'Do you want to know what that driver said in court?' Taylor asks, as if it really needs to be told. Then: 'MaDlamini, tell us what that man said?'

'He applied his brakes!'

'Applied brakes,' echoes Taylor, adding, 'what's the good of brakes if a car stops over a fallen victim?'

'The man has a black heart,' says MaDlamini.

'She lost a lot of money on that case,' says Taylor, as if he didn't hear what was said before that.

'And I never want to complain,' MaDlamini says, like a bride at the altar.

'But whoever thinks about these things? All people know is how to cheat! *Hawu!* . . . About that driver, know what happened? He was made to twist in the mud. He tried to plead for mercy. The judge stood his ground. "Guilty! Guilty!" he said . . . . The court fixed another day for sentence. My mind didn't wait for that day. I said to myself: Taylor, you must do something for MaDlamini. Don't wait until she's dead like you did in the case of Meisie. The time is now . . . There's damages coming from the injuries of your son. It is a lot of money. And you are sure going to get something . . . '

'I bought fruits for the boy in hospital,' MaDlamini says, as if she means she had spread her huge body across the city of Johannesburg to collect funds for the handicapped.

Taylor cuts into the feelings of MaDlamini: 'We had lived in this place for a long time without all the furniture we wanted.' There's a touch of bitterness in his voice. There's also some shame at his failings ... 'How could I have done much for the house when my health suddenly took a turn for the worse — when I wasn't even thinking about it? I never worked long with the IDENTITY.'

'I wanted a bedroom suite badly all my life,' says MaDlamini.

'I told her to go into town and choose a thing of her heart. And I meant it. She did. But she thought I would grumble. The furniture was expensive. But how could I be funny to a woman who had been a mother to my son? ... But money, I tell you ... My son was given 2 000 pounds damages ... Meisie's mother, sis!'

'It makes me mad too,' says MaDlamini.

'I couldn't go to court that day of the sentence. Everybody knew I wasn't well. MaDlamini went there to stand in for me. What does the ol' lady tell the court? Fanyana's father was a man called Mandlenkosi Thela in Zululand. When MaDlamini stands up to say King Taylor and Mandlenkósi Thela are names of the same person everybody just laughs. Think of it, they laughed. Why? D'you think it is because of one man with two names or is it because they can't think of a Mrs Taylor like MaDlamini? Another person says he is sure I didn't want to show my face in court because I had stolen the IDENTITY. What has that got to do with the 2 000? Now I think of it I can see it was all a trick, fixing things up for the ol'lady, not my son. But do you think they would laugh in my face? Never! I would have raised the corpse of Meisie from the grave. *Yebo!* I would have told them all that. And maybe more! After all, I came to Johannesburg and I pissed on their heads. That I did, and they all know it so well. Now I have my back turned so they think they can do that to me. What are they trying to do? Finish me off? Never! I'm from Majuba Hill! ... Can you believe it, I got not a penny from that money. 'Strue's living God, not a penny!

'We started this shebeen to pay for the bedroom suite. Think we had a chance to pay it off? One day the furniture people came into the house. I was seated just where I am now. I didn't move. What for? I pointed at the bedroom. They don't know me. I come from Majuba Hill. I looked at them as they took it away. I said: *Hamba nayo!* Ask her, I said it. Think I care ... People look at you on the outside, then they think they know you. Not me. A man is not a man because of what appears on the outside. In time I've come to know this truth . . .

'I want to go back to Majuba . . . '

MaDlamini leans on Taylor at this juncture. She tries to stand up by resting a hand on his shoulder. Both wobble drunkenly. Taylor exclaims:

'Ah! MaDlamini, this thirst . . . '

'Why do you think I stand up?' Her voice has an edge to it.

'Yes, I must go back to Majuba Hill . . . '

'I would ask: who is it has been standing in your way all this time?'

MaDlamini has mocked the moment, she has shuffled into the bedroom, touching here, touching there, flinging violently aside the curtain that hangs in the opening that leads into the bedroom. There is no doubt that this talk of her man going away to the other woman touches a flame in her bosom. And she can't keep that under control. Taylor gets the message because he merely says sadly, 'Such is life.' Then he turns to the music, the same number. Above the din of the music he continues:

'I have been making enquiries about the old flat where I used to work. Nobody is able to say whether or not it is still standing. You see, I must pave my way back to Majuba. I must find out if my family is still there. Once I heard they were moving people away from the foot of Majuba Hill into locations . . . A man can't leave *iGoli* to go to live under a tree. That kind of life was killed a long time ago.'

Taylor falls silent as if to listen to the clash of sounds from his favourite record. The music shouts, it runs, it stops and flows away.

'You want to know why I want to know about the old flat? The answer is simple. Nobody at Majuba knows King Taylor. That's why . . . There's a lot that has been happening in my mind. You see the 'pass' is me. Not the IDENTITY. The 'pass' is my skin-top. Yet no-one can touch the man underneath the skin. That is him saying, "Go back to Majuba" . . . I know it won't be easy-life for me. There are many reasons to laugh at me. But much more would be in store for me if I were to go. Thembekile is my wife, the mother of my children. She knows I am her husband, the father of her children. I paid lobola for her with cattle of four hoofs. That she knows . . . I know it won't be easy 'to bring from the dead' Mandlenkosi Thela. But that man has to rise from the grave. And he will. I swear by my father who lies at the foot of Majuba Hill.'

MaDlamini drags herself back into the company of her man. In one hand and under one armpit she carries two bottles of beer to quench the thirst. Henceforth not a word will be said. Only the clinking of glasses and the screeching of *Majuba! Jika Sibhekane!* The music sails into Xuma Street and beyond, in the same way that the cries and yells of warriors had risen above the slopes of the Hill. Then the cries were carried by dry air in the scorching heat. But on this day the music could not be dry. The sounds mingle with the fumes of liquor, are made wet on the palate of a man's tongue. And from his throat Taylor can be heard to hum, and then as if grousing he goes 'La-la-la' with the tune he knows so well. For him there is really no screeching. For him there are no agonised cries of clashing spears and gun echoes and horse-hooves. No! The man tries to articulate the crying joy of rediscovery. He has found himself before his own last trip!

'*Hawu!*' moans Taylor as if he's writing his own epitaph in Stirton-ville. Then his head dangles helplessly as he goes on humming. Now sleep hugs his wakeful state and he slides away. And he's gone to dreamland. MaDlamini remains looking out into Xuma Street. Maybe she sees beyond. But she has strength for only one note of resignation: '*E-eh!*'

Ahmed Essop/NOORJEHAN

When I began my career as a teacher, Noorjehan spent nine months in my matriculation English class. I shall always remember her as a very intelligent pupil, no more than five feet in height, with a smooth open forehead, hair auburn shading to brown in colour, parted in the middle and the two plaits gathered neatly by mother of pearl clasps on either side of her face. The beauty of her impeccably fair complexion was set off by the definiteness of her dark eyes. Her refined blooming appearance, the wraith of a perfume that seemed to be her constant companion, her literary sensibility, and that subtle accord that exists between a gifted pupil and a tutor, always filled me with a singular happiness.

Then suddenly, in early October, Noorjehan left school. A friend of hers told me that her parents had decided to keep her at home. That was all I learnt and she was no longer a presence. About a fortnight later I received a letter from her, brought by a maidservant to my home.

'You must have wondered,' she wrote,'why I left school at this time of the year. The truth is, my parents are convinced that I shall soon receive a marriage proposal and that in anticipation I should prepare myself. You will appreciate that I have no choice but to obey.

'Last month the go-betweens of the boy (or man?) interested in marrying me came to have a look at me. At first they spoke to my parents in the lounge while I was told to stay in my room. Later my mother asked me to prepare tea and serve the guests. This was a way of allowing them to scrutinize me. There were two women and a man. One of the women smiled at me and the other asked me a few idle ques-

92

tions.

After they had left, my father said that it would not be long before
I was married. I protested, overwhelmed by the prospect of a sudden
change in my life. My mother declared that God would punish dis-
obedient children, and in any case who was I to object to the wishes of
those who did everything for the happiness of their children.

Is it possible for you to come and speak to my father and try to
dissuade him from forcing me into a marriage I do not want. Forgive
me for troubling you, but could you come?'

I went to Noorjehan's home. She lived in a small semi-detached
house, the outside painted lime-green. Her father asked me to enter
after I had declared my identity and offered the explanation that I had
come, in the ordinary course of my professional duties, to inquire
about the absence of one of my pupils.

'She left for a very good reason,' said her father, a tall, austere-
looking hawk-nosed man. 'Noorjehan is going to be engaged shortly.'

I said that perhaps it would be wise to allow her to complete her
matriculation before she was betrothed, but he waved an impatient
hand at me and said:

'Teachers are understandably concerned about their charges, but
parents know what is best for their children.'

I then said that it did not seem to me reasonable to provide girls
with a modern education and then expect them to follow tradition in
their private lives.

To this he did not answer but looked at me impassively.

I left. I did not see Noorjehan while I was in the living-room.
Outside, as I reached the front gate and turned to close it, I saw her
standing at a bedroom window with one hand holding aside the froth of
a lace curtain. She smiled tepidly and fluttered her fingers good-bye.

After a few days I received another letter from her.

'I am to be engaged at the end of November. The go-betweens were
here again to arrange a time and date. While they talked to my parents I
sat miserably in my bedroom. You can imagine my feelings when
people are closeted, seemingly for hours, deciding on the course of my
life. I felt as if I was living two lives, one isolated in the bedroom and
later in the kitchen preparing tea for the visitors, the other captured in
the living-room, the subject of much talk. All that talk about "me" gave
"me" a kind of significance that frightened me.'

After her engagement she wrote again:

I was engaged two days ago. My future husband came with his

family and friends. He brought the usual gifts (which remain in their boxes, unopened) and presented me with a diamond ring which stands on my dressing table and which I cannot, perhaps never will bring myself to wear. What point is there in telling you what he looks like since he is a stranger to me and I cannot love him.

'After they had left I went to my bedroom and cried bitterly. My mother came and tried to comfort me by saying that a girl must marry and what difference does it make whether she marries now or later, or whether she marries a certain man or some other man. "I never saw your father," she said, "until the day of the wedding, and we have been happy. You are very lucky. His family is very wealthy. Your father is only a shop assistant." '

Shortly afterwards, in another letter, Noorjehan made the following confession:

'However much I would like to please my parents, I cannot see myself being married to a man I neither love nor hate, whose welfare will become an object of my life-long devotion. Such a marriage for me will be a marriage of self-obliteration. I am just not made for this kind of transaction. For some time now a terrible and desperate longing (growing out of my misery and helplessness) seizes me, the longing for *"my* prince" to rescue me. Perhaps this longing for a "prince" is generated by the memory store in me of the magic world of fairy stories told to me during my sapling days at school; or perhaps I am being silly, romantic and sentimental. But you will admit that the girl who meets her "prince" in the end is lucky.'

After several weeks Noorjehan wrote again:

'My wedding-day is to be arranged this coming week-end. I know what it will involve. All sorts of preparations will begin, invitations will be sent out, my trousseau will be in the hands of a busy seamstress, everyone will be excited while I will be regarded as an outsider who has little relation to the event. It is in the wedding trappings and its props that people will be interested. When I think of that day I am seized by a strange indefinable fear, you know the sort of fear that comes to one sometimes in dreams when one senses an oblique danger.'

I felt sorry for Noorjehan. I could understand her emotional predicament. I had known her to be a girl of precocious intelligence and sensitivity. Now, under pressure from her parents and the conventions of their society, she was reduced to the level of a sacrificial victim. Marriage transactions, although wilting under the force of twentieth century changes, were still conducted, and I had known of girls who had been pressured into marriage when they were yet mere slips, hardly ready for its coital demands.

On Friday morning I received a very brief letter from her:

'What must I do? What must I do to escape my fate? There is no one to help me. If only my . . .' The letter trailed off without mentioning the redemptive possibility.

Late in the afternoon I received an urgent message from her to meet her at Park Station at seven in the evening.

It was a cold evening — a chill wind had come up from the south — as I waited for her outside the station. Soon a taxi came to a halt and she alighted. I immediately noticed that she had undergone a transformation in her appearance. She had lost weight, seemed a little older and bore a solemn look.

'Thank you for coming,' she said in a soft voice.

She wore a green trouser suit. On her wrists were several silver and brass bangles and she wore a necklace of oyster-white beads.

As I felt that it would be callous to ask her immediately where she planned to go, I said it would be warm in the station restaurant.

We sat at a table next to a window. From where we sat we could see the movements of pedestrians in the street, the beams of glossy cars, the mendicant signs of varicoloured neon lights, and frosty street lamps.

'I suppose no one knows that you have left home,' I said in a conspiratorial voice, stirring the sugared coffee.

'Only my teacher knows,' she answered, 'and he should also know that I am taking the 8.30 train to Cape Town.'

'Cape Town?'

'I have an uncle there. I hope he will help me. And even if he does not, who would want to marry a girl who has run away from home . . . ?'

I drank some coffee, musing what the future held in store for my former pupil and acutely pained by her unhappiness. An inner flow of life seemed to be sustaining her in her flight to seek some other world where she could refashion her life.

'Noorjehan,' I said, 'don't you think you should tell your parents that you will not go through with a wedding.'

'You know that my feelings don't count with them.'

I sensed her inordinate bitterness and disappointment at what her parents had done to her young vulnerable life.

'I must go away,' she said softly, sipping coffee.

I looked out of the window at the medley of lights in the street and the rectangular gems adorning terraces of windows.

'When do you intend to marry?' she suddenly asked in a sharp hysteria-tainted voice.

Her question, so irrelevant to the situation and so unexpected, left me looking at her in bewilderment and curiosity.

'Not yet,' I said, recovering, 'but I intend to get engaged soon.'

She went on sipping coffee. I detected a tremor in her hand as she held the cup to her lips. It ignited within me a fervent sense of being implicated in her life, and aroused a strange, almost occult feeling that I was withhholding some mysterious power in me to protect her and restore her to happiness.

She looked at her watch and said that half an hour remained before her train arrived.

'Please write to me,' I said.

'I promise to keep my teacher informed like a dutiful pupil,' she said, forcing a tepid smile and replacing the cup in the saucer.

'Noorjehan, I hope you will be happy.'

'Thank you,' she said, taking her handbag and standing up. 'I think we should wait on the platform.'

We walked towards the platform and stood there looking at the movements of passengers and porters, the gliding black engines as they entered the station or departed, the hissing of steam and the glowing of furnaces, and at the swift passage of electric trains.

When the train for Cape Town arrived I found an empty compartment for her. I sat down beside her and spoke of some people I knew in Cape Town.

'I shall be glad to meet them,' she said. 'I spent some school holidays there once, so I should be able to find them.'

'Please go to them if you need any help,' I said, taking my note-book out of my pocket and jotting down a few names and addresses on a page.

When I looked up to hand her what I had written, I saw her holding her embroidered handkerchief to her eyes.

'You will be happy again, Noorjehan,' I said.

I looked around the compartment, at the green leather seats, the cramped space, the oval mirror above the washstand. She would be incarcerated in here for many hours, carrying with her the memory of unfeeling parents and the fear of an uncertain future in a distant city.

She took the handkerchief away from her face, pushed back a few strands of hair with her fingers and looked at me with her dark moist eyes.

As it was about time for the train to depart, I alighted and stood on the platform next to her compartment window.

Punctually at half-past eight the train gave its initial jerk and then began to move slowly. Noorjehan gave me her hand for a moment, then lifted it and shouted in a strident schoolgirl's voice: 'Good-bye sir! Good-bye sir!' as the train gathered speed and left the station.

Stunned by the formality of her last words, recalling the academic atmosphere of the class-room, I failed for a moment to register her meaning. Then I was overwhelmed by the rebuke implicit in them, and experienced a trenchant sense of guilt for having been so blind to the romantic image of me which she had conceived.

Her words resonated in my mind as I made my way home. I began to feel that they were not only a rebuke, but a cathartic rejection of me from her innermost self.

Mafika Pascal Gwala/SIDE-STEP

She was a tall, skinny thing with drooping shoulders, yet her face was beautiful. She was twelve, but for her height one would have guessed her age to be seventeen. Everybody called her Tiny.

Word had it that Tiny had been born prematurely as a punishment: her parents, it turned out, had been first cousins. That was the explanation bold mothers gave for Tiny's frail features. Nobody clearly knew how far the story went. Like in any other township, people spoke. People heard and people passed on the little they had grasped. It kept them going. And more than that, the Ndwandwes kept to themselves.

It was a neighbourhood of strugglers who flung themselves on the mercy of Mr. Ndwandwe in spite of the high liquor tips they had to pay him. For Ndwandwe was a clerk for a legal firm in town. He made it a point that business with his clients ended at the office, though this principle did not stop him from touting for more clients after office hours. The people kept Ndwandwe out of their way as far as was possible, and any man could tell you that Ndwandwe was a fly-catcher, sticky and deadly.

Ndwandwe's wife, young and slender, and a woman of modern tastes, worked as a typist for a herbalist. Mrs. Ndwandwe was also the type of woman who, in spite of her liberal outlook, made sure she aired puritanical views whenever she was in young company and treated 'young life' like sour grapes.

The children grew up in such an atmosphere. I lodged at the house next to the Ndwandwes. Every time I walked past the Ndwandwes' house, Tiny would be standing looking through the window, watching passers-by. Occasionally she would show her tongue at young men and boys who walked past that way.

'She's a fast one that child,' a friend once remarked. These approaches did not exclude me from her many victims. And they went on until one day matters came to a pretty pass. I was taking out a girl friend, Busie by name. Tiny was watering flowers along the fence close to our gate. When our eyes met she curled her lips, though her looks were full of mischief. Just as I was pulling the gate open, a splash of water blinded my eyes. I wanted to fist her nose in.

'You skinny swine, what's wrong with you?' I barked at her.

Tiny had dropped the hose and suppressed her laughter. Quickly she picked the hose up.

'Sorry, *boet* Dan. I did not mean it.' Not the least remorse. Instead there was sarcasm in her teasing eyes.

'Let me get you a towel.' She ran into the house.

Busie just stood as if glued to the ground. With drops of water sprinkled on her shoes, she just broke into indignant laughter. We did wait for that silly Tiny. I had to change my wet skipper shirt. In the room Busie could not hide her anger any longer:

'Why do you get used to drips like that? You are always with kids, now you see what they do to you?' But she was being snobbish in a pungent sense, and I told her so.

'I just don't care a brass farthing whether she is your sideline or not; but just warn her, I'll squeeze her bloomin' thing if it itches.

'You are acting innocent eh? That bloody thing there is after you. But I just can't imagine her, a sick-looking thing like her, being my star.' If the child was after me, well, it made things easier for me later. When a woman gets jealous she is hard to convince, and Busie was no exception.

Ndwandwe and his wife hardly ever spent their Saturday afternoons at home. One could always find them at the swimming pool or at the tennis court. On Sundays too they often visited relatives or went for a drive with the family. Tiny, who had grown too naughty, was excluded for her 'wet blanket behaviour,' as her mother put it. Tiny would then remain with the house servant, to stare at the street crowds and play pop records. The children from next door were not allowed into the house because Mrs. Ndwandwe did not like to see them 'dirty' the house.

One day Tiny came up to my room and started a long chat on how fed up she was with pop music. Everyone was digging jazz, her school-friends were, why couldn't she?

'Sure,' I said. There was no law against listening to jazz.

The problem was that her father would not want to buy her jazz records. Then she told me a long rigmarole of a story of how her parents seemed to love classical music when they couldn't really make head or tail of it.

'They just sit like dumbs and ask us all to sit quietly after supper. I get constipated, really.'

But I'm not one to encourage a child to criticize her parents. Let her find the truth herself. As for Tiny, the truth was just around the corner.

From that day Tiny borrowed jazz discs from me, which I generously gave to her. A friendship developed, not in the 'you-know-what' manner. Whenever she came into my room she would look around for something to rouse her curiosity. There seemed to be booby-traps she was setting against every move I took.

'Lend me that magazine *boet* Dan.' She was pointing at the *Esquire* lying on my bed.

'I want to read something.' There were magazines strewn all over on the bed and on the floor, with Tiny kneeling on the edge of the bed, reading one of them.

'You know my father has taken a girl-friend? I'm so glad.' I pretended I wasn't getting her.

'Why, my mother, isn't she his girl-friend? They behave like young lovers even in front of us. How I hate seeing them kiss in our presence, and rolling on the bed in broad daylight.'

I tried to taunt her. 'Right child, collect your dream-lovers. All those long-faced, long-haired figures on these pages. Which one of them is your man?'

Tiny just ignored me. I told her I was expecting a woman any moment, so would she please leave.

She got up, threw herself on the bed — pressing the mattress down, every corner of it.

'Does this bed make any noise at night?' Then she continued rather detachedly, 'I wonder how many pudding dishes have been cooked in this oven.'

'You'll come to know that when you've grown up.'

She now sat on the deck-chair beside the bed, the heap of magazines on her thighs. Her thighs were exposed intentionally, her dress was not mini.

'When I've grown up! Do you think I am a child?' Furiously she grabbed the magazines and frou-froued out of the room.

The next Saturday afternoon I had friends around. A booze come-together. It was then that I decided to fetch my records from Tiny. Now Tiny and I had not been on speaking terms, though I hate to say it. She couldn't come to a settlement with the idea that at thirteen she was still a child. To me at least. And I'm the last man to risk going in for rape. The law has not caught up with me yet, and I want things that way as long as I can keep on running. Apart from that, I knew Ndwandwe well; the bastard would try to wring every ounce of my flesh if he ever got the upper hand of me.

At the door I was met by the house servant, MaZungu, an elderly auntie who did all the household chores. MaZungu was cursing bitterly, 'Such a lazy child, all she knows is how to lift her legs. This thing will never get a husband. Who'll marry such a thing, tell me?' I proceeded to the sitting room. That topic was not my bone to chew.

Tiny lay face-down on the divan. All in black. Black slacks and a black Banlon. Her arms were wound tightly around a cushion, clutching it as if it were the last thing on earth. My rubber soles did not screech (though they were getting worn out) until I stood close to her. Then I noticed, her teeth were thrust deep into the edge of the cushion. I gave her a slight spank on the shoulders.

'You disturbed me.' That's all she was in a position to say, in her mellow voice.

It was three days later and I hadn't seen Tiny since that Saturday. Tiny's mother knocked on my door.

'Is Tiny not in here?' she queried. Her voice was a little off-beat. Seems I was the first suspect because Mrs. Ndwandwe made a search in my room.

'She has been missing since we got up this morning. I just thought — that she must have overslept in your room.' But I'm not that kind of sucker. I don't let them oversleep.

They looked for Tiny all over the township. No sign of Tiny. Her escape was even publicized through the F.M. Radio. All to no avail. Tiny was doing Form I at that time.

After this happening, I gradually got to know the Ndwandwes better. Mrs. Ndwandwe often invited me to have tea with her. Her husband was now working till late, she told me. Tea is not in my line. Booze does a better job. But I could not refuse an 'invitation', never. Call it weak-mindedness if you like.

'Look Dan, I'm thirty today, but I never suspected my daughter could leave me, just like that.' The puritan in her had gone now, her voice was deeply sensual and I listened with two minds as she poured out all her personal problems. Digging them from the well of her childhood dreams, I would say. She also bored me to death with her mamby-pambies on what she termed a 'psychological analysis' of a growing child. She hardly understood it. She was inclined to smile all the time too. But all her smiles were gew-gaw, beneath lay a diabolical love of self-justification.

I ran into Tiny six months later in a busy Maritzburg street. There was an experienced look in her face now. She told me she was a domestic servant in Scottsville.

'How I long to see home again, but I hate the sight of it.'

'It's your own doing, why did you leave home?' I asked her.

'What did you expect me to do? Tiny don't do this, don't do that. Tiny do this and do that,' she replied.

It was now her turn to put off my advances. Her bullying man-friend always spent the night in her room, so we couldn't make it.

Then she tried to touch me for fifty cents. It was ten days before month-end, but there was a go-getter attitude in her manner of asking. She appeared to be a regular hustler. I didn't have to rebuff her. My pockets were soak-empty.

As we parted, I wondered how many men she had entertained with her freedom.

Mtutuzeli Matshoba/TO KILL A MAN'S PRIDE

Every man is born with a certain amount of pride in his humanity. But I have come to believe that this pride is only a mortal thing, and that there are many ways to destroy it. One sure way is to take a man and place him in a Soweto hostel.

At the mention of the word 'hostel' those who have never been near the Soweto version, or live in places where all people are treated as people, if there is any such place in the world, will immediately think of an establishment along Salvation Army lines. They would be infinitely far from the truth. A nearer comparison would be a Nazi concentration camp. North of our location lies our own Auschwitz. From its long grey structures the chimneys jut out of asbestos roofs into the sky; row upon monotonous row of low-built rough brick is packed into a triangular patch north of Mzimhlope and the adjacent Killarney, south east of Meadowlands. These three locations are separated from the hostel by one street on two sides; the third side faces the golden mine dunes across a rocky veld depression with an almost dry stream meandering in the middle from a small dam, which is more like a swamp, in Florida.

The hostel is, by conservative estimate, the home of some twenty thousand migrant labourers from all parts of Southern Africa, some of whom begin the trek as far away as Malawi and Zambia. Since the Kliptown floods at the beginning of 'seventy-seven, the families whose shanties were swept away in the deluge have been 'located' in a section of the hostel complex near Meadowlands. (This section was evacuated in 'seventy-six after certain tragic events about which I shall find the opportunity one day to tell you.) There they waited, a family to a five by three metre cubicle, until the WRAB could figure out what to do with them. Opposite Killarney a space just big enough for two soccer fields side by side was left vacant when the hostel was built. That is all the whole complex can boast by way of recreation facilities. There was also a bottle store, a beer lounge for fifty people all seated around rusty metal tables, and a *mai-mai* (sorghum beer) beerhall, an open square with benches along the walls and under a sort of continuous verandah. Along a street off the Soweto highway were prospering shops where the hostel inmates used to buy food. Today, the ruins of these buildings are ghastly monuments of the day of fire in June 'seventy-six.

It was there, in room 413, that my friend Somdali stayed. We had met at work. I had just been hired and was still keeping to myself, working at the tedious paper guillotine impatiently, with repeated glances at the clock high up on the wall. Lunch-time was forty-five minutes away and it seemed to me that Detail Die-cut Limited worked to a different time scale. The minutes were crawling, and Pieters had just come to instruct me about something I knew, for the thousandth time. Perhaps he underestimated my intelligence; but more likely he was 'breaking me in', measuring my tolerance. The die-cutting machines were whining incessantly and above their noise the maddening sound of Springbok Radio screeched out of a small home-made soundbox hanging from the whitewashed concrete roof which was supported by colossal, whitewashed cylindrical pillars. The walls too were white-washed. The thirty or so factory 'girls' were working noisily at their tables behind me, chattering and giggling as if trying to outdo the machines and the radio.

Tea-break, my first there, had been an ordeal of eyes studying me from behind large mugs and the tins that were used as teacups. Fortunately, the 'girls' had their own tea-room, otherwise it would have been worse. There were sixteen 'boys', including myself, around the long unvarnished table. I was sitting at the far side, a pungent toilet door behind me — not the type that you sit on, but a hole in the floor for squatting over. I could never bring myself to use it during all the eight months I spent working there. The tea was the only thing the firm could offer. You bought your own bread and anything that you could afford to go with it. Since I hadn't known that, and hadn't had a cent in my pocket when I was taken on in the morning, I was not eating. After being tipped by a neighbour who worked next door to Detail that one 'boy' had severed his fingers with the guillotine and there might be a 'space', I had borrowed a twenty cent piece for the train ticket and rushed there. So now I sat at the end of the table, not knowing what to do with my hands and feeling like a specimen for human study and contemplation while the others were hurriedly eating their first meal of the day. The 'girls' were chatting and giggling at the tops of their lungs in the other room. One of the 'boys' suggested that John had cut his fingers on purpose to get workers' insurance money. They talked about it until the buzzer sounded after fifteen minutes.

At lunch I had nowhere to go. I decided to familiarise myself with the neighbourhood. It was one of those rusty industrial outskirts of town where one sees no one but grease-stained overall-clad mechanics and handy-men. Nothing but trucks and vans off-loading semi-processed goods. Our firm was at the southern end of Mooi street, under a maze of highways, with Heidelberg road forming a T with Mooi street, and running into mine dunes. I followed Mooi street in the direction of Carlton Centre. I had an hour, a hungry hour to kill. Not that my empty stomach worried me; well, it worried me only because it was an uncomfortable sensation which could not be totally ignored. Someone was walking beside me. His tall shadow had fallen in line with mine. Both of us had our hands in our pockets. I moved aside to give him way to pass but he did not.

'*Hawu, sawubona mfowethu.*' He extended his massive hand to greet. It was one of the 'boys' from the firm; tall, receding forehead, smooth dark skin and one eye. In the one eye and the wide grin I could read recognition, although I had never seen the man myself. His Elmer skipper that was no longer its original white but brownish, and the flimsy dark trousers that came to just above his naked ankles, were worn without any thought of physical decoration, but only to cover the body. I gave him my hand.

'Seems you don't recognise me, but I know you. I have seen you at Mzimhlope.' He was telling the truth.

I felt slightly embarrassed at not knowing a man who knew me. It's always like that. Anyway he did not know me by name either. 'I can't even recognise you. Let alone place you,' I answered, also showing my teeth.

'My name is Somdali. I also stay at Mzimhlope,' he said by way of introduction.

'Mzimhlope? Which side?' I was asking with due regard for his feelings, not wishing to make him feel awkward. I had already placed him in 'Auschwitz' from his appearance and the way he spoke with a deep Zulu accent. People born and bred in Soweto speak every language in a characteristic way.

'The northern side of the station,' and seeing that he had finally to divulge the guarded domicile, he amassed enough courage to tell me, 'in the hostel.'

'Oh, I see. My name is Mtutu. I stay in . . . in the location.'

'Yes. I have seen you there, when I'm going to and from the station.' They hold a servitude, a right of way in the location and are hardly worth a second glance from the location residents, except maybe the dark night's children who never fail to collect the dues on Fridays and month-ends, or the fallen women who provide the hosteliers with female company for sale.

I did not have anything to say. We went a few paces before he continued. 'You were lucky to arrive first. One guy cut his fingers with the guillotine yesterday. That thing thing needs to be operated with care, it's dangerous. You've filled that guy's space.' I did not comment. 'They're going to teach you the machines too.' I let him go on. 'But you won't be paid before you're registered. They first take a person for trial.'

That was interesting. 'How long is the trial?'

'Two, three weeks — Pieters decides. But *ag*, it's only a way to get free labour out of the people they employ before they register them. Pieters is the owner of the firm. He takes the good-looking girls away in his VW station wagon 'to clean his house' before he registers them. You should see him among the girls — acts like a bull that has been kept alone for months, when it is released among a herd of cows. Some of the girls are married. When their husbands want to talk to them on the phone, or come looking for them at lunch or after work, he refers to them as 'boyfriends'. Otherwise he has a little sense of humour when he has not got out on the wrong side of his bed in the morning. His assistant is aloof and has an affair with one of the two Indian girls in the office.'

'How much is the starting pay?'

'Twenty-five rand a week. Thirty for those who have been with the firm over three years. The women, I don't know.'

He told me a little more about himself, that he had come from Mondlo near Vryheid in Natal to work in Johannesburg with a forged pass eight years before, that he had been with Detail for two years and (he must have guessed I was curious to know) that he had lost his eye in a stick-fight competition when he was a teenager, an unfortunate accident for which no-one could be blamed. 'Your mouth is dry. You

106

must be hungry.'

'I'm used to it, *mfo*. Don't worry,' I said politely.

'Say it again, *mfowethu*. We are all used to it at one time or another of our lives. But I have fifty cents here. Let's go buy some *magewu*.'

That was how I struck up a friendship with the man from the hostel. At the end of the first week he lent me money to buy a weekly ticket, gave me cigarettes every day without being asked; we ate and talked together during lunch and entrained together at Mzimhlope and Faraday Stations.

Tell me — who could deny such a man friendship? I could see that people we met who knew me always wondered what I was up to with a 'country boy', but I knew better. However I never invited him home — what could I invite him for? To remind him that he also had a family he was denied? And it was not until after I had been registered that he invited me to the hostel 'just to see where I live'.

Registration for work is such an interesting example of a way of killing a man's pride that I cannot pass it by without mention. It was on Monday, after two weeks of unrewarded labour and perseverance, that Pieters gave me a letter which said I had been employed as a general labourer at his firm. I was to take the letter to the notorious 80 Albert Street. Monday is usually the busiest day there because everybody wakes up on this day determined to find a job. They end up dejected, crowding the labour office for 'piece' jobs.

That Monday I woke up elated, whistling all the way as I cleaned the coal stove, made fire to warm the house for those who were still asleep, and took my toothbrush and washing rags to the tap outside the toilet. The cold water was revivifying as I splashed it over my upper body. I greeted 'Star', also washing at the tap diagonally opposite my home. Then I took the washing basin, half-filled it with water and went into the lavatory to wash the rest of me. When I had finished washing and dressing I bade them goodbye at home and set out, swept into the torrent of workers rushing to the station. Somdali had reached the station first and we waited for our trains with the hundreds already on the platform. The guys from the location prefer to wait for trains on the station bridge. Many of them looked like children who did not want to go to school. I did not sympathize with them. The little time my brothers have to themselves, Saturday and Sunday, some of them spend worshipping Bacchus.

The train schedule was geared to the morning rush hour. From four in the morning the trains had rumbled in with precarious frequency. If you stay near the road to the hostel you are woken up by the shuffle of a myriad footfalls long before the first train. I have seen these people on my way home when the nocturnal bug has bitten me. All I can say is that an endless flow of resolute men hastening in the inky, misty morning down Mohale street to the station is an awesome apparition.

I had arrived ten minutes early at the station. The 'ninety-five' to George Goch passed Mzimhlope while I was there. This train brought the free morning stuntman show. The daredevils ran along the roof of the train, a few centimetres from the naked cable carrying thousands of electric volts, and ducked under every pylon. One mistimed step, a slip — and reflex action would send his hand clasping for support. No comment from any of us at the station. The train shows have been going on since time immemorial and have lost their magic.

My train to Faraday arrived, bursting along the seams with its load. The spaces between the adjacent coaches were filled with people. So the only way I could get on the train was by wedging myself among those hanging on perilously by hooking their fingers into the narrow runnels along the tops of the coaches, their feet on the door ledges. A slight wandering of the mind, a sudden swaying of the train as it switched lines, bringing the weight of the others on top of us, a lost grip — and another labour unit would be abruptly terminated. We hung on for dear life until Faraday.

In Pieters' office. Four automatic telephones, two scarlet and two orange coloured, two fancy ashtrays, a gilded ball-pen stand complete with gilded pen and chain, two flat plastic trays, the one on the left marked IN and the other one OUT, all displayed on the bland face of a large highly polished desk. Under my feet a thick carpet that made me feel like a piece of dirt. On the soft opal green wall on my left a big framed 'Desiderata' and above me a ceiling of heavenly splendour. Behind the desk, wearing a short cream-white safari suit, leaning back in a regal flexible armchair, his hairy legs (the pale skin of which curiously made me think of a frog's ventral side) balanced on the edge of the desk in the manner of a sheriff in an old-fashioned western, my blue-eyed, slightly bald, jackal-faced overlord.

'You've got your pass?'

'Yes, mister Pieters.' That one did not want to be called *baas*.

'Let me see it. I hope it's the right one. You got a permit to work in Johannesburg?'

'I was born here, mister Pieters.' My hands were respectfully behind me.

'It doesn't follow.' He removed his legs from the edge of the table and opened a drawer. Out of it he took a small bundle of typed papers. He signed one of them and handed it to me. 'Go to the pass office. Don't spend two days there. Otherwise you come back and I've taken somebody else in your place.'

He squinted his eyes at me and wagged his tongue, trying to amuse me the way he would try to make a baby smile. That really amused me, his trying to amuse me the way he would a baby. I thought he had a baby's mind.

'*Esibayeni*'. Two storey red-brick building occupying a whole block. Address: 80 Albert street, or simply 'Pass Office'. Across the street, half the block (the remaining half a parking space and 'home' of the homeless methylated spirit drinkers of the city) taken up by another red-brick structure. Not offices this time, but '*Esibayeni*' (at the kraal) itself. No question why it has been called that. The whole black population of Johannesburg above pass age knows that place.

Like I said, it was full on a Monday, full of wretched men with defeated eyes sitting along the gutters on both sides of Albert Street, others grouped where the sun's rays leaked through the skyscrapers and the rest milling about. When a car driven by a white man went up the street pandemonium broke loose as men, I mean dirty slovenly *men*, trotted behind it and fought to give their passes first. If the white person had not come for that purpose they cursed him until he went out of sight. Occasionally a truck or van would come to pick up labourers for a piece job. The clerk would shout out the number of men that were wanted for such and such a job, say forty, and double the number would be all over the truck before you could say 'stop'. None of them would want to miss the cut, which caused quite some problems for the employer. A shrewd businessman would take all and simply divide the money he had laid out among the whole group, as it was left to him to decide how much to pay for a piece job. Everybody was satisfied in the end — the temporary employer having his work done in half the time he had bargained for, and each of the labourers with enough for a ticket back to the pass-office the following day, and maybe ten cents worth of dishwater and bread from the oily restaurants in the neighbourhood, for three days. Those who were smart and familiar with the ways of the pass-office handed their passes in with twenty and/or fifty-cent pieces between the pages. This gave them first preference, and they could choose the better jobs.

The queue to *'Esibayeni'* was moving slowly. It snaked about thirty metres around the corner of Polly street. It had taken me more than an hour to reach the door. Inside the ten-foot wall was an asphalt rectangle, longitudinal benches along the opposite wall in the shade of narrow tin ledges, filled with bored looking men, toilets on the lower side of the rectangle, facing wide bustling doors. It would take me another three hours to reach the clerks. If I finished there just before lunch-time, it would mean that I would not be through with my registration by four in the afternoon when the pass office closed. Fortunately I had twenty cents and I knew that the blackjacks who worked there were nothing but starving leeches. One took me up the queue to four people who stood before a snarling white boy. Those whose places ahead of me in the queue had been usurped wasted their breath grumbling.

The man in front of me could not understand what was being bawled at him in Afrikaans. The clerk gave up explaining, not prepared to use any other language than his own. I felt that at his age, about twenty, he should be at RAU learning to speak other languages. That way he wouldn't burst a vein trying to explain everything in one tongue just because it was his. He was either bone-headed or downright lazy or else impatient to 'rule the Bantus'.

He took a rubber stamp and banged it furiously on one of the pages of the man's pass, and threw the book into the man's face. 'Go to the other building, stupid!'

The man said, 'Thanks,' and elbowed his way to the door.

'Next! *Wat soek jy?*' he asked in a bellicose voice when my turn to be snarled at came. He had freckles all over his face, and a weak jaw.

I gave him the letter of employment and explained in Afrikaans that I wanted E and F cards. My use of his language eased some of the tension out of him. He asked for my pass in a slightly calmer manner. I gave it to him and he paged through. 'Good, you have permission to work in Johannesburg right enough.' He took two cards from a pile in front of him and laboriously wrote my pass numbers on them. Again I thought that he should still be at school, learning to write properly. He stamped the cards and told me to go to room six in the other block. There were about twelve other clerks growling at people from behind a continuous U-shaped desk, and the space in front of the desk was overcrowded with people who made it difficult to get to the door.

Another blackjack barred the entrance to the building across the street. 'Where do you think you're going?'

'*Awu!* What's wrong with you? I'm going to room six to be registered. You're wasting my time,' I answered in an equally unfriendly way. His eyes were bloodshot, as big as a cow's and as stupid, his breath was fouled with *'mai-mai'*, and his attitude was a long way from helpful.

He spat into his right hand, rubbed his palms together and grabbed a stick that was leaning against the wall near him. 'Go in,' he challenged, indicating with a tilt of his head, and dilating his gaping nostrils.

His behaviour perplexed me, more than angering or dismaying me. It might be that he was drunk; or was I supposed to produce something first, and was he so uncouth as not to tell me why he would not allow me to go in? Whatever the reason, I regretted that I could not kick some of the *'mai-mai'* out of the sagging belly, and proceeded on my way. I turned to see if there was anyone else witnessing the unnecessary aggression.

'No, *mfo*. You've got to wait for others who are also going to room six,' explained a man with half his teeth missing, wearing a tattered overcoat and nothing to cover his large, parched feet. And, before I could say thanks: 'Say, *mnumzane*, have you got a cigarette on you? Y'know, I haven't had a single smoke since yesterday.'

I gave him the one shrivelled Lexington I had in my shirt-pocket. He indicated that he had no matches either. I searched myself and gave the box to him. His hands shook violently when he lit and shielded the flame. *'Ei! Babalaz* has me.'

'Ya, neh,' I said, for the sake of saying something. The man turned and walked away as if his feet were sore. I leaned against the wall and waited. When there were a good many of us waiting the gatekeeper grunted that we should follow him inside to another bustling 'kraal'. That was where the black clerks shouted out the jobs at fifty cents apiece or more, depending on whether they were permanent or temporary. The men in there were fighting like mad to reach the row of windows where they could hand in their passes. We followed the blackjack up a sloping cement way rising to a green double door.

There was nowhere it wasn't full at the pass-office. Here too it was full of the same miserable figures that were buzzing all over the place, but this time they stood in a series of queues at a long counter like the one across the street, only this one was L-shaped and the white clerks behind the brass grille wore ties. I decided that they were of a better class than the others, although there was no doubt that they also had the same rotten manners and arrogance. The blackjack left us with another one who told us which queues to join. Our cards were taken and handed to a lady filing clerk who went to look for our records.

I was right! The clerks were, at bottom, all the same. When I reached the counter I pushed my pass under the grille. The man who took it had close-cropped hair and a thin sharp face. He went through my pass checking it against a photostat record with my name scrawled on top in a handwriting that I did not know.

'Where have you been from January until now, September?' he said in a cold voice, looking at me from behind the grille like a god about to admonish a sinner.

I have heard some funny tales, from many tellers, when it comes to answering that question. See if you can recognise this one:

CLERK: *Heer, man. Waar was jy al die tyd, jong?* (Lord, man. Where have you been all the time, *jong?*)
MAN: I . . . I was mad, *baas.*
CLERK: Mad!? You think I'm your uncle, *kaffer?*
KAFFER: No *baas,* I was mad.
CLERK: *Jy . . . jy dink . . .* (and the white man's mouth drops open with no words coming out.)
KAFFER: (Coming to the rescue of the *baas* with an explanation.) At home they tell me that I was mad all along, *baas.* 'Strue.
CLERK: Where are the doctor's papers? You must have been to hospital if you were mad! (With annoyance.)
KAFFER: I was treated by a witchdoctor, *baas.* Now I am better and have found a job.

Such answers serve them right. If it is their aim to harass the poor people with impossible questions, then they should expect equivalent answers. I did not, however, say something out of the way. I told the truth. 'Looking for work.'

'Looking for work, who?'

'*Baas.*'

'That's right. And what have you been living on all along?' he asked, like a god.

'Scrounging, and looking for work.' Perhaps he did not know that among us blacks a man is never thrown to the dogs.

'Stealing, huh? You should have been caught before you found this job. Do you know that you have contravened section two, nine, for nine months? Do you know that you would have gone to jail for two years if you had been caught, *tsotsi?* These policemen are not doing their job anymore,' he said, turning his attention to the stamps and papers in front of him.

I had wanted to tell him that if I had had a chance to steal, I would not have hesitated to do so, but I stopped myself. It was the wise thing to act timid in the circumstances. He gave me the pass after stamping it. The blackjack told me which corridor to follow. I found men sitting on benches alongside one wall and stood at the end of the queue. The man in front of me shifted and I sat on the edge. This time the queue was reasonably fast. We moved forward on the seats of our pants. If you wanted to prevent them shining you had to stand up and sit, stand up and sit. You could not follow the line standing. The patrolling blackjack made you sit in an embarrassing way. Halfway to the door we were approaching, the man next to me removed his upper clothes. All the others nearer to the door had their clothes bundled under their armpits. I did the same.

We were all vaccinated in the first room and moved on to the next one where we were X-rayed by some impatient black technicians. The snaking line of black bodies reminded me of prisoners being searched. That was what 80 Albert Street was all about.

The last part of the medical examination was the most disgraceful. I don't know whether it was designed to save expense or on some other ground of expediency, but on me it had the effect of dishonour. After being X-rayed we could put on our shirts and cross the corridor to the doctor's cubicle. Outside were people of both sexes waiting to settle their own affairs. You passed them before entering the cubicle, inside which sat a fat white man in a white dust-coat with a face like an owl, behind a simple desk. The man who had gone in ahead of me was zipping up his fly. I unzipped mine and stood facing the owl behind the desk, holding my trousers with both hands. He tilted his fat face to the right and left twice or thrice. 'Ja. Your pass.'

I hitched my trousers up while he harried me to give him the pass before I could zip my trousers. I straightened myself at leisure, in spite of his *'Gou, gou, gou!'* My pride had been hurt enough by exposing myself to him, with the man behind me preparing to do so and the one in front of me having done the same, a row of men of different ages parading themselves before a bored owl. When I finished dressing I gave him the pass. He put a little maroon stamp somewhere in amongst the last pages. It must have meant that I was fit to work.

The medical examination was over and the women on the benches outside pretended they did not know. The young white ladies clicking their heels up and down the passages showed you they knew. You held yourself together as best as you could until you vanished from their sight, and you never told anybody else about it.

'*Maar*, my friend. Why don't you come with me to the hostel one day? Just to see where I stay, and meet some of the guys who come from Natal with me. Are you afraid?' Somdali asked as we went through the barriers at Faraday station.

It was the third week after I had been to the pass office. I was even beginning to get used to the twenty-five rand and few cents in a brown envelope that the Indian lady bookkeepers in the office had given me, and which made me feel very ashamed each time I received it. I felt like a dupe when I had to go to the office to sign for chicken feed after working honestly for a whole week and taking Pieters' scorn without any complaint. He seemed to think that we, the workers, depended on him for a living — and to forget that he, in turn, depended on our labour for his easy life. Maybe this was because he knew that the greater demand was for jobs, for work, not for labour. Everybody was at his mercy. Somdali had been right about the bull-like behaviour of our boss. He behaved like a sheik in a harem. None of the women liked it, but they had to hide their disapproval as long as they wanted to remain working. We only gritted our teeth and let him continue.

I could not refuse Somdali's invitation. It was not an invitation to a cocktail party but it was an invitation right enough. Such are the invitations of the simple. Apart from the fact that he was my friend, in the evenings I usually had nothing to do at home but listen to the hysterical screams of my sisters' babies, while being asked to shift this way and that in the doll's house. And the hostel was no longer danger-ous: 'seventy-six had come and gone. Before Somdali invited me there, the hostel was to me a place I knew of and didn't know about. I knew it must be hell to live there — family men without families, married men without wives. That was how I had seen it, and that was where my concern ended. But when it comes to the misery of life one has to partake to really understand. The deepest pangs of the man caught up in squalor are never really felt from a safe distance. Most people shrink from experiencing what it feels like to be down, licking the base of the drain. Somdali's invitation was my chance to get to the core of hostel life.

In order for you to understand why I had never cared about the hostel, I think a brief description of how I viewed the hostel from afar will be necessary. At first the security of the hostel was tight with watchmen at every gate, preventing outsiders from entering the premises. Perhaps someone still had a little conscience, and wished to try and hide the shameful place. As time went on this security slackened until there was free traffic between the location and the hostel, although only men went there — it would have been sheer madness for a woman to go into that encampment of deprived men. However, even then it was the location drunks who went there after the poisonous brew of yeast, brown bread, brown sugar and water, *mbamba* or *skokiaan* and other variations of the same thing, which were readily available and out of sight of the people of the location. We only went there to sell something, a watch maybe, the hosteliers being ever prepared to 'snatch a bargain', or to use the showers and quickly return to the location.

The few inmates with a venturesome spirit or having relatives 'outside', most of whom had been discovered there in the Golden City by the tracing of lineage, went out to mix with the location people. Black people seem to believe that they are all related to each other in this way. This way you can never be lost, wherever you go, because everybody with the same surname or clan-name as you is regarded as a relative and is obliged to you. Others formed bands who invaded the location at night solely to rape and kill, so that there was someone lying dead somewhere in the small location once in every week. This gave the hostel people a formidableness that made it difficult to befriend them or to sympathise with their terrible lot.

The bulk of the inmates chose to stay 'inside' at weekends, filling in the emptiness of their lives with alcohol and traditional song that brought them nostalgia for the places of their birth, the barren hopelessness of which had driven them to gather scraps in the human jungles of Johannesburg. Murder was also rife inside. Dehumanized people lose their concern for life: 'We live like hogs, wild dogs or any other neglected animals. The pets of *abeLungu* live better than we,' Somdali would say to me on a day when he was in a really depressed mood. Normally he never complained.

'Okay Somdali, I'll go with you today. It's still early,' I said and saw that he was pleased.

At the station a man named Joe, who was already quite familiar with Somdali from dice games in the hostel, joined us. Somdali and Joe were friends, only that was rather costly to the former. What kept them going was that Somdali provided beers. Innocent Somdali was not aware of the exploitation and derived great satisfaction from living with *amajita*, as he would say. There was no need to wise him up. I could not help laughing inside when I heard Joe promising to get Somdali a woman and to lead the latter to a 'spot'. The expeditions always ended up with both of them drunk and Somdali claiming that he had been pickpocketed at the 'spot', but not sore about it, perhaps considering it as part of the sacrifice of learning to live Soweto-style. The three of us went up Mohale street with the wave of countless people, turned down Carr street and fifty metres later crossed the new Soweto highway where it started skirting Mzimhlope.

We entered the first 'street' to our left. It was the first time that I had been to the hostel to visit someone (I had gone there on impersonal matters) and naturally my senses were sharp. The first thing that told you you were in a different place was the smell hanging in the air, the stench of rotting rubbish, urine, dirty water and neglected toilets, an unhygienic mucky atmosphere that almost made you puke. If you've ever been near a pigsty, then you have the right idea. Not that I rate the location much better, but at least the location smells of life, not neglect. As we went deeper into the hostel I was disgusted to think that it was humans who let other humans live like that, in the lowest state of dereliction: and yet their sweat fuelled the economy of the country to keep it going. The so-called last bastion against roving Marxism; a bastion of men scraping small sooty enamel pots to cook the tomatoes, onions and mealie meal they had in plastic carriers. A bastion of men wasting away on *skokiaan*, a bastion of men washing overalls in the water-troughs; a bastion of men walking in the open in their underpants. Don't count me in, and count Somdali out too.

The first dormitory was fifty short paces long. Three doors. A gap. Another pile of brownish, greyish bricks and undulating asbestos on top, this time the toilets. Six basins in a row in an enclosure with no door and the wall going only halfway up so that a passerby could see a person sitting inside. Adjacent to this: high narrow troughs, apparently to wash dishes in. Behind this: low, deep cement troughs for washing clothes in. The longitudinal half of this place an empty room with eight showers. A man was vigorously rubbing soap on his naked glistening body under one of them. The long dormitories alternated with the toilets. A man obeying the call of nature in the middle of the night had to walk outside for not less than fifteen paces — well, like in the location. The wise thing to do was to be armed when going to the toilet.

There had been an attempt to make the place homely, maybe when it was still new. Peach trees lined our way on both sides and through the gaps between the buildings I saw that there were garden patches with wilting plants, mostly maize and potatoes. The grass behind and between the buildings grew waist high. The stench was unbearable.

At length, after jumping and stepping around the puddles, we came to where Somdali stayed. He pushed the metal door inwards without knocking. The noise it made put our teeth on edge. He went in ahead and as we followed, my foot sank into stagnant water just in front of the door. There was a buzz of agitated insects.

When you go into a place where people are living, you expect to find something, at least, which indicates that this is so. But in the hostel you are utterly disheartened. The door opened into a medium-sized room. The floor was bare, dust-laden cement. Near the wall facing the door, which had two squares cut into it for windows that had never been cleaned since the hostel was built, were two tables made of cement slabs on metal stilts coming out of the floor. The benches on opposite sides of the tables were also made of cement slabs resting on sewerage pipes. Two old men in denim overalls sat at one table talking in a dull murmur and apparently drinking from a plastic container between them. They did not even raise their eyes to see who was coming in. Against the side walls were long steel cabinets from which the green paint had peeled long ago and which rust now covered almost completely. They extended from the front wall half the length of the side walls to two openings on the left and right. The walls were not plastered and the asbestos roof rested on rafters that were coated with thick layers of soot and spider-webs. The soot might have come from a brazier during winter.

We followed Somdali to the opening on the right, into a closet for four people sleeping in the corners. The first opening led to another, into a closet exactly the same as the one we had passed, except that it was the last and had only one opening to it. Eight men on either side of the central room, which meant sixteen men to one door and, there being three doors in the long dormitories, forty-eight men to one unit fifty paces long. There is absolutely no privacy there. You sleep in your corner of the closet, on the door-like lid of a brick kist in which you are supposed to keep your possessions, a metre from the man next to you and the men below you.

The last closet was full of men huddled around a small one-plate stove hardly a foot high from which a thin battered chimney pipe rose

117

to a small hole in the roof. The sun was setting and it was cold in the 'house', although the middle of summer was not long gone. Worn, dirty shreds and blankets were heaped on the wooden lids and from the smutty rafters hung all sorts of dust-covered rags, jackets, overcoats, jerseys and whatever you may care to name. There was even a bicycle suspended with a wire, and two electric guitars. A smell of rotting food, sweat and the coal-smoke from the miniature stove stifled the air. Suddenly the naked bulb blinked alive and shed a light that made the room eerie, casting darkness in the corners.

'This is my bed, *majita,* make yourselves at home,' Somdali said and took off his jacket which he added to the clothes hanging near his 'bed'. We sat on the kist, Joe settling down beside me without showing any sign of surprise at the unspeakable living conditions. As I said, he was used to personal visits to the hostel. As for me, I was shocked.

After hanging his coat Somdali turned to greet the others. When we had come in they had just glanced at us and resumed their conversation. The African way of entering the company of others is for the new-comer to announce himself by greeting first. It is the *'umthakathi'* (wizard) who arrives unseen. *'Sonibonani ekhaya* (Good evening at home).'

'Awu, Somdali! You are back from *esiLungwini. Athin'ama Bhunu?* (What do the Boers say?)' They greeted him enthusiastically, as if they were noticing Somdali for the first time.

'What can they say, but continue to give us the scorpion's bite? Er, *madoda,* I have brought you a friend of mine that I work with . . .' and he introduced me, starting with my first name and inserting the possessive preposition 'ka' before my surname. 'Well, this *skelm,* Joe, you know.'

One man held my hand and introduced himself. The others followed suit. I counted eight of them. Somdali came to sit next to me. 'You seem not to be at ease, my friend. Relax. You must be shocked by this stable when you see it for the first time. You'll get used to it, *mfo-wethu.'*

'Let's hope I will. But I doubt it,' I replied.

'This is our reward for working for the whites. They don't care how you live, as long as you turn up for work the following day,' said Somdali bitterly.

'They don't know. Otherwise they'd be ashamed of themselves,' I answered, thinking that no normal human being could consciously tolerate other people living that way.

'You think so?' Somdali seemed to disagree. 'What do you say of the very idea of building such a place, of removing men from their families after taking their livestock and what little land they had, and burying them in filth? Is that not meant to kill a man's pride in himself?'

I understood what Somdali meant. Before I could make that known in so many words he went on, with gall in his voice, 'If you take a man, a married man, from his wife it's tantamount to castrating him. A bullock is castrated to make it strong for labour purposes.'

'Yes, Somdali is right, *ndodana* (son).' It was old Khuzwayo, the grey-head sexagenarian Somdali had told me was like a father to them in their labour camp dens. 'Come nearer boy, I want to see you when I talk to you. Fana, sit yourself somewhere.' Fana stood up from the tin of paint he was sitting on. I replaced him beside the old man. The little stove was beginning to glow on the sides, a solitary pot filling it's whole face and boiling furiously. The heat-wave was too much for me, so I shifted a little backward. The old man also positioned himself to look directly into my face. His Bushman-like features were attractive.

'*Ya, ndodana ka . . . ?* (Yes, son of?)' I answered him by finishing his greeting with my name. I did this twice before he heard me well. 'You defend *abeLungu* by saying they do not know? Now, my boy, tell me this: is this — the way we live, all of us blacks — our rightful legacy from the ancestors, or from Tixo who made heaven and earth?' He paused, looking at me. 'Or is it an apportionment that our conquerors think fit for us?'

'It is the latter, *baba*,' I replied without certainty, as I did not know what old Khuzwayo was getting around to. Everybody was listening. Doubtless they were all sensitive about the question of their status in the social stratification. They knew that a man could not sink lower down than they were, and the only way they could let off steam was by damning the system that degraded them. To them every white man stood for the forces that held them down with their faces in the muck of the hostel. In other words, their hopelessness bred a volcanic racism.

'That is right, my boy. You are following my words well. You see, they have laid claim to everything that you can turn your eyes to see. If everything had gone according to their desires they would have owned even us black people, to till the soil for them until the end of the world. But one human being cannot be owned by another. And since they are unable to own us, all they lack is a way to justify genocide. You can remove a man from the face of a piece of paper, scratch his name out and pretend that he does not exist, but you cannot remove him physically from the face of the earth without murdering him. For he is born here and so he dies here, fighting perhaps for the one square metre he owns in the world. For man was created by Nkulunkulu so that he might avail himself of that which *umhlaba* (earth) was made to give. Man was not created to divide for others that which is bad and to keep that which is good for himself. We all die in the end and leave everything as we found it when we were born.'

'Ya. The old man is right, *mfowethu*. No man is ordained to determine the fate of another. If he has, by some vile means, usurped the other's right to self-determination, then peace is disturbed. When peace is disturbed it is always a sign that someone who is dissatisfied is trying to get his rightful share from the world.' So said the man who had introduced himself as Bongani. I had tried to vindicate their oppressors and they assailed me from all directions.

I attempted to manoevre out of the spot I was in by explaining exactly what I had meant. 'What I intended to say was that the majority of whites do not know how you live because the whole rotten situation is camouflaged. The harsh enforcement of the inhumane laws that result in such conditions produces a calm of sorts, and this deceives them into thinking that everybody is satisfied except a few anarchists and agitators who must be weeded out. I think that the people are very apt when they refer to the police as "the camouflage" these days, because they camouflage black vexations with brute violence — and whenever there is a marked "calm" the whites are made to believe that all is peaceful. Whatever the cause of strife was, it has been settled and things are under control. The means by which this has been brought about are made light of, or deliberately and unscrupulously suppressed. A counterfeit peace is produced for them. They don't know what is going on "in their own backyard." That's what I meant.'

They seemed satisfied with my clarification, for no one attacked me after that.

Old Khuzwayo had taken to me. He slapped my shoulder amicably. 'You know, my son, you know. For a moment I thought that you were lost. Your explanation takes my mind back to the end of the Second World War. When the time came to ask the German nation why they had allowed people to be decimated in front of their eyes, they shamefully claimed that they had not known what was taking place until it was too late to do anything about it but stand up in defence of the sovereignty of their country. It did not help them any because everybody was against them. Their country was divided among their enemies

120

because they allowed some fanatics to control their destiny. Blind obedience and gullibility are suicidal.'

I stayed longer than I had intended with Somdali and his mates. Bongani, who had been cooking — boiling an assortment of old vegetables into a thick soup — cut our topic short by announcing supper. Each man dived to where he kept his spoon and, at the drop of an eyelid, I was alone in front of the small stove. Even Khuzwayo had been surprisingly swift for his age. Joe came from the shadows to sit on the old man's plastic milk crate.

I saw why they had been so fast in their reactions to Bongani's call. They all ate together from the steaming pot. Three loaves of bread were placed on a sheet of paper that was spread on the dusty floor. They broke pieces from the loaves and scooped from the pot with their spoons. You could see that they were racing, each wanting to down more soup and pieces of bread than the next man. I don't wish to insult those brothers of ours, but have you ever seen the deadly excitement of a predator after making a killing? They even fought over space.

'Damn it, Fana, don't push!' snarled one of them.

'Give me space. How do you think I'll reach the pot?' retorted Fana with a full mouth.

'You're cheeky, you Fana. One day I'll beat it out of you,' the other one threatened.

Old Khuzwayo ruled for peace. 'Awu, don't fight over food like puppies, boys. You're spoiling everybody's meal. And while you're busy fighting, the food is getting finished.'

Supper over, Somdali sent Fana to buy him 'mai-mai' from the opposite dormitory. Bongani went to wash the pot and the spoons in the sink outside. Another one took a broom to sweep where they had been eating. 'No, boy. You'll sweep tomorrow morning. The dust will take time to settle down,' said Somdali, preventing him. He collected only the crumbs they had made. There was a certain organisation in the way they lived. The young ones did the chores.

When Bongani returned he removed the guitars from their perches and gave one to Fana. They connected the guitars to an amplifier with a PM 10 and strummed for some seconds. Then, with extraordinary dexterity, they played a moving 'mbaqanga' (a fast African beat that is still a favourite with country people). The sound of an electric guitar in that gloomy lair, with the men sitting around the small stove and listening sorrowfully to the melodious twangs, the overhanging dust-covered rags, the bicycle, the shadows cast by the dim, stained light bulb, mesmerised me in a way which I fail to find words to describe. Somdali was drinking his beer in slow sips. He passed the can to the next man, who took a few draughts and also passed it on. If you did not want to drink you gave the can to the man beside you. The music paused while Bongani and Fana drank. They started another song immediately after that.

'What's the time, Somdali?' I asked, thinking that at home they would be wondering why I had not returned from work. I was three hours late already.

'I don't know, my friend. You want to go now? *Madoda,* any of you got a watch?' None had, so one of the younger men had to go and ask the time in the opposite house, and bring another can of beer.

'Yes, *ndoda,* I should be running away before my people decide to go looking for me at the police-stations.' It was after nine. I bade everybody goodnight and stood to go. Joe did the same. Somdali took us out. 'So you've seen where I stay, my friend. Hope you come by yourself when you've got time. So long.'

'Sweet, Somdali. See you tomorrow morning,' I said, and we parted.

As we came out of the gaping fence onto the highway, I remarked about our visit to Joe.

'You know, Joe, I've never spent such a long time in the hostel. Jesus, man, these people live like animals. To travel the whole distance from where they come from to stay like this!'

'Ya. It's bad, sonny. Think of the many other such places in Soweto alone. How many are there? Let's see — It's this one, Dube, Nhlazane, Merafe, Nancefield,' counted Joe.

'And Diepkloof. All about the same size. Hundreds of thousands of disgruntled men, leaving hundreds of thousands of starving families in the so-called homelands. That's not counting us location people, because we're not much better off than the hostel residents except in that we are allowed a temporary sojourn with our families.'

'Not counting the rest of South Africa either. It's not only Johannesburg. All over the country there are people who have been uprooted from normal family life to slave in the cities. Take Somdali's bitterness and multiply it about twenty million times and see if you don't arrive at a very sad and volcanic state of affairs,' said Joe, and I silently agreed with him.

At home I thought about the hostel before I dozed off. The more I recalled all the details of my visit the more I felt depressed. My last thought was that the world was still too far from perfection and that those who hoped for world peace at this point in time were building castles in the air.

It would not be the last time I visited Somdali. Something about the dirt and the desolation of the hostel attracted me strongly towards the place. Instead of going there for vice, like many of the location people, I went there out of sympathy with my friends and maybe that is why I felt so strongly about the way they lived. What's more, sharing the emptiness of the life of Somdali and his comrades filled, for me, the listless evenings on street corners, outside the shops and at the station. Every day we gave vent to our feelings and it was amazing how therapeutic the exercise was for me. It gave me the satisfaction of knowing much more about life than those who prefer the escapism of artificiality.

As I continued going there, I discovered that song was the only solace of those lonely people. At least two days a week they sang traditional choral music. After supper they would assemble in the adjoining closet and start singing with the conscientiousness of a stage group rehearsing for a fête. Hearing this, Mbobo and others would come from the opposite house and join in the singing. Some of the songs were performed with graceful dances, so elegantly carried out that I wondered where they could all have learnt the same paces. When they sang, it was from the core of their souls, their eyes glazed with memories of where they had first sung those lyrics; and interruptions were not tolerated. Sometimes I was so moved by their music that I yearned to join them, and because I did not know the songs I sailed away in my mind for paradises that I conjured up, where people sang their troubles away. After an evening of invigorating talk and untainted African traditional song I went away feeling as if I had found treasure in a graveyard. Those men might be buried there in the labour camps, but they are still people and, because they live in the throes of debasement, human adaptability has given them a most simple and practical approach to life, and none of the illusions of people who live comfortable lives or strive only for that throughout their time on earth, never achieving it but ending up drowning their frustrations in the pleasures of the flesh, half-immersed in intoxicants and half out of their minds half the time, until their humanity rots inside them. I would rather depend on a poor man for help, because a rich man, never having known hunger himself, will let you go away with an empty stomach.

The weekends were most exciting. They made me think of words I heard from a friend (I don't know where he picked them up). He would look at some of the people we worked with, who came from the rural areas and say, 'You can take the man out of the country, but you can never take the country out of the man.' On Friday the dreariness was stirred by a din that reached a crescendo on Sunday afternoon.

A typical weekend went like this: after looking in at home on Friday, I would go up to the hostel in the company of Joe or some of the guys who went there to augment their scanty paypackets with Soweto's favourite game of chance, shooting craps (dice). Somdali was a loyal worshipper of Bacchus. I would find him sitting like a lord in the shadows of his cist with two or three bottles of beer between his legs, the rest of a whole crate inside the multi-purpose 'bed'. When I came in he would greet me like a long-lost friend, as if we had not been together only an hour or so before.

'Aah, son of my mother! You came just in time. Borrow a mug from one of our brothers here and let us drink to our ancestors. Bongani, give him something to drink with.'

'*Heer*, Somdali. You're drinking the sweat of your brow? Is this what you have been working for, the whole week?' I would reply jokingly, and accept the mug that Bongani handed to me.

'Of course; what do you think? It's Friday today; everybody drinks white man's beer and feels rich. Come on, use your mouth for what it should be used now, not for preaching.'

When Joe was with me, he did not wait to be invited, but took a container and gulped down as much as he could before Somdali protested that he was drinking as if it was his last day on earth.

Meanwhile, the game would be warming up in the main room. 'Five I do, five I do . . . *Eê*, pop! *Eê*, six three!' we would hear them singing out with great gusto. On that evening the stove would burn itself to ashes with no one tending it. Fridays they did not dine together. Everyone ate an almost substantial meal in one of the city '*chesa-nyamas*' and returned to the hostel replete. Old Khuzwayo never returned on weekends because of the boisterousness, which was too much for his aged nerves. He slept in the sky slums on the roof of the Golden City. When we felt that the game was hot enough, we went in for the gambit. Sometimes we won and at other times we lost, but mostly we lost. The foolish lost their whole pay envelopes there and it was such a pity to watch them begging to be advanced more money, only to lose that as well. Depending on the amount of money involved, it was possible for the game to last the whole night. The winners never hung around the game long, but went off to drink their crumpled scoops in one of the countless haunts of vice. When you are poor there is no form of entertainment that you can afford to drown your misfortunes in besides over-indulgence of one kind or another.

At Msomi's you got everything: cigarettes, dagga, any concoction you wanted, and the profligate women whose sole source of income was peddling themselves to the famished hostel men. The latter were only too eager to part with a little hard-earned cash for the company of anything in skirts, no matter what she was like. Msomi's traffic in vice was booming and there was no fear of interference from the police, any sign of whom in the hostel invoked among the inhabitants a primordial bloodlust. Stoning and hacking to death of 'sellout intruders', as they referred to them, occurred from time to time.

When it got late I went home or somewhere else in the location. The difference was striking. In the location the presence of womenfolk and children contributed a certain amount of warmth and a reason for living; a man's delight is a loving woman and growing children.

Saturday morning was always a drab spectacle. Many woke up with a whole day to themselves. Before the beerhall was destroyed, everybody swarmed there to sink what had remained of their Friday earnings in beer. There was nothing else they could do. When the bar went up in flames the Msomis saw a chance to go into business supplying their hostel mates with debauchery. However, even before that, as soon as the sun surfaced in the east on Saturdays everybody came out of their lairs to soak up the mild morning beams. They made me think of a plague-stricken concentration camp although I had never seen one. That is why when I learnt of Auschwitz, the Nazi camp in Poland, I simply dubbed the hostel 'our Auschwitz'. Grim-looking men sat or stood against the wall drinking from tins at every house. Some did their washing at the troughs and others clustered together playing dice. Door to door merchants had their colourful goods draped over their shoulders and arms with the rest of their stocks in bulging paper bags. The clothing they sold ranged from men's underwear to overcoats, and even female garments which were bought and locked up in the cists until such time as the buyer took them home to present to his family. The street vendors would be preparing their make-shift shops to start selling everything from sheep entrails to chicken pieces that hummed with green flies, while the rib-cages of mongrels kept themselves at a safe salivating distance. As the day got older, the tempo would increase to a fast drunken frenzy until the night came to cover it all up.

Then, on Sunday, a sleeping social consciousness, underlined by a strong traditional inclination, showed itself. The men drank together according to their places of origin. Don't mistake this for a reflection of tribalism. It was only their recollection of how they used to spend their Sundays in the different country areas they came from — not necessarily Sundays, but those days that were traditionally set aside for social gatherings where the young and nimble entertained their elders with dances to the sound of tom-toms and songs which were sung by the great-grandfathers and handed down from father to son.

Sunday morning was no different from a Saturday except that you could see that something important was being prepared for. The few converts wore their 'Zionist' uniforms of blue on snow-white and clutched their staffs and bibles to join other worshippers in the locations. Groups of dancers wearing distinctive garb left the hostel singing, whistling, waving their dancing sticks and pausing at every busy street corner to treat the location people to some dancing and singing. The disappointing part was that many location people regarded it as backwardness. 'You'll never see whites doing such things where they stay,' they would say. Why should the whites do them? *Mos* they're not black like I am. And who told you that your whites are the measuring standard of right and wrong? I wanted to ask the critics but chose not to because I knew their minds had been stolen from them in order to 'civilize' them. Other groups came from other hostels to ours in the same fashion, their sorrows forgotten for a while.

At two in the afternoon, after preparing themselves, the groups went out to the 'market-place' (an open space near where the beerhall used to be and where most of the vendors sold their assortments of goods). The first sound of the tom-tom and the flutes of the Pedis brought people to watch from all corners of the hostel.

The baPedi formed a line and swayed gracefully from side to side, blowing their flutes in typical fashion while others played the drums of diminishing size; the biggest of them made out of a paraffin drum and the smallest, the size of a gallon of paint.

A most exciting entertainment was provided by the foot-stomping Zulus. They dressed in traditional attire and danced to the sound of a single drum with amazing rhythm. They sat or knelt in formations of four, five or six, according to the size of the competing group, clapping hands in unison with the drum and singing or humming in high spirits. They kept themselves going with long draughts from a big black clay vessel which was refilled from large plastic containers. The competitors took the 'stage' like waves, those in front vigorously stomping the ground with their tyre sandals until you thought you could feel it

vibrating. Their feet rose above their heads and came down thunder-
ously. Endurance and physical fitness is basic to the African 'ballet',
and a weakling does not waste his time going on the stage. As I say, the
dance was performed with superb rhythm. If you missed a step you
were penalized by having to leave the stage to await your partners, and
your group lost points for that.

The drum, the clapping hands, the songs, shouts of '*Usuthu!*' and
the rising and falling legs went on and on, the muscular and wiry black
bodies glistening with sweat until sunset, when the sun would lie on
Meadowlands like a glowing half-circle, and the smoke from the
chimneys would blanket the slumbering Soweto.

Bob Leshoai/THE MOON SHALL BE MY WITNESS

Mahlomola location is situated on the eastern border of the city of Bloemfontein. It is populated by black people from almost all parts of South Africa. In the majority are the Barolong, a very gentle and peace-loving people. The second largest population group are the Basotho, who migrate from Lesotho to work in the gold mines.

Further east of Mahlomola, a distance of about twenty minutes' walk, are two other townships. The larger one, much younger and neater than Mahlomola, is Bochabela which sprawls over a large area to link with Digaratene, a rather neat municipal complex which acts as a curtain to hide the ugly and violent slum location, Kaffirfontein. North of Bochabela, beyond the tarmac road that goes to Durban, is the second location, Heatherdale, occupied by the 'coloureds'.

Running from south to north is a shallow stream, Bloem Spruit, which separates Mahlomola from Bochabela and Heatherdale. During the dry winter season Bloem Spruit can be crossed at almost any point but in summer it has many stagnant pools full of frogs and crabs, and covered with slimy spirogyra. Bloem Spruit, its bed dry in the winter, is a place where young girls are deflowered in broad daylight by red-eyed dagga-smokers: the name is thus doubly ironic. At night it becomes the hiding place for would-be murderers, robbers and adulterers. During the wet season people commute across it by means of a narrow ford of granite stones placed at random, making the crossing exercise rather hazardous. The children of both sides of the Spruit sometimes meet at this ford to compete in crossing it, especially when the stones are hidden below the water. An ugly and sinful winter spot provides great fun for the children in summer. The stagnant pools become swimming places for the youth when the Bloemfontein sun scorches fiercely from the cloudless blue skies.

There were once two friends who lived in Mahlomola, by the names of Ou Breench and Skeelie. They had grown up together and were in their mid-twenties. Unlike his friend, Ou Breench had married a beautiful young wife by the name of Dintsejang. She had a dark coffee-coloured complexion and a pair of large laughing white owl's eyes. The hair on her head was black and long. Don't talk about her breasts, which stood out like hillocks. She walked in a deliberate style, always aware of the men who gazed at her in admiration.

Sometimes an admirer would follow her to make the usual nonsensical enquiries. Always when this happened she would stop with her head to one side and her large eyes coquettishly directed at her confused admirer. Then she would bite her fingernails playfully with her large milky teeth. The victim's heaving chest would lead her on to tease him by drawing ugly figures in the sand with her big toe while swaying from side to side like a reed in the wind, with the poor admirer talking his tongue off. And when she had played her game to the finish she would suddenly dash off, twittering with expressive laughter. It was a dangerous game, but she loved it.

Ou Breench was brought up by his grandmother, MmaSelala. He loved her fondly and as a child he sat with her outside her mud house to listen to the stories she told. She also taught him the names of the stars such as Selemela, the Seven Sisters; and the bright Morning Star — The Scatterer of Adulterers — and the Southern Cross. She taught him about the moon and the effect it had on the seasons and people. She told him about the woman in the moon, the rainbow and the rain and wind clouds.

On such an evening he would ask — as he would often do because he liked the story:

'Grandmother, how did you say that woman got to the moon?'

And she replied, 'Go away; go away from me; you have heard the story countless times, haven't you?'

And then she would slap him lightly and fondly on the shoulder and say to him, 'She had hatred in her heart, my child.'

Then he would draw nearer and fondly say, 'Please granny, just this once and I promise never to pester you again.'

'Alright now, open your ears' — playfully and fondly pulling at his lobe — 'open them and listen.'

Then he would tug at her shawl and draw nearer, smacking his lips the way the old men do when they are about to take a long and deep draught of *seqhaqhabolo*.

'As I told you before, she had hatred in her heart because her neighbour had built herself a beautiful hut.'

'I would have built myself a better house!'

'So you would? Well, she allowed herself to be full of hatred and jealousy, and like you, she was going to build herself a better house.'

'By the way, you say she was a widow?'

'Yes, and of course! The rains were near and she had to prepare the place where she would build the hut, and also plant her crops before the rains came.'

'I hear, grandmother! So every Sunday morning she went to gather firewood!'

'That's right. But who is telling the story, you or me?'

'I am sorry, I'll not talk again.'

'And the villagers warned her not to do this because Sunday was a church and prayer day.'

'But she ignored them.'

'Quite right, my child, as you have just ignored your promise.'

'I really promise now!'

'It is bad to have hatred in one's heart, my child. One Sunday morning while the moon was still on the horizon, as she walked home with a bundle of wood on her head and her baby on her back, she was snatched away by something and flung against the moon there. And there she is with the wood on her head and her baby on her back.'

'Terrible!'

'Yes child of my child, it's terrible to have hatred in one's heart.'

Skeelie was Ou Breench's friend: very little else is known about him. He appeared to be a very serious and good young man and the people of Mahlomola liked him very much. There were stories about his mother having died when he was a baby; there were also tales that he had had a grandmother who always mumbled to herself.

A year after the death of Ou Breench's grandmother, his wife, Dintsejang, saw him off at Bloemfontein station on his way to the mines in Johannesburg. Skeelie was also there. The third class Mbombela coaches were crammed with other men from Lesotho and the Cape. As the train puffed its way out of the station, for some inexplicable reason Skeelie ran after it waving at the men leaning out of the windows shouting and singing vulgar songs. As he reached the edge of the platform he saw Ou Breench blowing a kiss at his wife. He was suddenly seized by a fit of jealousy; he cupped his hands and shouted, 'Hey, you, Ou Breench, tonight I shall sleep in your bed!' And he waited for an answer. And then it came over the clanging wheels and the railway lines and the crude laughter of men who know what happens to unprotected women while their husbands are busy acquiring silicosis in the gold mines many miles away. He stood and watched and listened until the clanging and the crude laughter died away in the distance. Then he turned round as the red tail lights of the Mbombela disappeared around the bend. Dintsejang had not heard the remark and together they trudged their way back to Mahlomola. She was speaking all the time about her husband, but Skeelie walked in silence with his hands deep in his trouser pockets. When they reached Mahlomola there were only a few candles or paraffin lamps burning in the houses, visible through the curtainless windows. Occasionally, as they passed close to a window, they saw the naked body of a man or woman silhouetted against the opposite wall as he or she prepared to creep into the sleeping rags on the cold earthen floor. After leaving her at the door of her mud house, her *motlhomahatshe,* he sauntered to his own hovel deep in thought.

That night Skeelie could not sleep, for his mind was full of thoughts about Dintsejang. Day after day he tried to repress his growing affection for her, but it was difficult. Soon he succumbed and broached the subject of an illicit love affair. When a young wife is torn away from her husband after sharing a bed for only one year, it is difficult for her to resist temptation. Skeelie knew this and he was going to take advantage of the situation. Dintsejang also knew that her husband would be away for a long time, for many cruel months. She had tried to dissuade him from 'joining', but he desperately wanted to go to Johannesburg to bring back from the City of Gold, like those before him, nice clothes, a bicycle and a gramophone. It did not take long before she yielded to Skeelie's temptations. At first they tried to be very cautious, to hoodwink the bumpkins of Mahlomola, as they called them; but when the heart is aflame with love it is very difficult to control its emotions. Soon the women began to ask questions and to speak in innuendos.

'I say, Mmakakana, we hear there's a human bitch around here; I tell you we see wonders, I tell you.'

And, of course, Mmakakana, not to be beaten in this gossip game retorted with, 'Ah, you mean this has not been known to you? Kakana's father, late one night, saw the bitch sneak into the bull's den.'

'That's nothing! Sello's father, coming home late, stood outside the bull's window. He says from the bull's breathing and the bitch's whimpering and wild talk there was no doubt about the kind of business taking place in there.'

Before she hastily parted from her friend, Mmakana warned, 'Please don't say you heard it from me! Some of us don't want to be beaten by our husbands.'

'Me too, you have not heard it from me,' replied Sello's mother.

And so the letters from Dintsejang to Ou Breench became fewer and shorter until his heart began to feel heavy with sadness. Meanwhile the gossip grew in Mahlomola and the bitch and the bull became more and more reckless. The months dragged painfully for Ou Breench, and eventually though there were only thirty days left to the end of his contract, they seemed like thirty years. When he finally arrived from the mines with new dresses and shoes for his wife, a gramophone and a shiny bicycle decorated with mirrors and rubber pieces at the bottom end of each of the mudguards, his heart felt lighter and happier. Dintsejang greeted him warmly and Skeelie shook his hand vigorously. But as the days went by he noticed that his friend's eyes always avoided his, and then he recalled the words screamed at him the night he left for the mines.

In Mahlomola location it is very difficult to conceal scandalous happenings. The people go about their work, but nevertheless, they soon smell a rat. Before Ou Breench's return his wife's misconduct was openly discussed. Skeelie's strange behaviour towards his friend confirmed his suspicions. Ou Breench did not suspect any more — he was now sure. Don't the Basotho wisely say that the one who crawls is better able to see the one who creeps? Don't actions speak louder than words? Hatred slowly crept into his heart, and so he sent his wife home to her relatives in Thaba Ncho so that he could freely plan his vengeance and strategy. At last, while she was away, he hit upon a plan and resolved to carry it out.

It was a nagging thought and Ou Breench didn't want to believe it. Yet it sounded so clearly in his ears again that night as he sat under the tall trees behind his mud house. It was as though his long dead grandmother was speaking the words from her grave. The moon was full and the trees cast weird shadows on the walls of Bloem Spruit. That day the sun had burned like an oven and though it was long past sunset, the heat still lingered in the stones and in the walls of the mud houses. It was to avoid the heat in his mud house that Ou Breench was sitting outside wearing only an old pair of pants and a vest. His mind was also burning as the heat of the sun had burnt. He had been thinking all day.

The breeze from the Spruit didn't help him at all and the rustling of the leaves annoyed him.

He punched the palm of his hand with his fist and exclaimed, 'I don't believe it, I don't!' But the words came to his unbelieving ears wafted on the gentle breeze. He could hear his grandmother's voice speak the words to him as she had done when he was young. 'It's a terrible thing my son, child of my child, a terrible thing to have hatred in one's heart.'

He leapt to his feet and screamed to the pale moon above fleeting through the fleecy clouds. 'It's not true! It's not a terrible thing if there's a reason for it!'

The moon dipped behind the clouds and raced on its nightly mission as though running from his evil thoughts. He scowled at it for an answer to ease his mind, but like a ghost it just raced away behind the fleecy clouds. The gentle breeze sang through the trees and again he heard his grandmother's voice, the voice he didn't want to hear. 'It drives one to commit acts one will regret.'

He was still looking at the moon with clenched fists and vengeance in his eyes. He was grinding his teeth like one engaged in a life and death struggle. Then the moon appeared again from a rent in the clouds. He felt the tenseness of his body ease; his knit brows and clenched fists relaxed and he smiled to himself and spoke to the moon. 'How long did you think you could hide behind those fleecy clouds up there?' There was no reply from the moon and it just went on gliding, like a phantom. Now behind the clouds, now visible through the rents; silently it rode on, watching the earth below.

Ou Breench went back to his seat and buried his head in his hands and tried not to listen or think. But the cool breeze tickled his senses and forced him to listen. And again he unmistakably heard the words in the sound of the wind.

'But I must make him pay with his blood,' he screamed as he jumped to his feet and walked into his mud house with great determination in his strides. He hurriedly pulled a small blanket over his shoulders, put on his grass hat and picked up his stick. As he felt its shape and size in the darkness of the house he stood still — staring vaguely ahead with the terrible killer in his hands. Its round head felt bigger than usual, and its weight too felt greater. As he chuckled with satisfaction there was a loud gust of wind outside which shook the trees and in the rustling of the leaves he could clearly hear the words he so much tried to forget,

'And it drives one to commit acts one will regret.'

He slid the round-headed killer under his blanket and walked out of the house closing the door gently behind him. Outside the house, he stood and looked here, there and everywhere, but the night was silent except for the wind. He breathed with greater ease and now began to examine the killer in the moonlight. It was a terrible weapon! And the pale moon hid behind a thick cloud as though afraid of it. His grass hat cast a dark shadow over his face, and only his sharp eyes played like two will o' the wisps in the dark. He paced slowly to the trees behind his house and stood there with one foot on the log he had been sitting on a while ago.

He listened intently to the faint sounds from Bochabela location where he knew Skeelie had gone to attend a Saturday night *stokvel* beer party. He knew that all who were at the party were carelessly imbibing large quantities of *Sebapa le Masenke, Qhomaka* and *Lekau la Poo.* Skeelie would be half-dead and mad when the drinking, singing and dancing were over. Soon his keen ears told him that the merriment was fizzling out, for now and again a drunk lonely wanderer from Bochabela stumbled home. He could also hear the faint goodbyes from across the Spruit wafted by the wind. His eyes also told him that the latenight fires were dead in Bochabela. He could imagine the loud laughter of the naughty boys as they urinated onto the dying coals. He could almost smell and taste the burning ammonia as it rose with the steam from the coals, recalling how he, as a boy, had put out countless fires in the same manner. And he also knew that burning ammonia didn't smell good at all.

Another stumbling passerby woke him from his reverie, and he remembered that he was standing there that night poised to put out another fire — life! A cold shiver shook his body. It was now very quiet and the candle lights in Mahlomola were all extinguished. The people were sound asleep; and now he emerged from the shelter and darkness of the trees and briskly but noiselessly walked to the ford where he knew Skeelie would cross. He hid in one of the hollows on the bank of the Spruit where the women of Mahlomola dig out the soil with which they smear the floors and walls of their mud houses.

He did not wait long, for Skeelie was soon heard, and then seen as he staggered towards the ford. He was singing a funny song which evidently greatly amused him, for now and again he would stop to laugh and remark about the words of his song. And then he would start again,

A re yeng, a re yeng, a re yeng Matikiring!

And then, beating out a rhythmic step with his feet,
Le kile la se bona kae ntja e goga peipi!
And then he laughed in the pale moonlight. Ou Breench waited with bated breath, clenching his teeth furiously.

When Skeelie reached the ford he put his right foot cautiously on the first stone and laughingly said, 'By my grandmother this water is cold,' as he felt it with his index finger. Now he put forward the left foot and laughed loudly as he succeeded in balancing on the stone. Then he sang again,
A re yeng, a re yeng, a re yeng Matikiring,
Le kile la se bona kae ntja e goga peipe?
Then he beat out a rhythmic shuffling step on the stones. He was amused when he did not lose balance and he swore vigorously, 'Here is my cross, 'strue's God, *die Here weet, Mme a ntsetse,* I would not have been my father's son had I fallen into this cold water!' Then he howled into the night, 'By my ancestors, I swear it!'

He began to laugh again and felt very proud of his achievement. He picked his way cautiously over the stones. Once on the other side he kicked up a little dust with his dancing feet as he sang,
A re yeng, a re yeng, a re yeng Matikiring,
Le kile la se bona kae ntja e goga peipi?
Now he laughed loudly and said, *'Ke nna mor'a Phakoe, motho o motle ha a boleloa ke batho!'* He trotted smartly, close to the hollow in which Ou Breench was hiding. With his back to it he pulled out his penis, leaned back so that it pointed upwards and began to urinate into the water. The urine made a rainbow-like curve in the air and dripped into the water to Skeelie's satisfaction, and then he sang out again,
Sontaga aant kereke toe gaan
Met die lang maneer
En die abalakie
Die robalatsabi
Die wisarana fink
You fink I'm will?
I dinow . . .
Ou Breench was rather fascinated by the urinating act and the singing as he quietly prepared to leap out of the hollow. Skeelie, oblivious of the enemy, took up the chorus of his new song.
Girls come along,
Stand by the corner
Do not aan

Die robalatsabi
Die wisarana fink
You fink I'm will?
I dinow!

He had finished urinating and was laughing, still leaning back and struggling to close the fly of his trousers. Ou Breench leapt from the hollow like a cheetah and stopped Skeelie's foolish laughter abruptly by hitting him a vicious blow on his forehead with the murderous club. Skeelie fell on his face like a log. Ou Breench was now mad with rage and rained blow after blow on the befuddled man as he yelled, 'Take that one, and that one and this one, you dirty pipe-smoking dog!'

'Please don't kill me,' the dying man screamed.

'I joo, Mme wee! People come to my rescue!'

'That one too! It'll teach you to leave other people's wives alone in the other world.' It was a stunning blow executed with all the power he could marshall.

And then Skeelie realised who his attacker was and he screamed through his reeking breath, 'Ou Breench, spare my life, I pray you.'

'Take this one too, son of a dog!'

'You kill me, Ou Breench, you kill me! Oh my God the world reels! I vomit!'

But the blows just rained down interspersed with, 'That, and this one too, you vomiting dog!' And then when he lay still, the angry attacker stood over him to finish him should he try to rise, but he merely rolled over onto his back. His watery eyes were open but they did not see. His body shook violently. He clenched his fists, bit his teeth and hissed feebly, 'Ou Breench, my dear friend, you have killed me — finished me in this lonely place, but the moon shall be my witness.'

He died a terrible death, that man. Ou Breench gave himself up to the police, and after a lengthy trial, he was found guilty of manslaughter and sentenced to ten years' imprisonment with hard labour. After his release, the people of Mahlomola and Bochabela were still talking about Skeelie's terrible death; they warned their children never to go to the Matikiring because the system, they said, was evil and exposed men and women to horrible temptations.

Miriam Tlali/THE POINT OF NO RETURN

S'bongile stopped at the corner of Sauer and Jeppe Streets and looked up at the robot. As she waited for the green light to go on, she realised from the throbbing of her heart and her quick breathing that she had been moving too fast. For the first time since she had left Senaoane, she became conscious of the weight of Gugu, strapped tightly on her back.

All the way from home, travelling first by bus and then by train from Nhlanzane to Westgate station, her thoughts had dwelt on Mojalefa, the father of her baby. Despite all efforts to forget, her mind had continually reverted to the awesome results of what might lie ahead for them, if they (Mojalefa and the other men) carried out their plans to challenge the government of the Republic of South Africa.

The incessant rumbling of traffic on the two intersecting one-way streets partially muffled the eager male voices audible through the open windows on the second floor of Myler House on the other side of the street. The men were singing freedom songs. She stood and listened for a while before she crossed the street.

Although he showed no sign of emotion, it came as a surprise to Mojalefa when one of the men told him that a lady was downstairs waiting to see him. He guessed that it must be S'bongile and he felt elated at the prospect of seeing her. He quickly descended the two flights of stairs to the foyer. His heart missed a beat when he saw her.

'*Au banna!*' he said softly as he stood next to her, unable to conceal his feelings. He looked down at her and the baby, sleeping soundly on her back. S'bongile slowly turned her head to look at him, taken aback at his exclamation. He bent down slightly and brushed his dry lips lightly over her forehead just below her neatly plaited hair. He murmured 'It's good to see you again, Bongi. You are *so* beautiful! Come, let's sit over here.'

He led her away from the stairs, to a wooden bench further away opposite a narrow dusty window overlooking the courtyard. A dim ray of light pierced through the window-panes making that spot the only brighter area in the dimly-lit foyer.

He took out a piece of tissue from his coat-pocket, wiped off the dust from the sill and sat down facing her. He said:

'I'm very happy you came. I . . . '

'I *had* to come, Mojalefa,' she interrupted.

'I could not bear it any longer; I could not get my mind off the quarrel. I could not do any work, everything I picked up kept falling out of my hands. Even the washing I tried to do I could not get done. I *had* to leave everything and come. I kept thinking of you . . . as if it was all over, and I would not see you nor touch you ever again. I came to convince myself that I could still see you as a free man; that I could still come close to you and touch you. Mojalefa, I'm sorry I behaved like that last night. I thought you were indifferent to what I was going through. I was jealous because you kept on telling me that you were committed. That like all the others, you had already resigned from your job, and that there was no turning back. I thought you cared more for the course you have chosen than for Gugu and me.'

'There's no need for you to apologise, Bongi, I never blamed you for behaving like that and I bear you no malice at all. All I want from you is that you should understand. Can we not talk about something else? I am so happy you came.'

They sat looking at each other in silence. There was *so* much they wanted to say to one another, just this once. Yet both felt tongue-tied; they could not think of the right thing to say. She felt uneasy, just sitting there and looking at him while time was running out for them. She wanted to steer off the painful subject of their parting, so she said:

'I have not yet submitted those forms to Baragwanath. They want the applicants to send them in together with their pass numbers. You've always discouraged me from going for a pass, and now they want a number. It's almost certain they'll accept me because of my matric certificate. That is if I submit my form *with the number* by the end of this month, of course. What do you think I should do, go for registration? Many women and girls are already rushing to the registration centres. They say it's useless for us to refuse to carry them like you men because we will not be allowed to go anywhere for a visit or buy anything valuable. And now the hospitals, too . . .'

'No, no wait . . . Wait until . . . Until after this . . . After you know what the outcome is of what we are about to do.'

Mojalefa shook his head. It was intolerable. Everything that happened around you just went to emphasize the hopelessness of even trying to live like a human being. Imagine a woman having to carry a pass everywhere she goes; being stopped and searched or ordered to produce her pass! This was outrageous, the ultimate desecration and an insult to her very existence. He had already seen some of these 'simple' women who come to seek work from 'outside', proudly moving in the streets with those plastic containers dangling round their necks like sling bags. He immediately thought of the tied-down bitch and it nauseated him.

S'bongile stopped talking. She had tried to change the topic from the matter of their parting but now she could discern that she had only succeeded in making his thoughts wander away into a world unknown to her. She felt as if he had shut her out, aloof. She needed his nearness, now more than ever. She attempted to draw him closer to herself; to be *with* him just this last time. She could not think of anything to say. She sat listening to the music coming from the upper floors. She remarked:

'That music, those two songs they have just been singing; I haven't heard them before. Who composes them?'

'Most of the men contribute something now and again. Some melodies are from old times, they just supply the appropriate words. Some learn 'new' tunes from old people at home, old songs from our past. Some are very old. Some of our boys have attended the tribal dancing ceremonies on the mines and they learn these during the festivities. Most of these are spontaneous, they come from the feelings of the people as they go about their work; mostly labourers. Don't you sometimes hear them chanting to rhythm as they perform tasks; carrying heavy iron bars or timber blocks along the railway lines or road construction sites? They even sing about the white foreman who sits smoking a pipe and watches them as they sweat.'

S'bongile sat morose, looking towards the entrance at the multitudes moving towards the centre of town and down towards Newtown. She doubted whether any of those people knew anything of the plans of the men who were singing of the aspirations of the blacks and their hopes for the happier South Africa they were envisaging. Her face, although beautiful as ever, reflected her depressed state. She nodded in half-hearted approval at his enthusiastic efforts to explain. He went on:

'Most of the songs are in fact lamentations — they reflect the disposition of the people. We shall be thundering them tomorrow morning on our way as we march towards the gaols of this country!'

With her eyes still focussed on the stream of pedestrians and without stopping to think, she asked:

'Isn't it a bit premature? Going, I mean. You are *so* few; a drop in an ocean.'

'It isn't numbers that count, Bongi,' he answered, forcing a smile. How many times had he had to go through that, he asked himself. In the trains, the buses, at work . . . Bongi was unyielding. Her refusal to accept that he must go was animated by her selfish love, the fear of facing life without him. He tried to explain although he had long realised that his efforts would always be fruitless. It was also clear to him that it was futile to try and run away from the issue.

'In any case,' he went on, 'it will be up to *you*, the ones who remain behind, the women and the mothers, to motivate those who are still dragging their feet; you'll remain only to show them why they must follow in our footsteps. That the future and dignity of the blacks as a nation and as human beings is worth sacrificing for.'

Her reply only served to demonstrate to him that he might just as well have kept quiet. She remarked:

'Even your father feels that this is of no use. He thinks it would perhaps only work if all of you first went out to *educate* the people so that they may join in.'

'No, father does not understand. He thinks we are too few as compared to the millions of all the black people of this land. He feels that we are sticking out our necks. That we can never hope to get the white man to sit round a table and speak to us, here. All he'll do is order his police to shoot us dead. If they don't do that, then they'll throw us into the gaols, and we shall either die there or be released with all sorts of afflictions. It's because I'm his only son. He's thinking of *himself*, Bongi, he does not understand.'

'He *does* understand, and he loves you.'

'Maybe that's *just* where the trouble lies. Because he loves me, he fails to think and reason properly. We do not agree. He is a different kind of person from me, and he can't accept that. He wants me to speak, act, and even think like him, and that is impossible.'

'He wants to be proud of you, Mojalefa.'

'If he can't be proud of me as I am, then he'll never be. He says I've changed. That I've turned against everything he taught me. He wants me to go to church regularly and pray more often. I sometimes feel he hates me, and I sympathise with him.'

'He does not hate you, Mojalefa; you two just do not see eye to eye.'

'My father moves around with a broken heart. He feels I am a renegade, a disappointment; an embarrassment to him. You see, as a preacher, he has to stand before the congregation every Sunday and preach on the importance of obedience, of how as Christians we have to be submissive and tolerant and respect those who are in authority over us under all conditions. That we should leave it to 'the hand of God' to right all wrongs. As a reprisal against all injustices we must kneel down and pray because, as the scriptures tell us, God said: 'Vengeance is Mine'. He wants me to follow in his footsteps.'

'Be a priest or preacher, you mean?'

'Yes. Or show some interest in his part-time ministry. Sing in the church choir and so on, like when I was still a child.' He smiled wryly.

'Why don't you show *some* interest then? Even if it is only for his sake? Aren't you a Christian, don't you believe in God?'

'I suppose I do. But not like *him* and those like him, no.'

What is *that* supposed to mean?'

'What's the use of praying all the time? In the first place, how can a slave kneel down and pray without feeling that he is not quite a man, human? Every time I try to pray I keep asking myself — if God loves me like the bible says he does, then why should I have to carry a pass? Why should I have to be a virtual tramp in the land of my forefathers, why? Why should I have all these obnoxious laws passed against me?'

Then the baby on Bongi's back coughed, and Mojalefa's eyes drifted slowly towards it. He looked at the sleeping Gugu tenderly for a while and sighed, a sad expression passing over his eyes. He wanted to say something but hesitated and kept quiet.

Bongi felt the strap cutting painfully into her shoulder muscles and decided to transfer the baby to her lap. Mojalefa paced up and down in the small space, deep in thought. Bongi said:

'I have to breast-feed him. He hasn't had his last feed. I forgot everything. I just grabbed him and came here, and he didn't cry or complain. Sometimes I wish he would cry more often like other children.'

Mojalefa watched her suckling the baby. He reluctantly picked up the tiny clasped fist and eased his thumb slowly into it so as not to rouse the child. The chubby fingers immediately caressed his thumb and embraced it tightly. His heart sank, and there was a lump in his throat. He had a strong urge to relieve S'bongile of the child, pick him up in his strong arms and kiss him, but he suppressed the desire. It was at times like these that he experienced great conflict. He said:

'I should never have met you, Bongi. I am not worthy of your love.'

'It was cruel of you Mojalefa. All along you knew you would have to go, and yet you made me fall for you. You made me feel that life without you is no life at all. Why did you do this to me?'

He unclasped his thumb slowly from the baby's instinctive clutch, stroking it tenderly for a moment. He walked slowly towards the dim dusty window. He looked through into the barely visible yard, over the roofs of the nearby buildings, into the clear blue sky above. He said:

'It is because I have the belief that we shall meet again, Bongi; that we shall meet again, in a free Africa!'

The music rose in a slow crescendo.

'That song. It is so *sad*. It sounds like a hymn.'

They were both silent. The thoughts of both of them anchored on how unbearable the other's absence would be. Mojalefa consoled himself that at least he knew his father would be able to provide the infant with all its needs. That he was fortunate and not like some of his colleagues who had been ready — in the midst of severe poverty — to sacrifice all. Thinking of some of them humbled him a great deal. S'bongile would perhaps be accepted in Baragwanath where she would take up training as a nurse. He very much wanted to break the silence. He went near his wife and touched her arm. He whispered:

'Promise me Bongi, that you will do your best. That you will look after him, please.'

'I *shall*. He is our valuable keepsake — your father's and mine — something to remind me of you. A link nobody can destroy. All yours and mine.'

He left her and started pacing again. He searched hopelessly in his mind for something to say; something pleasant. He wanted to drown the sudden whirl of emotion he felt in his heart when he looked down at S'bongile, his young bride of only a few weeks, and the two-month-old child he had brought into this world.

S'bongile came to his rescue. She said:

'I did not tell my mother that I was coming here. I said that I was taking Gugu over to your father for a visit. He is always so happy to see him.'

Thankful for the change of topic, Mojalefa replied, smiling:

'You know, my father is a strange man. He is unpredictable. For instance, when I had put you into trouble and we realised to our horror that Gugu was on the way, I thought that he would skin me alive, that *that* was now the last straw. I did not know how I would approach him, because then it was clear that you would also have to explain to your mother why you would not be in a position to start at Turfloop. There was also the thought that your mother had paid all the fees for your first year and had bought you all those clothes and so forth. It nearly drove me mad worrying about the whole mess. I kept thinking of your poor widowed mother; how she had toiled and saved so that you would be able to start at university after having waited a whole year for the chance. I decided to go and tell my uncle in Pretoria and send *him* to face my father with that catastrophic announcement. I stayed away from home for weeks after that.'

'Oh yes, it was nerve-racking , wasn't it? And they were all so kind to us. After the initial shock, I mean. We have to remember that all our lives, and be thankful for the kind of parents God gave us. I worried *so* much, I even contemplated suicide, you know. Oh well, I suppose you could not help yourself!'

She sighed deeply, shaking her head slowly. Mojalefa continued:

'Mind you, I knew something like that would happen, yet I went right ahead and talked you into yielding to me. I was drawn to you by a force so great, I just could not resist it. I hated myself for weeks after that. I actually despised myself. What is worse is that I had vowed to myself that I would never bring into this world a soul that would have to inherit my servitude. I had failed to "develop and show a true respect for our African womanhood", a clause we are very proud of in our disciplinary code, and I remonstrated with myself for my weakness.'

'But your father came personally to see my people and apologise for what you had done, and later to pay all the *lobola* they wanted. He said that we would have to marry immediately as against what you had said to me — why it would not be wise for us to marry, I mean.'

'That was when I had gone through worse nightmares. I had to explain to him why I did not want to tie you down to me when I felt that I would not be able to offer you anything, that I would only make you unhappy. You know why I was against us marrying, Bongi, of course. I wanted you to be free to marry a 'better' man, and I had no doubt it would not be long before he grabbed you. Any man would be proud to have you as his wife, even with a child who is not his.'

He touched her smooth cheek with the back of his hand, and added:

'You possess those rare delicate attributes that any man would want to feel around him and be enkindled by.'

'Your father would never let Gugu go, not for anything, Mojalefa. He did not name him 'his pride' for nothing. I should be thankful that I met the son of a person like that. Not all women are so fortunate. How many beautiful girls have been deserted by their lovers and are roaming the streets with illegitimate babies on their backs, children they cannot support?'

'I think it is an unforgivable sin. And not all those men do it intentionally, mind you. Sometimes, with all their good intentions, they just do not have the means to do much about the problem of having to pay *lobola*, so they disappear, and the girls never see them again.'

'How long do you think they'll lock you up, Mojalefa?' she asked, suddenly remembering that it might be years before she could speak to him like that again. She adored him, and speaking of parting with him broke her heart.

'I do not know, and I do not worry about that, Bongi. If I had you and Gugu and they thrust me into a desert for a thousand years, I would not care. But then I am only a small part of a whole. I'm like a single minute cell in the living body composed of millions of cells, and I have to play my small part for the well-being and perpetuation of life in the whole body.'

'But you are likely to be thrust into the midst of hardened criminals, murderers, rapist and so on.'

'Very likely. But then that should not deter us. After all most of them have been driven into being like that by the very evils we are exposed to as people without a say in the running of our lives. Most of them have ceased to be proud because there's nothing to be proud of. You amuse me, Bongi. So you think because we are more educated we have reason to be proud? Of what should we feel proud in a society where the mere pigmentation of your skin condemns you to nothingness? Tell me, of what?'

She shook her head violently, biting her lips in sorrow, and with tears in her eyes, she replied, softly:

'I do not know, Mojalefa.'

They stood in silence for a while. She sighed deeply and held back the tears. They felt uneasy. It was useless, she thought bitterly. They had gone through with what she considered to be an ill-fated undertaking. Yet he was relentlessly adamant. She remembered how they had quarrelled the previous night. How at first she had told herself that she had come to accept what was about to happen with quiet composure, 'like a mature person' as they say. She had however lost control of herself when they were alone outside her home, when he had bidden her mother and other relatives farewell. She had become hysterical and could not go on pretending any longer. In a fit of anger, she had accused Mojalefa of being a coward who was running away from his responsibilities as a father and husband. It had been a very bad row and they had parted unceremoniously. She had resolved that today she would only speak of those things which would not make them unhappy. And now she realised with regret that she was right back where she had started. She murmured to herself:

'Oh God, why should it be us, why should we be the lambs for the slaughter? Why should you be one of those handing themselves over? It's like giving up. What will you be able to do for your people in gaol, or if you should be . . . '

She could not utter the word 'killed'.

'*Somebody* has got to sacrifice so that others may be free. The *real* things, those that really matter, are never acquired the easy way. All the peoples of this world who were oppressed like us have had to give up *something*, Bongi. Nothing good or of real value comes easily. Our freedom will never be handed over to us on a silver platter. In our movement, we labour under no illusions; we know we can expect no hand-outs. We know that the path ahead of us is not lined with soft velvety flower petals: we are aware that we shall have to tread on thorns. We are committed to a life of service, sacrifice and suffering. Oh no, Bongi, you have got it all wrong. It is not like throwing in the towel. On the contrary, it is the beginning of something our people will never look back at with shame. We shall never regret what we are about to do, and there is no turning back. We are at the point of no return! If I changed my mind now and went back home and sat down and deceived myself that all was alright, I would die a very unhappy man indeed. I would die in dishonour.' He was silent awhile.

'Bongi, I want to tell you my story. I've never related it to anyone before because just *thinking* about the sad event is to me a very unpleasant and extremely exacting experience . . . He was picking his way carefully through memories.

'After my father had completed altering that house we live in from a four-roomed matchbox to what it is now, he was a proud man. He was called to the office by the superintendent to complete a contract with an electrical contractor. It had been a costly business and the contractor had insisted that the final arrangements be concluded before the City Council official. It was on that very day that the superintendent asked him if he could bring some of his colleagues to see the house when it was completed. My father agreed. I was there on that day when they (a group of about fifteen whites) arrived. I had heard my parents speak with great expectation to their friends and everybody about the intended 'visit' by the white people. Naturally, I was delighted and proud as any youngster would be. I made sure I would be home and not at the football grounds that afternoon. I thought it was a great honour to have such respectable white people coming to *our* house. I looked forward to it and I had actually warned some of my friends . . .

'After showing them through all the nine rooms of the double-storey house, my obviously gratified parents both saw the party out along the slasto pathway to the front gate. I was standing with one of my friends near the front verandah. I still remember vividly the superintendent's last words. He said: 'John, on behalf of my colleagues here and myself, we are very thankful that you and your kind *mosade* allowed us to come and see your beautiful house. You must have spent a *lot* of money to build and furnish it *so* well. But, *you should have built it on wheels!*' And the official added, with his arms swinging forward like someone pushing some imaginary object: 'It should have had *wheels* so that it may *move* easily!' And they departed, leaving my petrified parents standing there agape and looking at each other in helpless amazement. I remember, later, my mother trying her best to put my stunned father at ease, saying: *'Au, oa hlanya, mo lebale; ha a tsebe hore ontse a re'ng. Ntate hle!'* (He is mad; just forget about him. He does not know what he is saying!)

'As a fifteen-year-old youth, I was also puzzled. But unlike my parents, I did not sit down and forget — or try to do so. That day marked the turning point in my life. From that day on, I could not rest. Those remarks by that government official kept ringing in my mind. I had to know why he had said that. I probed, and probed; I asked my teachers at school, clerks at the municipal offices, anyone who I thought would be in a position to help me. Of course I made it as general as I could and I grew more and more restless. I went to libraries and read all the available literature I could find on the South African blacks.

I studied South African history as I had never done before. The history of the discovery of gold, diamonds and other minerals in this land, and the growth of the towns. I read of the rush to the main industrial centres and the influx of the Africans into them, following their early reluctance, and sometimes refusal, to work there, and the subsequent laws which necessitated their coming like the vagrancy laws and the pass laws. I read about the removals of the so-called 'black spots' and why they were now labelled that. The influenza epidemic which resulted in the building of the Western Native and George Goch townships in 1919. I dug into any information I could get about the history of the urban Africans. I discovered the slyness, hypocrisy, dishonesty and greed of the law-makers.

'When elderly people came to visit us and sat in the evenings to speak about their experiences of the past, of how they first came into contact with the whites, their lives with the Boers on the farms and so forth, I listened. Whenever my father's relations went to the remote areas in Lesotho and Matatiele, or to Zululand and Natal where my mother's people are, during school holidays, I grabbed the opportunity and accompanied them. Learning history ceased to be the usual matter of committing to memory a whole lot of intangible facts from some obscure detached past. It became a living thing and a challenge. I was in search of my true self. And like Moses in the Bible, I was disillusioned. Instead of having been raised like the slave I am, I had been nurtured like a prince, clothed in a fine white linen loincloth and girdle when I should have been wrapped in the rough woven clothing of my kind.

'When I had come to know most of the facts, when I had read through most of the numerous laws pertaining to the urban blacks — the acts, clauses, sub-clauses, regulations, sections and sub-sections; the amendments and sub-amendments — I saw myself for the first time. I was a prince, descended from the noble proud house of Monaheng — the true Kings of the Basuto nation. I stopped going to the sports clubs and the church. Even my father's flashy American 'Impala' ceased to bring to me the thrill it used to when I drove round the townships in it. I attended political meetings because there, at least, I found people trying to find ways and means of solving and overcoming our problems. At least I knew now what I really was . . . an underdog, a voiceless creature. Unlike my father, I was not going to be blindfolded and led along a garden path by someone else, a foreigner from other continents. I learnt that as a black, there was a responsibility I was carrying on my shoulders as a son of this soil. I realised that I had to take an active part in deciding (or in insisting that I should decide) the path along which my descendants will tread. Something was wrong: radically wrong, and it was my duty as a black person to try and put it right. To free myself and my people became an obsession, a dedication.

'I sometimes listen with interest when my father complains. Poor father. He would say: "Mojalefa *oa polotika*. All Mojalefa reads is politics, politics, politics. He no longer plays football like other youths. When he passed matric with flying colours in History, his History master came to my house to tell me how my son is a promising leader. I was proud and I moved around with my head in the air. I wanted him to start immediately at University, but he insisted that he wanted to work. I wondered why because I could afford it and there was no pressing need for him to work. He said he would study under UNISA and I paid fees for the first year, and they sent him lectures. But instead of studying, he locks himself up in his room and reads politics all the time. He has stopped sending in scripts for correction. He is morose and never goes to church. He does not appreciate what I do for him!" Sometimes I actually pity my father. He would say: "My father was proud when Mojalefa was born. He walked on foot rather than take a bus all the way from Eastern Native Township to Bridgman Memorial Hospital in Brixton to offer his blessings at the bedside of my late wife, and to thank our ancestors for a son and heir. He named him Mojalefa. And now that boy is about to sacrifice himself — for what he calls 'a worthy cause'. He gives up all this . . . a house I've built and furnished for R21 000, most of my money from the insurance policy my good old boss was clever enough to force me to take when I first started working for him. Mojalefa gives up all this for a gaol cell!" '

There were tears in the eyes of S'bongile as she sat staring in bewilderment at Mojalefa. She saw now a different man; a man with convictions and ideals; who was not going to be shaken from his beliefs, come what may. He stopped for a while and paused. All the time he spoke as if to some unseen being, as if he was unconscious of her presence. He went on:

'My father always speaks of how his grandfather used to tell him that as a boy in what is now known as the Free State (I don't know why) the white people (the Boers) used to come, clothed only in a "stertriem", and ask for permission to settle on their land. Just like that, bare-footed and with cracked soles, begging for land. My father does not realise that *he* is now in a worse position than those Boers; that all that makes a man has been stripped from under his feet. That he now has to *float in the air*. He sits back in his favourite comfortable armchair in his livingroom, looks around him at the splendour surrounding him, and sadly asks: "When I go, who'll take over from me?" He thinks he is still a man, you know. He never stops to ask himself: "Take *what* over . . . a house on wheels? Something with no firm ground to stand on?" ' He turned away from her and looked through the dusty window pane. He raised his arms and grabbed the vertical steel bars over the window. He clung viciously to them and shook them until they rattled. He said:

'No Bongi. There is no turning back. Something has *got* to be done . . . something. It cannot go on like this!'

Strange as it may seem, at that moment, they both had visions of a gaol cell. They both felt like trapped animals. He kept on shaking the bars and shouting:

'Something's *got* to be done . . . Now!'

She could not bear the sight any longer. He seemed to be going through great emotional torture. She shouted:

'Mojalefa!'

He swung round and faced her like someone only waking up from a bad dream. He stared through the open entrance, and up at the stair leading to the upper floor where the humming voices were audible. They both stood still listening for a while. Then he spoke softly yet earnestly, clenching his fists and looking up towards the sound of the music. He said:

'Tomorrow, when dawn breaks, we shall march . . . Our men will advance from different parts of the Republic of South Africa. They will leave their pass-books behind and not feel the heavy weight in their pockets as they proceed towards the gates of the prisons of this land of our forefathers!'

Bongi stood up slowly. She did not utter a word. There seemed to be nothing to say. She seemed to be drained of all feeling. She felt blank. He thought he detected an air of resignation, a look of calmness in her manner as she moved slowly in the direction of the opening into the street. They stopped and looked at each other. She sighed, and there were no tears in her eyes now. He brushed the back of his hand tenderly over the soft cheeks of the sleeping Gugu and with his dry lips, kissed S'bongile's brow. He lifted her chin slightly with his forefinger and looked into her eyes. They seemed to smile at him. They parted.

149

Mothobi Mutloatse/THE TRUTH, MAMA

'Where will we be going to this Christmas, Mama?' That was chubby, six-year-old, inquisitive Busisiwe, interrupting her mother as she wrapped up her provisions for someone special. Somebody very dear and yet so far, from the Serowe family of six . . . its head.

The father of Busi, five-year-old Nthato, seventeen-year-old Matimba and nineteen-year-old Xoli.

The husband of Morongwe. Phuthuma . . .

All Ma-Nthato — as she was affectionately known in the neighbourhood of Jabavu because of Nthato's pranks and antics — could mumble, was something like: 'There's no need to go anywhere this year.'

Back came Busi's question: 'Why Mama?'

Ma-Nthato frowned: 'Oh . . . because there's nowhere we can go to this time.'

Xoli, the eldest of the children and a high school student at Morris Isaacson — before the State took over forty schools, that is — looked up from the copy of *Ebony* he was absorbed in, and challenged his mother. Not so gently though:

'Mama, why can't you tell her the truth?'

'I can't as yet Xoli, and you know it.'

'Know what, Mama?' Busi queried further.

Just then, Matimba, who'd come in from attending one of the ghetto educational courses at the Early Learning Centre (Entokozweni) in Moletsane, intervened.

'What is going on in here, Ma?'

Xoli intercepted: 'She's selling Busi, here, a dummy.'

'Watch your language, Xoli. Very soon you will be sorry,' Ma-Nthato chided him.

But Xoli was not to be discouraged easily. Politely, he told his sister, Matimba, an ex-student at Naledi High (ex, again, because of the legalised hijacking of her school): 'Mama is playing a game of hide and seek with Busi. She refuses to tell her why we won't be going out this Christmas.'

Suddenly Ma-Nthato, to avoid an intense cross-examination by Xoli, and possibly Matimba, announced that the children would have to excuse her there and then. She had to leave for Modder Bee Prison.

Slip of the tongue: prison.

This was the first time in three weeks, since the disappearance of her husband — a few days after what was being referred to as the 'crack-down' — that she had mentioned the word 'prison' in the presence of all the children, though both Matimba and Xoli, as the elder children, had visited their father twice.

Ma-Nthato had decided, much against Xoli's protestations, not to tell the smaller children where their father was.

'How long mother, do you think that you can hide the truth from them? And do you think it is wise?' Xoli had asked then.

All this returned in a flash to her, as well as to Xoli, when she slipped up by referring to Modder Bee Prison by name.

Each time she left with *umphako* and kisses for everyone (except Xoli who argued that kisses were reserved for his girl friend only), Ma-Nthato would innocently but deliberately lie that she was visiting Ntate — the children's father — at his place of employment!

But now *nta etswile pepeneneng.* The cat was out of the bag!

For all to see — and diagnose clinically. As well as ethically.

Xoli took advantage of the situation and went on the encitement path.

'There's no way in which you can duck this one, Ma. You will have to tell them the truth. The whole, absolute truth — before they learn it from awkward quarters.'

'Will you stop harassing me,' Ma-Nthato protested, trying hard to conceal her embarrassment. She momentarily stole a glance at the expressions on all her children's faces to assess the situation.

When she saw, and, in a way smelled the curiosity, the unquenched curiosity in them, she decided to tell the truth. And let nature take its course.

But the difficult part was, how to tell it without losing face at the same time for having delayed the truth so long. And yet, there was no valid reason for doing so in the circumstances. Or was there?

She realised then that she would have to tell the truth in a skilful manner — to appease Xoli for instance, though she doubted that Xoli would ever be satisfied with anything less than his father's release.

The silence that ensued was trying. And piercing.

'We're still awaiting your explanation, Ma,' Matimba reminded her, disturbing Ma-Nthato's day-dreaming.

'Here's a chair, Mama,' Xoli said, matter-of-factly.

Busi, who had been quiet all along, opened the home inquisition with the obvious. 'What are you going to do at Modder Bee — isn't it a jail where criminals are kept? Like we were told by our teacher in Sunday School?'

Ma-Nthato heaved a sigh — she was near a mental breakdown as she sat down — with her children encircling her as they would their granny when she taught them history the human way each time they visited her.

'Where do I begin?' Ma-Nthato asked.

'You begin from the beginning,' retorted Xoli.

'Naturally,' added Matimba.

The smaller children were amused by this style of dialogue.

'Ma,' Xoli continued, 'simply tell them where Baba is, why he is there, and how long he anticipates being there. Don't make a short story long. Simply give them the facts. It is much better that they hear this news from no one but you. They are certainly going to be more relieved than shocked. That's my own opinion, though.'

Matimba appealed to her mother to speak the truth 'and it shall set you free.'

Naive as it may seem, the last remark by Matimba acted as a catalyst to Ma-Nthato. At least, she thought to herself, they are asking for an explanation from me because they dearly miss their father!

'Well, children . . . the truth is,' she heard herself say, not believing that the words were really coming 'your father is, in fact, at Modder Bee Prison.'

'And so he's a criminal,' Busi let go.

'No, he's not actually.'

'And so what is he doing there?' Nthato asked sharply.

'This is going to be a hell of a "court case",' Ma-Nthato mumbled to herself.

'What was that, Mama?' Matimba jumped in.

'Nothing, really, I was speaking to myself . . .'

'Is Mama sick then?' Busi wanted to know.

Xoli, who had been listening with arms folded as if he was the judge, explained: 'Mama is not sick . . . she's only concerned . . .'

Ma-Nthato did not know whether Xoli was being sarcastic or extra-sweet.

'Your father is not a criminal,' said Ma-Nthato quietly.

'If he's not a criminal what is he then? A worker at Modder Bee?'

'He does not work there,' Xoli put in. 'You know, as well as every-body does, that he was a teacher — until he resigned in protest against this monster that is Bantu Education, together with more than three hundred other teachers.'

Ma-Nthato took the cue: 'Your father was detained —'

Busi flashed back: 'What do you mean, "detained"?'

'Can you explain that for me, Xoli?' Ma-Nthato appealed.

'Unfortunately, Ma, this is not the right time and place for me to do so.'

'Aw, I see,' replied Ma-Nthato.

Was there a hint of sarcasm?

Nthato joined the band-wagon: 'Why was Ntate detained, Ma?'

Busi was not to be beaten to the punch: 'You wait your turn, Nthato: I was the one who was doing the asking. I want to know the meaning of "detained".'

'Children, can't we postpone this until I come back?'

'Noo!' was the chorus.

'The truth, Mama . . . Tell the truth here and now,' said Xoli, sort of matter-of-fact.

To start the ball rolling, he began humming, quietly the ghetto hymn, 'Senzeni Na?'

And, this time, Ma-Nthato was left with no alternative but to get the whole damned thing off her shoulders. Before the children unleashed real thunderbolts!

'Baba was detained — the police took him to Modder Bee under the Internal Security Act.'

'And what is that?' Busi inquired, with a worried expression.

Ma-Nthato looked at Xoli, but there was no sign of help ever coming from that end. So she essayed a lay person's interpretation of the law: 'It's a law under which people are arrested for politics.'

Like a fox-terrier, Busi shot back: 'And what is politics?'

'It is a long, long story.'

'Please tell us about it, Ma.' That was Matimba — of all people!

'Politics is saying something the Government doesn't like.'

'Who is this Govern-what?' Nthato chipped in.

'The Government are people who control this land.'

'What did Baba say that they didn't like?'

'Nthato, you sure ask too many questions . . .'

'But Ma, they have taken Baba away — what for, we don't know. What did Baba tell them that they didn't like?'

'He said, among other things, that he won't teach under Bantu Education any more.'

Busi got in before she was squeezed out again: 'But that is what we Ama-Azanians are fighting against. Everybody hates Bantu Education because all it produces is teargas.'

Matimba also wanted to know from her mother what the other reasons were for their father's detention.

Painstakingly, Ma-Nthato answered: 'I think it was because he said the Black man was well qualified enough now to run the Black man's affairs. Oh, children, you are torturing me.'

Even Xoli was touched.

He asked: 'Did Baba actually say so, Mama?'

'Y-y-yes,' sobbed Ma-Nthato. 'And he may be held for up to a year . . . that's why we cannot go away this Christmas, Busi.'

The tiny delicate creature, no, angel, was really moved.

'Mama, do you know what?'

'N-no, Busi.'

'I'm proud of my father . . . and of you too. Despite all the trouble we give every day before you leave for work in town, you still love us.'

'Care for us,' added Xoli as he slowly ambled towards his mother, arms outstretched.

'Christmas is no longer a time of enjoyment for us,' said Matimba in a soft tone. 'All our people have been detained.'

'All we can do is abstain from all pleasures — and remember all those who have been detained. And, like Biko, have died in detention.'

'Mother,' Xoli said as he embraced his tear-filled mother, 'I love you with all my heart. Forgive me for undermining you — for thinking poorly of you. I didn't know, I just didn't know how much all this was hurting you.'

Ma-Nthato smiled a little at Xoli and said: 'Your father would be proud of you now. In fact, he would have been disappointed if you had behaved otherwise. And were it not for your tough talk, I myself would have suffered a nervous breakdown long ago.'

In some surprise, Xoli found himself sobbing on his weeping mother. And the girls couldn't hold back their tears.

But then these were tears of togetherness. The family that would not allow detention to disrupt its unity.

Nor dampen its spirits.

Mango Tshabangu/THOUGHTS IN A TRAIN

When we ride these things which cannot take us all, there is no doubt as to our inventiveness. We stand inside in grotesque positions — one foot in the air, our bodies twisted away from arms squeezing through other twisted bodies to find support somewhere. Sometimes it is on another person's shoulder, but it is stupid to complain so nobody does. It's as if some invisible sardine packer has been at work. We remain in that position for forty minutes or forty days. How far is Soweto from Johannesburg? It is forty minutes or forty days. No-one knows exactly.

We remain in that position, our bodies sweating out the unfreedom of our souls, anticipating happiness in that unhappy architectural shame — the ghetto. Our eyes dart apprehensively, on the lookout for those of our brothers who have resorted to the insanity of crime to protest their insane conditions. For, indeed, if we were not scared of moral ridicule we would regard crime as a form of protest. Is not a man with a hungry stomach in the same position as a man whose land has been taken away from him? What if he is a victim of both!

We remain in that position for forty minutes or forty days. No-one knows exactly. We, the young, cling perilously to the outside of the coach walls. It sends the guts racing to the throat, yes, but to us it is bravery. We are not a helpless gutless lot whose lives have been patterned by suffering. The more daring among us dance like gods of fate on the rooftop. Sometimes there is death by electrocution but then it is just hard luck . . . He was a good man, Bayekile. It is not his fault that he did not live to face a stray bullet.

We remain in that position for forty minutes or forty days. No-one knows exactly.

156

We move parallel to or hurtle past their trains. Most often my impression is that it is they who cruise past our hurtling train. Theirs is always almost empty. They'll sit comfortably on seats made for that purpose and keep their windows shut, even on hot days. And they sit there in their train watching us as one watches a play from a private box. We also stare back at them, but the sullen faces don't interest us much. Only the shut windows move our thinking.

On this day it was Msongi and Gezani who were most interested in the shut windows. You see, ever since they'd discovered Houghton golf course to be offering better tips in the caddy business, Msongi and Gezani found themselves walking through the rich suburbs of Johannesburg. Their experience was a strange one. There was something eerie in the surroundings. They always had fear, the like of which they'd never known. Surely it was not because of the numerous policemen who patrolled the streets and snarled in unison with their dogs at Black boys moving through those gracious thoroughfares.

Msongi and Gezani were young no doubt, but this writer has already said that bravery born of suffering knows no age nor danger nor pattern. Fear of snarling policemen was out for these two young Black boys. Nevertheless, this overwhelming fear the like of which they'd never known was always all around them whenever they walked through the rich suburbs of Johannesburg. They could not even talk about it. Somehow, they were sure they both had this strange fear.

There was a time when they impulsively stood right in the middle of a street. They had hoped to break this fear the like of which they'd never known. But the attempt only lasted a few seconds and that was too short to be of any help. They both scurried off, hating themselves for lack of courage. They never spoke of it.

In search of the truth, Msongi became very observant. He'd been noticing the shut windows of *their* train every time he and Gezani happened to be in ours. On this day, it was a week since Msongi decided to break the silence. Msongi's argument was that the fear was in the surroundings and not in them. The place was full of fear. Vicious fear which, although imprisoned in stone walls and electrified fences, swelled over and poured into the streets to oppress even the occasional passer-by. Msongi and Gezani were merely walking through this fear. It was like walking in darkness and feeling the darkness all around you. That does not mean you are darkness yourself. As soon as you come to a lit spot, the feeling of darkness dies. Why, as soon as they hit town proper, and mixed with the people, the fear the like of which they'd never known disappeared. No, Msongi was convinced it was not they who had fear. Fear flowed from somewhere, besmirching every part of them, leaving their souls trembling; but it was not they who were afraid.

They did not have stone walls or electrified fences in Soweto. They were not scared of their gold rings being snatched for they had none. They were not worried about their sisters being peeped at for their sisters could look after themselves. Oh, those diamond toothpicks could disappear you know . . . Those too, they did not have. They were not afraid of bleeding, for their streets ran red already. On this day Msongi stared at the shut windows. He looked at the pale sullen white faces and he knew why.

He felt tempted to throw something at them. Anything . . . an empty cigarette box, an orange peel, even a piece of paper; just to prove a point. At that moment, and as if instructed by Msongi himself, someone threw an empty beer bottle at the other train.

The confusion: they ran around climbing onto seats. They jumped into the air. They knocked against one another as they scrambled for the doors and windows. The already pale faces had no colour to change into. They could only be distorted as fear is capable of doing that as well. The shut windows were shattered wide open, as if to say danger cannot be imprisoned. The train passed swiftly by, disappearing with the drama of the fear the like of which Msongi and Gezani had never known.

Achmed Dangor/WAITING FOR LEILA

It was winter. There were clouds gathering on Table Mountain, he knew that the night was going to be very cold.

BRRRAT-A-TAT-BRRR. Jackhammers picking like crows at his guts. All around him they were breaking down his city, brick by brick, stone for stone.

DISTRICT SIX — ROCK OF MY HISTORY!

LEILA! WHERE THE HELL ARE YOU?

For days now he had been waiting for Leila, even though he knew that his wait was in vain. She was going to be wed the next day.

Waiting in this hovel was painful. He looked around him: exactly as his parents had left it. Matchstick furniture, the glass showcase filled with cheap ornaments purchased on the Parade.

'Stroes merram, real bone china!'

On the wall hung the two mirrors inscribed with the Arabic legends: 'GOD IS GREAT', 'THERE IS ONLY ONE GOD'.

And behind the mirrors teemed the armies of cockroaches that had become his sole companions.

He shuddered. Infected with pestilence, like everything else. What a blerry slum this is!

The jackhammers stopped.

Must be six-o-clock already. Brrr! How cold it is. Only the skollies will be in the streets tonight. They are immune to the cold. This is what District Six does, hardens us. Hearts as empty as the shop windows in Hanover Street. In the shadow of Table Mountain, rats at the door of heaven.

He heard voices, a banjo strumming.

They're singing. The idiots! As if nothing's happened, as if nothing's happening. May God strike them dead.

Night was falling rapidly.

LEILA! LEILA!

Somewhere down in Roosstraat, you're sitting by the heat of the black stove, laughing. Warm and secure in the old homes of our mothers. And tomorrow you marry, *medora* on your head, your face veiled and hidden. Cosseted like a virgin, offered as noble sacrifice. And the willing smile on your face. Destiny! Destiny!

DESTINY *SE MOER*!

You're mine. Here in this room, beads of sweat down your back, the darkness of our bodies flickered on the wall. You moaned softly no, no, no. The breeze from the harbour brought the smell of diesel oil. Afterwards you lay exhausted, a pale flower, in the crook of my arm.

Perhaps it was then that you smelled the sheets. Indelible odour of my history. They sired me here, the last of five children. He with his merely adequate grunts. She my mother, Rose of the Strand 1947, received him with the same stoic incomprehension that enabled her to bear her children.

You saw the roaches scamper across the walls, a portent of my future. Love and life buried, here, in this, my last refuge.

Even my parents abandoned it.

When they left, my father announced, without emotion:

'We are going to Jo'burg. Jobs, a home, a new life.'

Only she, faded rose, pleaded with me to join them.

But I was adamant. This is my rock, I cannot leave.

She hugged me. Odour of faded carnality. I watched them leave in the overloaded taxi, struggling along behind the bus, the way the mist rolls and chases everything home.

OH MOTHER! This loneliness is in my belly, my hunger.

It was becoming quite cold now, but he dared not close the windows. The smell would drive him away.

A dead rat somewhere, rotting. Thousands of dead rats here in District Six. One can hear their sorrowful souls rustle in the darkness, lamenting the death of their beloved city. City of a thousand nations, disgorge your stinking belly. No white man will ever build his home here. Our ghosts are ineradicable.

It was silent outside, a ghost town. Most of the few remaining shops were closed. People now live in the Cape Flats. In Hanover Park, in Bonteheuvel, in homes with scraggy, sandy gardens that the ingenious white man had reclaimed from the sea.

GAMAT! YOU HAVE BECOME NEPTUNE'S TENANT. Pay your rent or he'll stick his trident up your arse.

But the smell was becoming unbearable.

Shall I go out and wander in the shadows?

Here was the fish shop. Snoek ten cents a piece. The shop assistant had a rose pinned to her bodice. Promise (òr remnant?) of a night's joy. I offer you a smile, a gesture of brotherly love. But you regard me with suspicion.

Salaam-a-leikum to you too. Go in peace, you worn-out old witch, thinking that I, I, am making eyes at you. My love is pure, I did not search for it in the shadowy faces that hide in darkened doorways.

LEILA — CHILD OF LIGHT. I first saw you in a crowd of pic-nickers, gambolling in the waves. The sea glistened on your olive skin, ripe as proud fruit. Oh Africa, cool paradise of Africa, why do you tighten the manacles so mercilessly?

But there was a foreigner — must have been Italian — accosting you with his smile. The remnants of a meal bristled in his moustache.

Blerry 'Talianer go back to Rome! A worse slum than mine. He moved away, feigned indifference. And I? All that I could offer you were my faded sheets.

The smell of decay seemed to have followed him, and he could not finish the salty sandwich the girl with the rose in her bodice had prepared. He flung it into the gutter and wiped his mouth.

Wine. I need some wine. As red and sweet as the flesh of a water-melon.

I remember you said I ate like a pig and that you hated me. We were on Strandfontein beach, where the sign says Whites Only. We were there not because we were daring in any way. We were there because of the heat, and the white quiet stretch of beach. The sea was cool, almost icy to the touch of our burning bodies.

'WAT' LEMOOOEN! FIVE BOB, NET FIVE BOB, SO ROOI SOOS DIE MOTCHIE SE LIPPE!'

You begged me to buy one, because of its swollen, ripe appearance. I tested the watermelon for ripeness by pressing it against the top of my head. It creaked, and then cracked.

A sudden, wild desire overcame me, as the sticky juice flowed into my hair. I raced towards the sea, gently cradling the fruit in my arms; the crack in its skin revealed itself to me, red and delicate, almost like the opening of your sex.

Trembling, I smashed the watermelon against a rock, and began eating, as voraciously as a starving animal. Bits of its flesh remained, impaled upon the rock. I could see the disgust in your eyes.

I remember only my own laughter, and the sweetness dripping from my mouth. I offered you a chunk of watermelon, oh love, like honey to a goddess.

'ANIMAL!'

Amen. Jus' a blerry educated skollie from Hanover Street. I looked around and saw three of my fellow men, skollies with *hang-gat broeke,* smiling at me.

'Ey you really enjoying it *hê*!'

I invited them to join me, communion with my own kind. We ate and spat the seeds into the air. The huge man, a grotesque tattoo on his chest heaving, spat the furthest, each feat accompanied by roars of raucous laughter.

A crowd of people, whites, had gathered around us. One could feel the tension. You had walked away and stood at the rear of the crowd. Then I saw the policeman, his peaked cap pulled low over his eyes.

'Pigs!' he screamed, and struck me across the back with his baton.

The pain seared through me.

'Hey! You don't have to blerrywell hit him!' the huge man growled at the policeman.

'Just get away from here before I bogger you up too!'

'Orraaight, don't piss in your *broeks!*'

'Go,' one of them whispered to me, 'we'll handle this burg.'

For a moment I watched them swagger through the crowd with indolent menace, almost daring the policeman to carry out his threat. Then I ran after you.

'Leila, Leila, Leila!'

The wind carried my jagged voice. That summer, those wonderful days, 'honey-sweating' in the heat of my room, I thought I had won, weaned you away from the suffocating bosoms of our mothers. How wrong I was.

In your home you were taught that watermelon, like life, had to be turned into *konfyt,* calcified, preserved in sugar, and eaten demurely. Wiping your hands afterwards with a clean white cloth. Joy was something you hid in the dark.

That's where you're hiding now.

He now stood before the shebeen which was situated off Hanover Street, in a side street that was no more than a wide alleyway. Someone shifted, almost unseen, in the shadows.

Better knock before he mistakes my intention.

'Who's there?'

'Me.'

'Who the *duiwel* is me?'

'Your most illustrious customer, champion of the faithless, last survivor of Kapini Street.'

'Stop talking *kak*! Who are you?'

'Sam. Samad, not Samuel, as the fate of my father's loin decreed.'

'It's that mad bogger from Kapini Street,' another voice rejoined from the shadows.

'What do you want?'

'Just a half bottle, not a ceremony.'

A latch shifted in its rusty scabbard.

The noises we inherited from our forefathers.

A head was thrust out of the half-opened door, its eyes searched the shadows.

'Okay — IN,' the voice hissed.

The door was shut, almost before Samad was inside. Old Harry, to whom the head and the darting eyes belonged, shuffled away, muttering darkly about the insane people that inhabited the District of late. In the pitch dark corridor, Samad, despite a conscious effort, could feel no fear.

Were it not for his fertile imagination, he would have been terrified, for he could only conjure up ghouls and djinns, not the real, living beasts that inhabited these evil portals.

Harry returned.

'Motchie wants to know if you've got money.'

'Ow, *Boeta* Harry, don't you trust me?'

'Not a blerry damn.' He broke into a smile that revealed a flaring harelip, barely hidden by his wild bushy moustache.

In my childhood I uttered a hundred prayers at the sight of such ugliness.

'Money, Money!' Harry said irritably . . .

Samad handed over the money, and soon, the bottle tucked under his arm, he was ushered out into the street of shadows.

Oh, for the days when there was summer in the streets . . . I remember, we walked that evening, apart, not touching. You were dressed in white, on your head was a lace mantilla you had bought from old Patel that afternoon.

'Ma-sha-Allah, THIS is how a Muslim girl must look.'

Beyond the enthusiastic voice, faint, disinterested eyes. His son (pale and beautiful, the legacy of generations of family inbreeding) stalked out of the shop in disgust at his father's coquettish sales talk. He stood outside, avoiding my eyes, head bowed, hands stuffed deep into his trouser pocket. But he too will end up like his father, his soul detached from his body — the way of all monied flesh.

Then, as we were walking, a City bus splashed mud all over us. The driver, stalled by the traffic, looked back at us, a wicked gleam in his eyes.

'YOU BASTARD!' I screamed.

'Can't your *jintoe* see where she's going?' he had retorted. He was still stuck in the traffic, and we grappled with the door of his cab. With a sudden jerk he had pulled away, leaving me to sprawl backwards into the street.

There was laughter in your eyes, in spite of the austere clamp of your lips. It was summer in the streets. You were finally beginning to enjoy our love.

Samad took a long swig at the bottle, and sat down on the kerb. That day Leila had disappeared. After many days Samad went down to Roosstraat, fearing that she was ill.

There were many young men at your house, suitors who wore spotless *kufiyas* over their Brylcream gladdies. Preening and arrogant young men, who spent their time playing dominoes, banging the tables with hefty fists.

They shone rudely of health, their wealth was unmistaken. They came armed with illustrious introductions:

'Taypie, son of Hajee Yusef.'

'Achmat Jabaar, son of Boeta Amin Jabaar.'

They drank the sweet milk your mother prepared, and with the kind of lusty harmony we are capable of, sang the songs of our tradition. Amidst it all I heard your guarded but happy laughter. While I, like a beggar, waited in the fallen house of my father, watching our kingdom decay into darkness.

Now, in the murky heart of District Six, in the netherworld of our lives, we snatch the fragile cloth from the corpses of our unused memories and clothe ourselves propitiously. We shall expire — *ons gaan vrek!* — and will be buried without the ceremonies of men. Without ash or prayer, we who slept to death behind our latticed minds.

Come, ghost of the twentieth century, open those darkened windows of grief, take the light that I, renegade, pagan from the skies, have to offer.

'Hey you *fokken dronklap*!' A man obviously disturbed by Samad's raving, stood at the railing of his balcony. His vest bore the stains of at least a week's honest sweat.

What grandeur in your broken backs!

'Go and do your *befokte* shouting somewhere else. A man can't even get a decent night's sleep here. *Voertsek.*'

A voice from within the hovel responded:

'I told you we have to get out of here, there's nothing decent left in this place.'

The man went indoors.

'Oh shut up. I told you — I'm not moving, this is my home!'

'Home *se voet*! Look at it,' the female voice said, disappearing into the inner recesses of the hovel. A lavatory cistern gurgled.

Samad tried to picture her, her huge buttocks spreading over the toilet seat, worn and rough from the many years of unremitting usage. In her mind the dim, oft suppressed fear of picking up some dreadful disease. This unconscious thought would fuel her agitation for the need to move from the District. To find a decent house, a home, with a toilet that only her family would use.

She no longer cares that this is his ancestral home, no more for her the warmth of the hovel, the brotherhood of poverty.

The light went out. The man emerged from the gloom.

'Hey, you still here? Fuck off before I come down there and break your neck!'

Farewell brother, a shadowy light creeps stealthily to your door.

Towards Upper Constitution Street. From the hill you can see the whole city.

Dark, brooding hulks in the harbour, alongside it, starkly contrasting, the expanse of beach. Because of oil pollution, the beach was no longer used for bathing.

There, three hundred years ago, Jan van Riebeeck, and privileged members of his entourage, gambolled in those white-headed breakers, enjoying the mysterious ecstasies of those glistening black thighs. And our whole history was buggered up.

Samad stood before the house of Suleiman the Dhukkum, who claims a kinship to Samad's great ancestor, Ben Yusuf, known as Benjamin the Mallaccan dhukkum.

This was once a house, humans lived here. Now it is boarded up, its ghosts preserved from our voracious vandals. There is something menacing about this place. Suleiman is watching me. I can hear his asthmatic wheeze.

'Leiman? Are you there?'

He is there, I can see his beady eyes in the darkness.

'Ah well, I drink alone tonight.'

Samad displayed the wine bottle, lovingly patting it.

Guardian of the ineluctable dark spirits, crawl out of your hole, you old fraud.

An old man, his lungs wheezing and hissing from the effort, emerged from his cave-like cellar.

'The noise, the noise, enough to waken the dead!'

'Salaam, . . .'

'Salaam, your breath stinks of wine.'

Samad took another long swig, as the old man looked on stoically stroking his milk white beard.

'How generous our young people have become.'

Samad extended the **bottle** to Suleiman, who was barely able to conceal his thirst.

The hunger in your rheumy eyes, you old crook.

Samad snatched the bottle away from the old man's lips.

'This time, it will be a spirit for a spirit.'

'Don't play with the dead.'

'You're an old fraud.'

'You saw nothing because you cannot see. The blindness is in your heart.'

'Spare me the blerry philosophies, you old crook.'

'You have no faith, you cannot see what you do not believe in.'

Samad grabbed the old man by the scruff of his filthy neck.

'This time I want to speak to them.'

'You're mad, mad,' the old man hissed.

Samad began to search the old man. A small packet, the size of a twenty-cent coin, under the collar of his jacket.

So this is where he hides the dagga on his skeletal frame.

'You're choking me.'

'Now I have you in my power, you blerry charlatan!'

'Please, please, . . .'

Samad put the bottle to Suleiman's lips. Just enough to wet the tongue.

The old man, coughing and choking, gradually regained his composure.

'What do you want?'

'I want to speak to them, to Benjamin the Mallaccan.'

'You are mad. Insane.'

'You're a liar and a thief.'

'Have you no respect?'

'Was Benjamin a fraud as well?'

'Don't mock the dead!'

Yes I know, you told me before. I will come to a bad end. An angel will come on the heavenly horse and strike my heart with lightning shafts. What else is new?

'Listen, old dog, times are bad with you. Not many customers know that the people are moving. Who do you cheat now, these gullible Portos who live in the 'poor' flats? Even they've seen through you. All you have left is me.'

'God help my soul.'

'Listen, when Leiman Hond has only Two-bob's dagga, things are pretty bad. Now I can give you dagga and wine. Or I can burn this blerry evil hell-hole. *Hêh*, we'll read about it in the *Herald* — "DHUKKUM DIES IN FIRE." He was drunk and fell asleep with his candle on. Who's going to believe that an angel came and fried your arse with shafts of lightning?'

'You fool! You mock everything!'

His eyes glowed like coals, the lips tight and hard, the nostrils flared. How fearsome he must have looked in his youth. Slowly his anger subsided, in his eyes a hidden gleam that Samad did not notice.

'I will give you what you ask.'

He crawled back into his hole, and re-emerged after a while with two bowls of cooked rice. He squatted on his haunches and placed the bowls before him. From his cavernous jacket pockets he produced a bottle of rose-water, some sweetmilk.

'Very special,' he said, holding the bottle up for Samad to see. Still Samad did not heed the sinister smile on the Dhukkum's face.

Now Leiman began to chant, slow and sonorous at first. It grew in intensity until the old man's voice was hoarse and rasping. His eyes were tightly shut.

The sky changed and the moon was hidden behind the clouds. Samad heard a rustling, and felt an intense coldness all around him. He was struck across the face by an iciness that was at once insubstantial, yet chilling.

'Leiman! You've really called them this time. Hey Leiman! Leiman!'

His screams echoed within the deserted building. But Leiman was in another world, his chanting had subsided to a low whisper, and he rocked himself, back and forth, rhythmically.

The shades and the shadows surged all around Samad, who was fighting to prevent his mind from being overwhelmed by terror and panic. His feet felt as if they were chained by some invisible force and he struggled for what seemed hours to walk to where Leiman sat entranced. All that remained of the bowls of rice were dried out kernels.

With a sudden movement Samad opened the bottle of wine and poured its contents over Leiman and the invisible circle that the cunning old man had created.

'NO! NO!' Leiman screamed, 'the wine is *haram.*'

'You wanted a libation *hê,* well here it is, wine sweeter than any milk that this old crook, or any cow, can concoct!' Within the circle Samad could see the shadowy, eyeless faces, some of which he vaguely remembered. They surged angrily towards him, then sniffing the wine, withdrew, howling like wounded children.

And then, like an insolent skollie, came Benjamin the Mallacan, dispersing the hysterical spirits before him. Black as the earth his skin glistened. Thus he had probably arrived more than two hundred years ago, proud and unsmiling, at the Cape of Storms.

Manacled, hand and foot, he had dragged his lithe body to the Kasteel, where for three years he had watched the moon's progress across the walls of his cell. Then he saved the Governor's child with a 'magic' potion that arrested the illness which was wasting away her body. Many say it was just a laxative, but Benjamin was rewarded. The beautiful Amina, and freedom, after a fashion.

Now, with the same decisiveness with which he had embraced Amina and his freedom, he swooped down into the circle. The wine seemed to be absorbed from the street into his body, and bursting into gales of laughter, he soared into the sky, followed by the babble of shrieking spirits who beat him with flailing, insubstantial arms.

Samad too was laughing, and thus incapacitated by the laughter of his ancestor rollicking in his throat, he did not notice Leiman sneak up behind him.

What a joyous gleam there was in the old man's eyes as he brought the empty wine bottle crashing down on Samad's head.

The dawn came, cold and dirty. People walked around Samad's inert body, grimacing in distaste. It took a kick from a policeman's hobnailed boot to convince a concerned passerby that Samad was not dead.

'Leiman you dog!'

'He's still drunk, the pig,' the policeman said contemptuously.

As Samad raised himself, he could hear, in the distance, the bull-dozers and the jackhammers hard at work.

'Listen, skollieboy, I give you five minutes to get your arse out of here,' the policeman said.

Mongane Wally Serote/WHEN REBECCA FELL

While there was something painful, there was also something soul-soothing at the home-workshop. There was restlessness. There was peace. There was nothing; but good Lord, there, my body and soul together were a tongue that licked the heaven of living. That is why the going away became the going back — and now, the looking back; at Dumile's home-workshop.

This is Parktown, up Jubilee Road. I forget the number. There stands the house, stone house, within it, a particular room. In there you could find him. Dumile, anywhere, and I mean just that, anywhere. On this evening, I found him under the bed. The room was black. That peaceful terror, hell, this man Coltrane, with his fingers from the heart was squeezing hard but tender soul out of the saxophone.

Oh man! when you cry you hurt, you console.

Talking of Dumile and that night. I knocked at the door. No answer. I tried the door and went in. The music met me and the darkness too. I stood there for a while, what I thought I do not know.

'Whosit?' What a voice it was! Such a shame I can't say what record was playing! God, I have forgotten, but I know it was Coltrane playing. 'Me,' I said. He mentioned my name and I said *ja*. 'The light-switch is on the floor next to the bed,' he said. I touched something stone-cold on the bed. I went looking for the switch.

'What are you doing?' The voice was impatient now. Silence except for the ruffling as I searched for the switch.

'Don't go on the bed: under!' The voice was angry now.

I quitted looking, just stood there.

'What are you doing?' The voice was pleading. 'What are you doing?'

the voice repeated. He called my name.

I answered.

'What are you doing?'

'Nothing.'

'Why? Look for the switch.' I heard rufflings. I lit. My eyes met the whole of him coming from under the bed. On the bed there was this plastic thing covering something body-size. There was also this board; huge. Pinned on it was a paper sheet, large. On it, drawn with charcoal, were men. You could see every muscle, tense, very tense. They had musical instruments, they were crying or screaming, as though they were rushing out of the paper. The clamour was for the skies. They were many men. They were naked and they were erect and there were no women and there were no skies and they sought something. Opposite this board were cattle. They were digging the ground like they were angry.

And I looked at him. Dumile. He had no shoes on. That meant a lot; home and working. His eyes were blood-shot, he looked tired.

'Hoozet?' He looked at me.

'Fine,' I said, and sat on the floor. I then remembered that I had been with someone. A white boy had brought me here.

I asked the boy to be at home. This was no place to satisfy white curiosity of black. The boy had turned pink. He wanted to go. I could not remain. I sensed that Dumile needed solitude. We left. Dumile said stay for a while but we left.

A friend and I went there, after two weeks I think. Dumile was fresh. He had on an Arrow shirt, green with red stripes, a B.V.D. 'skipper' peeping out of the neck. Blue trousers, brown Florscheim moccasins. He rayed with smiles. He was reading *Esquire* magazine. Immediately he saw us he said, 'Read this!' We read. It was something about a black girl in the States who was invited for lunch at the White House, but who threw black rejection at white 'come let's accept you.' We ate quinces and apples and we laughed and talked about the article.

We went to the room for tea. We talked and laughed and it was like the day should not come to an end. Eddy, a friend, asked Dumile about some of his works and Dumile was sort of evasive. He was steadily becoming not one of us. He went to the bed; I knew then, what it was I had touched the other day at night. He removed the plastic covering, slowly and carefully. He went out and came back with a plastic bucket and later brought a packet of cement.

'I want to stand this straight,' he said pointing at the figure on the bed and demonstrating with both hands.

'What's this?' Eddy can ask questions.

'Rebecca,' Dumile said looking at a foot that had broken. The other foot was a stump. It looked like the end of a guitar where you adjust the strings. Rebecca had a big navel, real huge. So was the stomach. The navel rested on a hand that spread from beneath the stomach to where the thighs met in the front. The weight of the stomach was heavy on the hand. Its muscles reflected the strain. She just lay there on the bed with one foot missing.

Eddy held her head. I held her body. Dumile, I don't know what he was doing, he seemed to hold everywhere. And we lifted Rebecca. She laid her whole weight on Eddy, and I went to help him and the weight was much too much for me and I held her arm which was like a trumpet — and it broke off!

'Heyee!' Dumile said, and he was sweating and looking awful. I was too sorry. I could say nothing. We all became real silent.

We put Rebecca's foot in the bucket and Dumile pushed an iron crowbar between her thighs to support her weight. She, slowly, sank. In minutes her head was off. I went to help reduce the weight from the iron which was peeping through Rebecca's neck. Something happened to my back. I cried with pain and gave in and Dumile rushed to help me. That's when Rebecca fell. He laid me down and rubbed me.

He said I should pump my back. As I stood there with my feet apart pumping my back, I caught Dumile's last look at Rebecca. Mothers know it, the look at the heap of soil that was once their son and daughter.

And when I stood up he wanted to know if I was well. Did I not need to rest? And when we went, he struggled to get us a lift back home despite our protests. In the car, he said he had thought about Rebecca for the last three years.

Now I ask why Dumile said that work was Rebecca. I don't know. I forgot to ask him. But I know it's from the Bible.

Charles Rukuni/WHO STARTED THE WAR?

It was seven in the morning. The Old Man sat alone at his *dare,* his legs almost encircling a fire that was too big for one person. On the fire was a small tin brim-filled with water that was beginning to simmer. The Old Man took the tin of water and sipped some. He gargled the water for a few minutes and spat it out to his right, rose up, walked about two paces from where he had been sitting and washed his face.

He replaced the tin in its usual place and went back to sit exactly the way he had been sitting before. He took out his pipe from his right shirt pocket, filled it with tobacco, fished a red ember out of the fire and lit the pipe. He puffed at his pipe for a few seconds and then began to smoke.

Though the Old Man had only left his hut at six-thirty, he had woken up around four. But because of the curfew he was not allowed to leave his hut until six in the morning.

'This damn bloody war,' the Old Man thought, 'when is it going to end? Or is it going to end at all?'

No one could answer him, so he began to think about the good old days. Not that he had anything to worry about at all. No. He was now used to it. What with boys on this side and soldiers on the other all demanding his loyalty to them and only them.

He was now living on a day-to-day basis, the way the Bible advocated. One day passed was one day gone, the following day would see for itself.

Ah! Sure! He had been a happy family man once, with three sons and one daughter. Not that he had thought of any family planning at all, but that was what God had given him. He wasn't a religious man

173

either, but he knew that God was there — whether he was the Bible's God or any other god, he didn't know and he didn't care.

His two elder sons had been educated to 'O' Level. The girl, though clever, had rushed to the altar after her Junior Certificate. No doubt he had raised his family well. But when he was beginning to think he could relax because he only had to pay fees for his youngest son who had gone on to 'A' Level, the war began.

The first blow came when his youngest son, then doing his final year, skipped the country to join the 'armed struggle' two months before the final examinations. This had grieved the Old Man very much at first. His youngest son on the threshold of going to university leaving school like that to go and handle a gun which any fool could? Why had he wasted his money like that?

His two elder sons had consoled him and explained why their younger brother had left. Though reluctant the Old Man had accepted the reasons given by his elder sons and he had almost forgotten about it now. The only time he thought about him was when he met his comrades or heard that security forces had killed 'so many terrorists', as the government agencies put it.

The second blow had been the tragic death of his second son. Ah! This bloody war! His son had bought a brand new Alfa Romeo and in the traditional manner he had decided to go and show his parents where his money was going. About twenty kilometres from home he had hit this landmine — planted by God-knows-who — and all they collected were scraps of metal and bones. And of course they did not know which bones were their son's because he had come home with three other friends. All killed.

His first-born had married and had three children now, but he was staying in Salisbury with his wife and children. Not that they liked the luxurious town life. Far from it: they could not even afford it but they were afraid of the war at home.

Though he did send the Old Man some money now and then, money was not what the Old Man wanted. He wanted human contact. A chat with his children but especially with his grandchildren. A family party over the holidays or something. But nothing was forthcoming. His family had, therefore, now been reduced to him and his wife — the way they were when they married, but with the sad and bitter difference that they were now both old.

'Ma-N-d-h-l-o-v-u,' the Old Man yelled.

'*He-vo*,' his wife answered in an equally high tone from her 'kitchen'.

174

'*Ahi!* Others are already drunk now. When am I going to have my breakfast?'

'Now now. *Sengibonda isitshwala sakona* — the pap will be ready in a minute. He-ee! Do you think that I am using electricity? This firewood is very wet and it is not producing any embers at all.'

The Old Man did not answer back. That was how his wife talked.

Breakfast for the Old Man was *chakaoma* — dry one — pap and some relish. Not that he could not afford to buy coffee, tea, sugar and bread. No. That was how he liked it. Tea and bread was women's stuff. In fact, that was what his wife had for breakfast.

Whilst his wife had three meals a day — tea and buttered or margarined bread for breakfast, pap and relish for lunch and the same for supper — the Old Man had only two meals a day: pap and relish, usually meat, for breakfast and the same for supper, though he usually had meat and meat only for supper.

MaNdhlovu brought the Old Man his breakfast, knelt in the traditional way and said: 'Here is your breakfast.'

'Thank you very much, mother-of-my-children,' the Old Man said.

MaNdhlovu turned to go. The Old Man did not say anything. He was already digging into the pap and enjoying himself.

'Won't you even invite me to join you?' MaNdhlovu asked.

'Why should I? You are going to have your tea and bread for breakfast. This is my only meal until supper.'

'How about if I have put in some *mupfuhwira* — love potion?'

'If you have put in some *mupfuhwira* that only shows you love me, doesn't it?'

'*Hevo,*' MaNdhlovu said and walked back to her kitchen.

The Old Man did not eat much. That was the problem with eating alone. But he did not leave a single piece of meat. He took the remaining pap and soup and poured it into his dogs' dish, called his dogs and let them eat.

'Ma-N-d-h-l-o-v-u,' the Old Man called again.

'What is it again?' MaNdhlovu answered.

'Come and collect your plates.'

MaNdhlovu, munching some bread, came to collect the plates, another piece of bread in her hand.

'Thank you very much, mother-of-my-children. Now what is left is a washdown,' the Old Man said.

'Washing down what? You have given all the pap to the dogs.'

'I am not a bag, dear. I have had enough. Now I have got to follow the others.'

'That's what you are always thinking about. Beer, beer, beer. It will kill you if you don't eat.'

'MaNdhlovu, how do you want me to eat? Like a young baby who only stops when he is told to?'

'No. Like a reasonable Old Man.'

'That's what I did. Anyway it's too early to have a quarrel. Can I have thirty cents for beer?'

'T-h-i-r-t-y cents! Do others buy beer at all or do they wait for you?'

The Old Man did not answer. That was how his wife always talked before he went off for a beer-drink. He rose up and called his dogs, took his walking stick and set off down the road.

'Now where do you think you are going?' MaNdhlovu yelled after him.

The Old Man did not answer. He walked on, whistling an unintelligible tune.

MaNdhlovu ran to the kitchen, collected the thirty cents and ran after the Old Man. The Old Man knew what was happening but he did not look back until MaNdhlovu caught up with him, now panting.

'Here you are,' she said, handing him the thirty cents.

The Old Man took the thirty cents and pocketed it, still walking.

They walked for some distance, both silent, then the Old Man said: 'Is that what you like? Running after me every time I am off for a beer-drink?'

MaNdhlovu did not answer. The Old Man stopped, looked at his wife for some seconds, tears nearly dropping down his cheeks, then hugged her.

'Sorry if I have hurt you, my dear.'

That was always how they parted.

'Come home early. Remember there is a curfew.'

'All right,' the Old Man said and walked away.

He was not back home until eight in the evening, though he was supposed to be indoors by six. All along the way he was singing:

> *Kill if you want to*
> *I am not the one who started the war*
> *After all what have I got to lose*
> *My sons are now beasts of the jungle with no home*
> *So what have I got to lose*
> *If I have anything to lose*

Why not spend my last days enjoying myself
After all they say there is no return where I go.

Columns

Obed Musi/COPS AIN'T WHAT THEY USED TO BE

The cat is out of the bag. And how! You might have been lulled by the nice words of reassurance that come out of the mouths of our rulers from time to time.

Indeed when they speak from their lofty heights our rulers get carried away. One utterance, an oft-repeated one, was that the law would go *kahle* on the pass laws.

If you believed this then you'll believe anything. The man who laid bare the facts was the Minister of Police and the scene was the House of Assembly the other day. He said some 30,000-plus Blacks had been hauled in under curfew laws — what we know as *nagpas* — during the past year.

That's why it is a wise man who tells his boss that, much as he would dearly love to stay on after *shayile* time, he dare not for fear of breaking the curfew laws.

Not that this is any difficulty in itself. All your boss has to do is to sign a slip of paper bearing the words 'South African Police, Please pass Native Bhekaphansi Naphezulu (with your identity number reflected) to his home. He has been working in my garden . . .'

'Strue, that's the wording favoured by many *mlungus* I've known. You are safe with this kind of paper. Ah, you ask, what happens if you don't have a job (remember there are about a million of us out of work right now)? Bearing in mind that if you have no job, then you have no employer to sign that piece of paper which will "pass" you home.

The answer is that you become a part of those statistics given by the Minister in Parliament that day.

I'm full of little anecdotes from my chequered past involving, half the time, the pass laws. It was in the 70s, and with bo-Dudu Phukwane, Nick Moyaka, Fats Bookholoane and other jazzmen we were returning from a gig aboard the good US merchant boat, the *African Moon*.

It was in Port Elizabeth and we were wending our way to the bus rank in Baakens Street for the Walmer buses. Not a wise thing to do at about midnight with the Baakens Street Police Station nearby.

As fate would have it a police van hove to and the usual South African opening gambit to a chance meeting ensued, and it went like this: *'Toe maan, julle nagpasse . . . waar is hulle!'*

We looked at each other. I was in no hurry to produce my press card for the simple reason that the Commissioner of Police had politely but firmly refused to sign it; none of us was any keener to produce a reference book because of such minor but disastrous defects in them like their not having been signed by our employers, Nick owing tax for donkey's years etc. All of us were generally not pleased by this set-up.

It was playwright Malefetse Bookholoane who walked up to the two cops and spoke thus, in a broad American accent: 'Hi Jack, waddya mean you wanta pess . . . go ahead go pess . . .'

The taller of the two cops looked at his companion and, shrugging his shoulders, remarked, *'Ek het jou gesê man. Dies net see kaffers. Los hulle.'* (For the uninitiated, *see kaffers* is an old slang word for Black sailors.)

That's how we got out of that one. But folks, a word to the wise here about pulling this stunt next time the cops stop you. Don't. Repeat, don't. You see, cops ain't what they used to be. No ways. If you meet up with a patrol van under similar circumstances, it won't help you any if you start jabbering away in a foreign accent. Chances are they'll mistake you for a visiting diplomat from Ruanda Urundi and ask you for your passport and boy, then you will be in a very tight corner indeed.

Since you are unlikely to have a passport or diplomatic immunity, stand by for an eardrum bursting with the words: *'Hoekom het jy nie gesê jy kom van oorsee, man?'* Heaven help you if it later comes out that you've never been beyond Gazankulu.

No, it doesn't do to flout the curfew laws. For instance, in Salisbury they shoot first and ask for your *nagpas* afterwards.

Hopefully we haven't reached that stage in this country. In fact in Bloemfontein — that centre of culture and agriculture — they have a bell that booms out at curfew time and heaven help any deaf darkie who is found wandering round town after that.

No wonder guys from Bloem used to love Gray's elegy which starts 'The curfew tolls the knell of parting day . . . '

That's why they say in Bloem you must always bear in mind John Donne's injunction: 'Ask not for whom the bell tolls . . . it tolls for thee . . . '

Jacky Heyns/OUR LAST FLING

I am sitting in my favourite un-licensed bar in District Six sipping a half-pint of the best from Paarl valley. I don't *have* to do my social drinking in a shebeen any more but my friends Vyf, Ooghare and Slim Jan are always casually dressed, which is frowned on by the doormen of the local one-star wine holes.

Vyf is a retired gentleman with a private income from fahfee and is so-named because he has five fingers only — three on one hand and two on the other. He never explains the fate of the missing five but it is said they were found trespassing while still attached to him — and summarily severed.

Ooghare is a fisherman, carefree, light-hearted and heavy-eyebrowed. Slim Jan is a part-time teacher. When he is not teaching, he works hard supporting the liquor industry.

The Aunty puts another bottle in front of us and my friends ask for an explanation for the contented smile on my dial.

I tell them: there is plenty of reason for all of us to have smug mugs these days. Surely, I say, they must also have this feeling that things are turning out fine. I say, just look around, and before you can adjust your mind to the beautiful happenings, something new is placed in view to dazzle the day.

My three mates look at me through glazed eyes, unimpressed. I push on, regardless.

Man, I say, racialism is fading out. Apartheid is being spelt in small letters these days, not being shouted out loud — only whispered. We blacks are wallowing in euphoric bliss.

Vyf suggests I say it in English. Slim Jan translates and Ooghare says for them to shaddup because he is listening to me and my bull.

I tell them that right now the whiteys are not having it so good. As we are sitting here chewing the fat, *they* are scratching head and biting nail. Many of their grand plans for separate development are not working out. Their job reservation, for example, if carried out, will bring the factories to a stop. They have to allow us in to do the job. Right?

Ooghare says he is working enough as it is. Slim Jan agrees with him and suggests that we change the subject and go to the bioscope or go down to the beach and look at the girls.

I say let's be serious. I say that at the present rate of change we will soon see the complete collapse of the colour-bar. We will soon celebrate a Great Day.

Ooghare says that is all right with him. He is all for celebrations, any kind. Vyf says it is a good idea and that we should start right away and order another bottle.

At this point Slim Jan shows his academic background and gets philosophical. He says the problem with black people is that they have no sense of responsibility. As long as they can have fun, any kind of roof over their heads, sex and a bottle of wine — then they are happy.

He says that is why the white man has got us where he wants us. He knows that he can keep us under control as long as he can keep us drugged with pleasure, says Slim Jan. Look, he says, they push us into black group areas and before we can complain they provide us with bioscopes, bars, dance-halls and sportsgrounds.

So that we can have a variety of entertainment we are given the CRC (Coloured Representative Council) during the year and at the end of the year the Coons.

Ooghare breaks in and asks what is wrong with that? He asks Slim Jan if he wants the black man to live like the white man. He says that when the poor white men go overseas as ambassadors, businessmen or sportsmen they are chaffed, chased and chopped at every stop-over place and destination. At every meeting they have to face demonstrations against apartheid.

Ooghare has been reading the newspapers and he shows this by saying that not only has the poor white man got troubles overseas but right here at home he is having sleepless nights.

He says that South Africa is surrounded by black people who are not friendly to our government and after all, he says, there are only a couple of million whites here who have to defend the country, while

15 million blacks sit around having fun.

Vyf pours another round and asks Slim Jan what he has to say about that.

Slim Jan takes it in his stride and says it is the white man's own fault that he is on his own in the world of worry. Instead of giving us a place in Parliament where we can share worldly problems, he gives us seats in the Nico Malan Theatre where we can enjoy ourselves even further with grand opera. Instead of allowing us to run for election to our city councils and provincial administrations where we can share the burdens of local government they give us the pleasure of multi-racial games.

He says the Whites have got us measured. They know how to keep us happy.

How many times, he says, have we been told that we are still adolescent, in a stage of development, you know, that we are not fully matured, you understand, to share and shoulder full citizenship, you follow?

Aunty brought another bottle. We drank and for a few seconds there was silence.

Then Vyf lifted his right hand with the two fingers and said, to me: so much for your Great Day.

I said they just have to believe me. The writing is on the wall. Mr Vorster and company cannot go it alone. With Red China in Komatipoort, and Rhodesia as good as gone, it must be clear, even to a verkrampte ostrich with his head beneath Oudtshoorn soil, that the happiest situation for South Africa is one where all the people inside our borders are loyal and patriotic citizens. Mr V. and Co. know this better than I and therefore the Great Day will be here before another apartheid sign has a chance to rear its ugly head.

My three friends, together, ask; then what?

I tell them that we will then share the power of decision-making in this land of ours. On that Great Day, I tell them, we will all share the problems and the burden, not only of running this country, but of defending it against all, even at the price of our lives.

Slim Jan rises from the table and says I can keep the Great Day. He says it is too late in his life to become a full citizen. He prefers to spend the rest of his years with the discrimination he is accustomed to, his fun-filled existence free of the fears and responsibilities which the whites hold exclusively today.

Ooghare eyes me suspiciously and ventures the question of whether I mean that the end of racial discrimination is not only open doors at white cinemas, travel in any bus, live in a Sea Point flat and play with the girls on Clifton Beach?

He wants to know whether I mean that he has to be with Mr V. when Kenneth Kaunda, Idi Amin and Samora Machel come knocking at the door?

I say yes man, that is the score. Equal pay means equal work. He says he doesn't like it.

Vyf opens his eyes and asks: how much longer have we got?

Optimistic me tells him he can start waving the flag. Any day now we will read the newspapers, hear the radio and see on TV that we are free. No more apartheid.

Vyf says: Jeez, we can't waste time. Aunty, bring us a dozen bottles. We better have our last fling before the white man delivers the final screw called freedom.

Black Stan Motjuwadi/WHAT IS NOT WHITE IS DARKIE

I am with a group of egghead buddies at our favourite Kliptown joint sobbing into our drinks. Headmaster Mac throws out his arms nearly spilling his drink — 'A stinking fraud, man.'

'But what the hell do these guys in Pretoria take us for?' Peter the rep shouts without expecting an answer.

'They'll realise when it is too late. You know how I feel like.' Dr. M. for once loses his cool.

We are all beefing. Beefing about the deal proposed for us in the government white paper on the Theron Commission.

But it is Ou Willie, the unlettered sage of the Klip, who brings us all to our senses with his uncanny way of watering things down to their lowest denominator.

'Aag majieta, ons is fiea-go gerwa,' he puts it in township lingo. (Gents, we have been had.)

'Kyk, hoekom sê hulle die ding is a white paper? Wietie julle my man? Julle is geleer. Hoekom? Wit papier . . .' (Look, why do you think they call the thing a white paper? You are educated men. White paper. Why?) He rattles on in his township logic.

'White paper vir die lanies. Vokol vir jou.' (White paper for the whites. Nothing for you.) Ou Willie downs his shot, allowing his profundities to sink in with his intellectual drinking cronies.

'Mar julle outies wat van die skool af kom beat my. 'Strue.' Ou Willie, shaking his replenished glass in his hands, sways from side to side like he is in a swivel chair. And pauses. This he always does when holding court and warming to the subject.

He explains why he is always baffled by guys who are 'from school' with some education, which should qualify them to know better.

'Kyk doktor, jy principal, Mr. Social Worker daar. Die tyd wat miering geblas was op die Theron shandies. Waar was julle? Wie het gesê — gents stop! Gee die miering hier. Huises van mense word gevat van water and kinders gaan sat moet hongerte?'

(Look doctor, you principal, you Mr. Social Worker there. When money was being blown on the Theron bezusus where were you? Who said — hold it with that lolly. Give it here, where houses are being swept away by water and children are starving to death?)

Ou Willie crosses his legs and downs his drink, not waiting for an answer, assuming that all his questions are rhetorical.

'Die trouble met ons darkies is dat ons like mekaar class. Ons vergeet dat ons is an een ma se kinders. Is dar waar ons blind baaiza,' he goes on.

(The trouble with us darkies is that we like to classify each other. We forget that we are one mother's children. That's the blind way in which we blunder.)

'Ky hies ons hier. Ons moan want hulle wil ons noe a favour doen moet sulle vote. Wat van ons broes in Soweto? Wat maak laat ons dink ons is beter?'

(Here we are. We are moaning because they don't want to do us a favour with their vote. What about our brothers in Soweto? What gives us the idea that we are better?)

The way Ou Willie brushes his brow, refills and looks into space I know that he is convinced that he is on to something good.

'Ek meen ons almal darkies. Net nie julle. Ons broers in Soweto is ook net so moegoes.' Ou Willie sips his drink, rolls it over his tongue. (I don't mean only you. I mean all darkies. Our brothers in Soweto are suckers just the same.)

'Jy sien my mamlady is a Xhosa in Transkei. Ek het a blaa, a neef my ou Nyaozo in Benoni. My waar's never in die Transkei maar hy is a Xhosa.' (You see my mother is a Xhosa in the Transkei. I have a brother, a cousin Nyaoza in Benoni. He's never been to the Transkei but of course he is Xhosa.)

'Wat maak die moegie?' (What does the yokel do?) Ou Willie asks, not expecting an answer as usual. *'Wat hy hoor die Transkei kry daai independence van hulle. Hy swank vir my. "Ya Willie, nou is ons deur. Ons het onse independence. Onse eie khaya. Ons worrie nie weer. Waar gaan julle? Is shandies vir julle. Ons het nkululeko," hy pronk.'*

(When he hears that the Transkei is getting that independence of theirs he swaggers for me. We are through. Our worries are over. We have our own country. Where are you coloureds going? We have our freedom, he brags.)

'*A maand gaan verby. Twee. Wat wietie jy my?*' (A month passes. Two. What do you tell me?)

'*Hy kom by my kesta. "Mzala, mzala help my!" Hy huil net soos a chirrie. "Help my. Ek kaan nie by daai blerrie plek gaan. Ek ken skaars die plek. Sit my deer met a identity. Ek sal fix die chien wat jy soek".*' Ou Willie is on his knees, talking like a weeping girl with his face cupped in his palms.

(He comes to my home. 'Cousie, cousie help me,' he cries, just like a girl. 'I can't go to that bloody place. I hardly know it. Put me through with an identity card, I don't want this pass. I will fix you with the money you ask.')

'*Hoe like jy dit?*' (How do you like that one?) He throws out his arms.

Behind his back his pals always talk of how Ou Willie is a useless, drifting layabout who only has money when he is 'from' the unemployment pension office.

Ou Willie, like Andy Capp, always tells us how badly things are run. Only Ou Willie is in step. But like Andy, Ou Willie is a lovable bloody rogue. They don't have to take him seriously but they admit he makes good company.

Ou Willie smiles because he feels he has them twirling around his little finger. Then he leans forward and talks in hushed tones.

'Eengleesh never was my mother tongue. But that be the lingo you prefer. So I'll talk it. There's only one thing. We must know that we darkies is darkies. Darkies. What is not white is darkie. We must know that when we cry we all cry together. Same time.

'And then we laugh. Ah man! We blerrie laugh together like now. Doctor, you propose the toast.' A loud guffaw. 'I think they should have Ou Willie on the next commission they have.'

The doctor's voice is drowned by laughter in the smoke-filled room.

Messages

Toivo Herman ja Toivo/HERE I STAND

My Lord,

We find ourselves here in a foreign country convicted under laws made by people whom we have always considered as foreigners. We find ourselves tried by a Judge who is not our countryman and who has not shared our background.

When this case started, Counsel tried to show that this Court had no jurisdiction to try us. What they had to say was of a technical and legal nature. The reasons may mean little to some of us, but it is the deep feeling of all of us that we should not be tried here in Pretoria. You, my Lord, decided that you had the right to try us, because your Parliament gave you that right. That ruling has not and could not have changed our feelings. We are Namibians and not South Africans. We do not now, and will not in the future, recognise your right to govern us; to make laws for us in which we had no say; to treat our country as if it were your property and us as if you were our masters. We have always regarded South Africa as an intruder in our country. This is how we have always felt and this is how we feel now, and it is on this basis that we have faced this trial.

I speak of 'we' because I am trying to speak not only for myself, but for others as well, and especially for those of my fellow-accused who have not had the benefit of any education. I think also that when I say 'we', the overwhelming majority of non-White people in South West Africa would like to be included.

We are far away from our homes; not a single member of our families has come to visit us, never mind be present at our trial. The Pretoria gaol, the Police Headquarters at Compol, where we were interrogated and where statements were extracted from us, and this Court are all we have seen of Pretoria. We have been cut off from our people and the world . . . The South African Government has again shown its strength by detaining us for as long as it pleased; keeping some of us in solitary confinement for 300 to 400 days and bringing us to its capital to try us. It has shown its strength by passing an Act especially for us and having it made retrospective. It has even chosen an ugly name to call us by. One's own are called patriots or at least rebels; one's opponents are called Terrorists.

A Court can only do justice in political cases if it understands the position of those that it has in front of it. The State has not only wanted to convict us, but also to justify the policy of the South African Government. We will not even try to present the other side of the picture, because we know that a Court that has not suffered in the same way as we have, cannot understand us. This is, perhaps, why it is said that one should be tried by one's equals. We have felt from the very time of our arrests that we were not being tried by our equals but by our masters, and that those who have brought us to trial very often do not even show us the courtesy of calling us by our surnames. Had we been tried by our equals, it would not have been necessary to have any discussion about our grievances. They would have been known to those set to judge us.

It suits the Government of South Africa to say that it is ruling South West Africa with the consent of its people. This is not true. Our organisation, SWAPO, is the largest political organisation in South West Africa. We consider ourselves a political party. We know that Whites do not think of Blacks as politicians — only as agitators. Many of our people, through no fault of their own, have had no education at all. This does not mean that they do not know what they want. A man does not have to be formally educated to know that he wants to live with his family where he wants to live, and not where an official chooses to tell him to live; to move about freely and not require a pass; to earn a decent wage; to be free to work for the person of his choice for as long as he wants; and finally, to be ruled by the people that he wants to be ruled by, and not those who rule him because they have more guns than he has.

Our grievances are called 'so-called' grievances. We do not believe South Africa is in South West Africa in order to provide facilities and work for non-Whites. It is there for its own selfish reasons. For the first forty years it did practically nothing to fulfil its 'sacred trust'. It only concerned itself with the welfare of the Whites.

Since 1962, because of the pressure from inside by the non-Whites and especially my organisation, and because of the limelight placed on our country by the world, South Africa has been trying to do a bit more. It rushed the Bantustan Report so that it would at least have something to say at the World Court.

Only one who is not White and has suffered the way we have, can say whether our grievances are real or 'so-called'.

Those of us who have some education, together with our uneducated brethren, have always struggled to get freedom. The idea of our freedom is not liked by South Africa. It has tried in this Court to prove through the mouths of a couple of its paid Chiefs and a paid official, that SWAPO does not represent the people of South West Africa. If the government of South Africa was sure that SWAPO did not represent the innermost feeling of the people in South West Africa, it would not have taken the trouble to make it impossible for SWAPO to advocate its peaceful policy.

South African officials want to believe that SWAPO is an irresponsible organisation and that it is an organisation that resorts to the level of telling people not to get vaccinated. As much as White South Africans may want to believe this, it is not SWAPO. We sometimes feel that it is what the Government would like SWAPO to be. It may be true that some member or some members of SWAPO somewhere refused to do this. The reason for such refusal is that some people in our part of the world have lost confidence in the governors of our country and they are not prepared to accept even the good that they are trying to do.

Your Government, my Lord, undertook a very special responsibility when it was awarded the mandate over us after the First World War. It assumed a sacred trust to guide us towards independence and to prepare us to take our place among the nations of the world. We believe that South Africa has abused that trust because of its belief in racial supremacy (that White people have been chosen by God to rule the world) and apartheid. We believe that for fifty years South Africa has failed to promote the development of our people. Where are our trained men? The wealth of our country has been used to train your people for leadership, and the sacred duty of preparing the indigenous people to take their place among the nations of the world has been ignored.

I know of no case in the last twenty years of a parent who did not want his child to go to school if the facilities were available, but even if, as it was said, a small percentage of parents wanted their children to look after cattle, I am sure that South Africa was strong enough to impose its will on this, as it has done in so many other respects. To us it has always seemed that our rulers wanted to keep us backward for their benefit.

1963 for us was to be the year of our freedom. From 1960 it looked as if South Africa could not oppose the world for ever. The world is important to us. In the same way as all laughed in Court when they heard that an old man tried to bring down a helicopter with a bow and arrow, we laughed when South Africa said that it would oppose the world. We knew that the world was divided, but as time went on it at least agreed that South Africa had no right to rule us.

I do not claim that it is easy for men of different races to live at peace with one another. I myself had no experience of this in my youth, and at first it surprised me that men of different races could live together in peace. But now I know it to be true and to be something for which we must strive. The South African Government creates hostility by separating people and emphasising their differences. We believe that by living together, people will learn to lose their fear of each other. We also believe that this fear, which some of the Whites have of Africans, is based on their desire to be superior and privileged and that when Whites see themselves as part of South West Africa, sharing with us all its hopes and troubles, then that fear will disappear. Separation is said to be a natural process. But why, then, is it imposed by force, and why then is it that Whites have the superiority?

Headmen used to oppress us. This is not the first time that foreigners have tried to rule us indirectly — we know that only those who are prepared to do what their masters tell them become headmen. Most of those who had some feeling for their people and who wanted independence have been intimidated into accepting the policy from above. Their guns and sticks are used to make people say they support them.

I have come to know that our people cannot expect progress as a gift from anyone, be it the United Nations or South Africa. Progress is something we shall have to struggle and work for. And I believe that the only way in which we shall be able and fit to secure that progress is to learn from our own experience and mistakes.

Your Lordship emphasised in your Judgment the fact that our arms came from communist countries, and also that words commonly used by communists were to be found in our documents. But my Lord, in the documents produced by the State there is another type of language. It appears even more often than the former. Many documents finish up with an appeal to the Almighty to guide us in our struggle for freedom. It is the wish of the South African Government that we should be discredited in the Western world. That is why it calls our struggle a communist plot; but this will not be believed by the world. The world knows that we are not interested in ideologies. We feel that the world as a whole has a special responsibility towards us. This is because the land of our fathers was handed over to South Africa by a world body. It is a divided world, but it is a matter of hope for us that it at least agrees about one thing — that we are entitled to freedom and justice.

Other mandated territories have received their freedom. The judgment of the World Court was a bitter disappointment to us. We felt betrayed and we believed that South Africa would never fulfil its trust. Some felt that we would secure our freedom only by fighting for it. We knew that the power of South Africa is overwhelming, but we also knew that our case is a just one and our situation intolerable — why should we not also receive our freedom?

We are sure that the world's efforts to help us in our plight will continue, whatever South Africans may call us. We do not expect that independence will end our troubles, but we do believe that our people are entitled — as are all people — to rule themselves. It is not really a question of whether South Africa treats us well or badly, but that South West Africa is our country and we wish to be our own masters.

There are some who will say that they sympathize with our aims, but that they condemn violence. I would answer that I am not by nature a man of violence and I believe that violence is a sin against God and my fellow men. SWAPO itself was a non-violent organisation, but the South African Government is not truly interested in whether opposition is violent or non-violent. It does not wish to hear any opposition to apartheid. Since 1963, SWAPO meetings have been banned. It is true that it is the Tribal Authorities who have banned them, but they work with the South African Government, which has never lifted a finger in favour of political freedom. We have found ourselves voteless in our own country and deprived of the right to meet and state our own political opinions.

Is it surprising that in such times my countrymen have taken up arms? Violence is truly fearsome but who would not defend his property and himself against a robber? And we believe that South Africa has robbed us of our country.

I have spent my life working in SWAPO, which is an ordinary political party like any other. Suddenly we in SWAPO found that a war situation had arisen and that our colleagues and South Africa were facing each other on the field of battle. Although I had not been reponsible for organising my people militarily and although I believed we were unwise to fight the might of South Africa while we were so weak, I could not refuse to help them when the time came.

My Lord, you found it necessary to brand me a coward. During the Second World War, when it became evident that both my country and your country were threatened by the dark clouds of Nazism, I risked my life to defend both of them, wearing a uniform with orange bands on it.

But some of your countrymen, when called to battle to defend civilisation resorted to sabotage against their own fatherland. I volunteered to face German bullets, and as a guard of military installations, both in South West Africa and the Republic, was prepared to be the victim of their sabotage. Today they are our masters and are considered the heroes, and I am called the coward.

When I consider my country, I am proud that my countrymen have taken up arms for their people and I believe that anyone who calls himself a man would not despise them.

In 1964 the ANC and PAC in South Africa were suppressed. This convinced me that we were too weak to face South Africa's force by waging battle. When some of my country's soldiers came back I foresaw the trouble there would be for SWAPO, my people, and me personally. I tried to do what I could to prevent my people from going into the bush. In my attempts I became unpopular with some of my people, but this too, I was prepared to endure. Decisions of this kind are not easy to make. My loyalty is to my country. My organisation could not work properly — it could not even hold meetings. I had no answer to the question 'Where has your non-violence got us?' Whilst the World Court judgment was pending, I at least had that to fall back on. When we failed, after years of waiting, I had no answer to give my people.

Even though I did not agree that people should go into the bush, I could not refuse to help them when I knew that they were hungry. I even passed on the request for dynamite. It was not an easy decision. Another man might have been able to say 'I will have nothing to do with that sort of thing.' I was not, and I could not remain a spectator in the struggle of my people for their freedom.

I am a loyal Namibian and I could not betray my people to their enemies. I admit that I decided to assist those who had taken up arms. I know that the struggle will be long and bitter. I also know that my people will wage that struggle, whatever the cost.

Only when we are granted our independence will the struggle stop. Only when our human dignity is restored to us, as equals of the Whites, will there be peace between us. We believe that South Africa has a choice — either to live at peace with us or to subdue us by force. If you choose to crush us and impose your will on us then you not only betray your trust, but you will live in security for only so long as your power is greater than ours. No South African will live at peace in South West Africa, for each will know that his security is based on force and that without force he will face rejection by the people of South West Africa.

My co-accused and I have suffered. We are not looking forward to our imprisonment. We do not, however, feel that our efforts and sacrifice have been wasted. We believe that human suffering has its effect even on those who impose it. We hope that what has happened will persuade the Whites of South Africa that we and the world may be right and they may be wrong. Only when White South Africans realise this and act on it will it be possible for us to stop our struggle for freedom and justice in the land of our birth.

Desmond Tutu/NIGHTMARISH FEAR

6 May 1976

The Hon. Prime Minister Mr John Vorster
House of Assembly
CAPE TOWN
8000

Dear Mr Prime Minister

This will be my second letter ever to you. In 1972 after I had been refused a passport to take up a post as Associate Director of the Theological Education Fund, I appealed to you to intervene on my behalf with the appropriate authorities. Your intervention was successful because, soon thereafter, the then Minister of the Interior changed his mind and granted me and my family our passports. I am writing, therefore, optimistically in the hope that this letter will have similar happy results for all of us.

I am writing to you, Sir, in all deep humility and courtesy in my capacity as Anglican Dean of Johannesburg and, therefore, as leader of several thousand Christians of all races in the Diocese of Johannesburg. I am writing to you as one who has come to be accepted by some blacks (i.e. Africans, Indians and Coloureds) as one of their spokesmen articulating their deepest aspirations as one who shares them with equal steadfastness. I am writing to you, Sir, because I know you to be a loving and caring father and husband, a doting grandfather who has experienced the joys and anguish of family life, its laughter and gaiety, its sorrows and pangs. I am writing to you, Sir, as one who is passionately devoted to a happy and stable family life as the indispensable foundation of a sound and healthy society. You have flung out your arms to embrace and hug your children and your grandchildren, to smother them with your kisses, you have loved, you have wept, you have watched by the bed of a sick one whom you loved, you have watched by the deathbed of a beloved relative, you have been a proud father at the wedding of your children, you have shed tears by the graveside of one for whom your heart has been broken. In short, I am writing to you as one human person to another human person gloriously created in the image of the selfsame God, redeemed by the selfsame Son of God who for all our sakes died on the Cross and rose triumphant from the dead and reigns in glory now at the right hand of the Father; sanctified by the selfsame Holy Spirit who works inwardly in all of us to change our hearts of stone into hearts of flesh. I am, therefore, writing to you, Sir, as one Christian to another, for through our common baptism we have been made members of and are united in the Body of our dear Lord and Saviour Jesus Christ. This Jesus Christ, whatever we may have done, has broken down all that separates us irrelevantly — such as race, sex, culture, status, etc. In this Jesus Christ we are forever bound together as one redeemed humanity, black and white together.

I am writing to you, Sir, as one who is a member of a race that has known what it has meant in frustrations and hurts, in agony and humiliation, to be a subject people. The history of your own race speaks eloquently of how utterly impossible it is, when once the desire for freedom and self-determination is awakened in a people, for it to be quenched or to be satisfied with anything less than that freedom and that self-determination. Your people against tremendous odds braved the unknown and faced up to daunting challenges and countless dangers rather than be held down as a subjugated people. And in the end they emerged victorious. Your people more than any other section of the white community must surely know in the very core of their beings, if they were unaware of the lessons of history both ancient and modern, that absolutely nothing will stop a people from attaining their freedom to be a people who can hold their heads high, whose dignity to be human persons is respected, who can assume the responsibilities and obligations that are the necessary concomitants of the freedom they yearn for with all their being. For most blacks this can never be in the homelands because they believe they have contributed substantially to the prosperity of an undivided South Africa. Blacks find it hard to understand why the whites are said to form one nation when they are made up of Greeks, Italians, Portuguese, Afrikaners, French, Germans, English etc., etc.; and then by some tour de force Blacks are said to form several nations — Xhosas, Zulus, Tswanas etc. The Xhosas and the Zulus, for example, are much closer to one another ethnically than, say, the Italians and the Germans in the white community. We all, black and white together, belong to South Africa, and Blacks yield place to no-one in their passionate love for this our beloved land. We belong together — we will survive or be destroyed together. Recently a multi-racial soccer team represented South Africa against a visiting Argentinian side. The South African team won all hands down and perhaps for the first time in our sporting history South Africans of all races found themselves supporting vociferously the same side against a common adversary. The heavens did not fall down. Is it fanciful to see this as a parable of what will happen when all South Africans together are given a stake in their country so that they will be ready to defend it against a common foe and struggle for its prosperity vigorously and enthusiastically?

I write to you, Sir, because our Ambassador to the United Nations, Mr Botha, declared that South Africa was moving away from discrimination based on race. This declaration excited not only us but the world at large. I am afraid that very little of this movement has been in evidence so far. It is not to move substantially from discrimination when some signs are removed from park benches. These are only superficial changes which do not fundamentally affect the lives of blacks. Husbands and fathers are still separated from their loved ones as a result of the pernicious system of migratory labour which a D.R.C. Synod once castigated as a cancer in South African society, one which had deleterious consequences on Black family life, thus undermining the stability of society which I referred to earlier. We don't see this much longed-for movement when we look at the overcrowded schools in black townships, at the inadequate housing and woefully inadequate system of transport etc.

I write to you, Sir, to give you all the credit due to you for your efforts at promoting detente and dialogue. In these efforts many of us here wanted to support you eagerly, but we feel we cannot in honesty do this, when external detente is not paralleled by equally vigorous efforts at internal detente. Blacks are grateful for all that has been done for them, but now they claim an inalienable *right to do things for themselves,* in co-operation with their fellow South Africans of all races.

I write to you, Sir, because like you I am deeply committed to real reconciliation with justice for all, and to peaceful change to a more just and open South African society in which the wonderful riches and wealth of our country will be shared more equitably. I write to you, Sir, to say with all the eloquence I can command that the security of our country ultimately depends not on military strength and a Security Police being given more and more draconian power to do virtually as they please without being accountable to the courts of our land, courts which have a splendid reputation throughout the world for fairness and justice. That is why we have called and continue to call for the release of all detainees or that they be brought before the courts where they should be punished if they have been found guilty of indictable offences. There is much disquiet in our land that people can be held for such long periods in detention and then often either released without being charged or, when charged, usually acquitted; but this does not free them from police harassment. Though often declared innocent by the courts, they are often punished by being banned or placed under house arrest or immediately re-detained. How long can a people, do you think, bear such blatant injustice and suffering? Much of the white community by and large, with all its prosperity, its privilege, its beautiful homes, its servants, its leisure, is hagridden by a fear and a sense of insecurity. And this will continue to be the case until South Africans of all races are free. Freedom, Sir, is indivisible. The Whites in this land will not be free until all sections of our community are genuinely free. Then we will have a security that does not require such astronomical sums to maintain it, huge funds which could have been used in far more creative and profitable ways for the good of our whole community, which would take its rightful place as a leader in Africa and elsewhere, demonstrating as it will that people of different races can live amicably together. We need one another and Blacks have tried to assure Whites that they don't want to drive them into the sea. How long can they go on giving these assurances and have them thrown back in their faces with contempt? They say even the worm will turn.

I am writing to you, Sir, because I have a growing nightmarish fear that unless something drastic is done very soon then bloodshed and violence are going to happen in South Africa almost inevitably. A people can take only so much and no more. The history of your own people which I referred to earlier demonstrated this, Vietnam has shown this, the struggle against Portugal has shown this. I wish to God that I am wrong and that I have misread history and the situation in my beloved homeland, my mother country South Africa. A people made desperate by despair, injustice and oppression will use desperate means. I am frightened, dreadfully frightened, that we may soon reach a point of no return, when events will generate a momentum of their own, when nothing will stop their reaching a bloody denouement which is "too ghastly to contemplate", to quote your words, Sir.

I am frightened because I have some experience of the awfulness of violence. My wife and I with our two youngest children stayed for two months in Jerusalem in 1966 and we saw the escalating violence and the mounting tensions between Jew and Arab which preceded the Six Day War. I was in Addis Ababa when there was rioting in the streets, a prelude to the overthrow of the dynasty of Haile Selassie. I was in Uganda just before the expulsion of the Asians from that country and have returned there since and experienced the fear and the evil of things there. I have visited the Sudan, admittedly after the end of the seventeen years of civil strife, but I could see what this internecine war had done to people and their property. I have visited Nigeria and the former Biafra and have seen there the awful ravages of that ghastly civil war on property and on the souls of the defeated Biafrans. Last year I was privileged to address the General Assembly of the Presbyterian Church of Ireland in Belfast — and what I saw shook me to the core of my being. We saw daily on television in Britain horrific pictures of the pillage and destruction being perpetrated in Vietnam: children screaming from the excruciating agony of burns caused by napalm bombing, a people rushing helter skelter, looking so forlorn and bewildered that one wanted to cry out 'But is there no God who cares in heaven'. No, I know violence and bloodshed and I and many of our people don't want that at all.

But we Blacks are exceedingly patient and peace-loving. We are aware that politics is the art of the possible. We cannot expect you to move so far in advance of your voters that you alienate their support. We are ready to accept some meaningful signs which would demonstrate that you and your Government and all Whites really mean business when you say you want peaceful change. First, accept the urban black as a permanent inhabitant of what is wrongly called White South Africa, with consequent freehold property rights. He will have a stake in the land and would not easily join those who wish to destroy his country. Indeed, he would be willing to die to defend his mother country and his birthright. Secondly, and also as a matter of urgency, repeat the pass laws which demonstrate to Blacks more clearly than anything else that they are third rate citizens in their beloved country. Thirdly, it is imperative, Sir, that you call a National Convention made up of the genuine leaders (i.e. leaders recognised as such by their section of the community) of all sections of the community, to try to work out an orderly evolution of South Africa into a nonracial, open and just society. I believe firmly that your leadership is quite unassailable and that you have been given virtually a blank cheque by the White electorate and that you have little to fear from a so-called right wing backlash. For if the things which I suggest are not done soon, and a rapidly deteriorating situation arrested, then there will be no right wing to fear — there will be nothing.

I am writing this letter to you, Sir, during a three day clergy retreat in Johannesburg, when in the atmosphere of deep silence, worship and adoration and daily services of the Lord's Supper we seek to draw closer to our Lord and try to discover what is the will of God for us and what are the promptings and inspirations of God's Holy Spirit. It is during this time that God seemed to move me to write this letter.

I hope to hear from you, Sir, as soon as you can conveniently respond, because I want to make this correspondence available to the press, preferably with your concurrence, so that all our people, both Black and White, will know that from our side we have done all that it seems humanly possible to do to appeal, not only to the rank and file of Whites, but to the highest political figure in the land, and to have issued the grave warning contained in my letter. This flows from a deep love and anguish for my country. I shall soon become Bishop of Lesotho, when I must reside in my new diocese. But I am quite clear in my own mind, and my wife supports me in this resolve, that we should retain our South African citizenship no matter how long we have to remain in Lesotho.

Please may God inspire you to hear us before it is too late, and may He bless you and your Government now and always.

Should you think it might serve any useful purpose, I am more than willing to meet with you to discuss the issues I raise here as you say in Afrikaans, *onder vier oë.*

Since coming to this Cathedral last year, we have had a regular service praying for Justice and Reconciliation in this country every Friday. And at all services in the Cathedral we pray :

God bless Africa
Guard her children
Guide her rulers and
Give her peace,
For Jesus Christ's sake.

And:

  O Lord, make us instruments of Thy peace: where there is hatred,
  let us sow love; where there is injury, pardon: where there is
  despair, hope; where there is darkness, light; where there is
  sadness, joy.

  O Divine Master, grant that we may not so much seek to be
  consoled as to console, to be understood as to understand, to be
  loved as to love: for it is in giving that we receive, it is in pardon-
  ing that we are pardoned, it is in dying that we are born to eternal
  life.
                            Amen.

And we mean it.

Yours respectfully,

Desmond Tutu.

NOTES ON CONTRIBUTORS

Both JACKIE HEYNS and STAN MOTJUWADI work for *Drum* magazine as columnist and editor respectively; and together with OBED VEZI MUSI are among the best satirists in their field. They are an important link with an earlier generation of black writers.

Bishop DESMOND MPILO TUTU needs no introduction. Interestingly enough, he was a colleague of both Motjuwadi and the late Kid Casey Motsisi at a college called the Normal (recall *Casey and Company?*) Arguably, Baba Tutu could make it as a full-time essayist.

JAMES MATTHEWS, editor of the *Muslim News,* heads Blac Publishing House — apart from being the irrepressible 'Godfather' of black literature in Azania. Any anthology without Matthews, be it prose or poetry, is inadequate because the man, though writing since the '50s, is still as fresh as the *Staffrider* generation of writers. No wonder youngsters relate to him so easily. He may be on the other side of forty, but writing-wise he is still as vibrant as ever. In fact, one might say that he was born in the wrong decade!

And not far from Matthews is MAFIKA GWALA who, though he looks like a *laaitie,* is one of the most seasoned as well as one of the most prolific of our contributors. Gwala and Matthews are known to some as 'the terrible twins', and they have the experience to prove it. Incidentally, Gwala is preparing a collection of his biting (as always) essays and speeches on Black Consciousness, when he is not writing poetry and reviews for *Staffrider.* His book of verse *Jol'iinkomo* was published four years ago. Still has lots of unpublished short stories.

An associate member of the Matthews-Gwala alliance is MONGANE SEROTE, author of *Yakhal'Inkomo, Tsetlo, No Baby Must Weep* and

Behold Mama, Flowers, now living out in Botswana. Serote, like Don Mattera, has been and is still a particularly strong influence on today's writers.

Then there's MBULELO MZAMANE, essayist, short story writer and until recently lecturer in English at the University of Botswana. He is furthering his studies in England and will 'definitely' return to Africa South after completing.

BESSIE HEAD, author of numerous books and perhaps the best-known of the writers in this collection, lives in Serowe, Botswana, though born in Pietermaritzburg.

MOTEANE MELAMU, also formerly a lecturer in Gaborone, is now Botswana's roving ambassador.

Professor BOB LESHOAI, (there seems to have been an exodus from the Gaborone campus) has taught drama in Zambia and Tanzania; still writes short stories and plays. Works in Johannesburg in the educational section of a well-known firm.

SIPHO SEPAMLA has published several poetry books, one of which (*The Soweto I Love*) was banned in '78; completed his first novel, *The Root Is One,* in '79. Edits *S'ketsh* and *New Classic* magazines.

AHMED ESSOP won the '79 Olive Schreiner Award for his anthology *The Hajji And Other Stories.*

MIRIAM TLALI, author of *Muriel At Metropolitan* and columnist in *Staffrider,* has finished her second novel, *Amandla,* to be published this year.

MOTHOBI MUTLOATSE is a journalist on *The Voice,* editor of *Casey and Company*, and now amateur film-maker.

MTUTUZELI MATSHOBA, author of *Call Me Not A Man,* a collection of stories banned in '79; is also busy on his first novel.

XOLILE GUMA is a newcomer from Swaziland, just like his countryman CHICKS NKOSI.

Other new arrivals on the literary scene are CHARLES RUKUNI, BERENG SETUKE, KAIZER NGWENYA and MATHATHA TSEDU, all of whom are journalists.

MANGO TSHABANGU is a former actor and founding editor of *S'ketsh.*

ACHMED DANGOR is a poet who was unbanned in '78 and has just won the Mofolo-Plomer prize for a prose collection.

TOIVO HERMAN JA TOIVO, Namibia's Nelson Mandela, is also serving a long sentence on the Island of Makhanda.

Mutloatse, Head and Tlali attended the International Writing Programme in Iowa, USA, in '76, '77 and '78, respectively.

Maatla ke a mang?